SARAH A. DENZIL

ONE FOR
SORROW

ONE FOR SORROW

Sarah A. Denzil

Copyright © 2018 Sarah A. Denzil

Cover and book design by Mae I Design & Photography

ALSO BY SARAH A. DENZIL

Saving April
The Broken Ones
Silent Child

ONE FOR SORROW

TRUE CRIME JUNKIE

The Crime that Rocked Rotherham
by James Gorden

Not long after the water ripples disturbed the usually calm water of the family pond did the details of the crime unfurl. I remember the exact moment I saw the news. It remains completely clear in my mind, as all enormous moments do, like the moment I heard about 9/11 or Princess Diana's death. I remember the blue t-shirt I was wearing and the exact position in which I was sitting on the sofa, magazines on the coffee table alongside my Tardis mug.

The details from the police were still hazy at that point, but what I heard was enough to make me hug my niece and nephew a little more tightly the next time I saw them.

I like to think that the undulations circling over the surface of the duck pond are continuing to form a path, and that the distressing murder left behind a beautiful pattern. There are not many instances of goodness coming from badness, but I have hope that my town can be the exception, that we will breed strength, and that goodness will flow through the community.

I still have hope.

It was a bright summer's day on the twelfth of August, 2010. On the grounds of the Fielding property, the laughter of children filtered up the long lawns from the duck pond by the edge of Scholes Woods. There wasn't a cloud in the sky, and the grown-ups were sipping mojitos on the patio of their expansive property. David and Anna Fielding were entertaining guests. Riya and Jason Earnshaw had brought their six-year-old daughter Maisie for a business/play date. The Fieldings' eldest daughter, Isabel, fourteen, was watching the two younger children—including her brother Owen, eleven—while the adults discussed an investment into Jason Earnshaw's construction company.

The Fieldings and the Earnshaws were, and still are, respected members of the community. Anna was well-known at the local church, ran raffles to help the needy, and routinely helped at the food bank. David invested in many local businesses, aiding the economy of the town. Riya and Jason Earnshaw were known as good employers who created jobs in the area.

The day was perfect until the sound of children's laughter stopped. Jason Earnshaw would later tell the police that after a particularly animated conversation with the Fieldings, where David told the group a joke, they noticed that the children had gone very quiet.

Riya stood up on the patio and called Maisie's name. When there wasn't an answer, Riya and Anna hurried down the long lawn, which sloped downhill to the pond.

Isabel was the first to be found. She was walking up the lawn with her hands outstretched. Anna ran to her, asking her if she was hurt. Isabel shook her head, but she was soaked to the waist, and there was blood covering her hands and lips. Barely a second later, Jason Earnshaw recalled hearing the piercing scream of his wife. He sprinted down the hill to see his wife wading into the pond, her expensive sun dress ruined by the murky water. He hurried to her, splashing through the shallow water.

As the Earnshaws were wading through dirty water, David Fielding saw his son wander towards him from the trees. Owen Fielding walked with his head bent low, tears dripping from his nose. There was blood splattered on his trousers, but he was not wet, and he was not as covered in as much blood as his older sister. David rushed to Owen to check that the child was not hurt.

And in the centre of it all, at the very centre of the pond, a little girl lay face down. She was stripped to the waist—the police would find her daisy-print t-shirt caught on a bush in the forest a few hours later—with her hair fanning all around her. Her loose, dark curls were as soaked as her jeans.

Maisie Earnshaw was dead.

Murdered.

We know since the trial that Maisie was taken into the woods, hit with a rock, and mutilated with a knife. Her small body was then dragged out of the woods and displayed in the centre of the pond.

We know that Isabel Fielding was covered in Maisie's blood, and that she was soaked from the waist down.

We know that Isabel Fielding was convicted of Maisie Earnshaw's murder at the age of fourteen. She was taken to a juvenile detention centre where she was deemed to be suffering with a mental disorder.

After lengthy questioning, it was decided that Owen Fielding did not assist with the death of Maisie Earnshaw.

Rotherham continues to mourn the loss of an innocent. We have stood together to help heal the grief that has opened up within the community. Many of us feel a fraction of the intense pain that the Earnshaws must be feeling. We are all in it together, and we will continue on with the pain in our hearts, but we will be stronger and more unified because of it.

CHAPTER

I

I was unaccustomed to the icy bite of the northern wind. Even in early March, I'd woken to frost on the windscreen that morning and layered up my clothing. Wearing my fingerless gloves as I drove, intermittently breathing into my hands to warm them, I wondered if there was indeed some truth in the stereotype of hardy northerners and southern wimps. I cursed the broken heater in my old Punto and pressed on the accelerator, wishing to be somewhere warm.

In three hundred yards make a right turn.

Glancing from the sat-nav on my phone—adhered to the dashboard with a cheap rubber mat I bought online—to the long stretch of road before me, I wondered where exactly this right turn was. I'd been driving on the same straight road for ten minutes, heading from barren stretches of moorland to bountiful, green woodland. Trees surrounded either side of the narrow road, blocking out much of the early morning sun. I craned my neck to the right, searching for this mysterious turning. Before long I saw the tall gates—a shock of industrialisation in this untouched, rural environment—and made the sharp right turn towards the steel bars, coming to a halt next to the guard tower.

"What's your business at Crowmont Hospital today?" the guard asked in a voice too cheerful for eight in the morning. The man was stout, with hair greying at the temples and throughout his beard. Fine lines appeared around his eyes when he smiled, which conveyed the same genuine warmth I'd noticed amongst the people of Yorkshire. Northerners were far too friendly for this half-frozen wimpy southerner in need of a strong cup of tea, or better yet, an extra two hours in bed.

"I start work today," I said. "My name's Leah Smith. I'm the new nurse on Morton Ward."

Though I had travelled up for an interview, it had taken place at York Hospital rather than Crowmont. The usual wing used for interviews had been closed for refurbishments and the interviewers decided to find a more neutral location. The fact that I hadn't actually seen my new workplace added to the first-day nerves that tickled my abdomen.

The security guard mentioned my name into a walkie-talkie while I continued to breathe onto my gloves to warm my stiff fingers.

"Cold morning, eh?" he said, moving away from his guard station and towards the car.

I nodded. "I hope it's warmer inside than it is out."

"Aye, well. Not much warmer." He looked up and nodded towards the road leading through the trees. A tall metal fence ran alongside it, giving the impression of being inside some sort of steel labyrinth. "Follow the road till you get out of the trees. You'll see the hospital then. You want to take your first right and keep going till you see the carpark. There's another gate before the carpark, but Brian'll let you in. That's where Morton Ward is."

"Right. Thanks for your help."

"No worries. I'm Ian, by the way. I work here at the gate most mornings. I'll be seeing you later on." He tapped the roof of my Punto and stepped back as I pulled away.

While making my way through the strange, gated maze, I realised my fingers were trembling, and it wasn't solely from the cold. First-day nerves were getting the best of me, or perhaps the gravity of the place rattled me—not that it should. This wasn't my first time at a high-security psychiatric facility.

Just like Ian said, the road emerged from the trees, and I saw Crowmont Hospital for the first time. On the edge of the woods another set of gates parted to let me through, which Ian must've been able to operate from his tower. Then the road continued towards the hospital itself, set back away from the steel labyrinth of fences. It was almost like its own community, with outbuildings and carparks leading up to the main hospital wing, sprawling old Victorian mansion of a building, four storeys high with rows of narrow windows. Steep gables pointed up like filed teeth above the thin windows. Two sturdy pillars stood proudly on either side of the grand, wide doorway. I could not take my eyes from the dark limestone walls, and almost missed the turning Ian had told me about. It was only when I noticed the sign for the hospital that I remembered where I was and why I was here. The white and blue NHS sign grounded me back to reality. I was about to start a new job, to go with my new life in a new place. *North Yorkshire Healthcare* was printed along the white portion of the sign, with *Crowmont Hospital* underneath in the blue section.

I turned my steering wheel and followed the road towards the carpark, which was also gated, as Ian had forewarned. The security guard at this gate stepped towards the car with his walkie-talkie in hand.

"Brian?" I asked.

This man was fair-haired, with ruddy cheeks and burst blood vessels around his nostrils. I noticed faded tattoos along his knuckles, but I couldn't work out what they said.

"Aye. And you're the new nurse."

"Leah Smith." He most likely already knew my name but I blurted it out by way of greeting.

Brian's walkie-talkie burst to life, with the person on the other end asking for an update. Brian informed the person of my arrival and waited for the go-ahead to open the gate.

"Now I know you'll have been warned about the security measures already, but I'll go over it quickly," he said, obviously well-rehearsed from explaining the unusual system to visitors. "You'll get a pass at reception. They'll take your photograph an' all. Security inside will tell you the rest, but you'll have to be searched before you go on the ward. There's a list of restricted items that you can't take into the ward, and they'll assign you a locker to keep your belongings in."

"Thanks," I replied, appreciative of the heads-up. I knew security would be tight, but when it's your first day, it's nice to know exactly what to expect.

A new job in a new place, away from home. Adrenaline began to kick in, chasing away the cold. Blood pumping around my body replaced the cold stiffness in my muscles. Now my heart thudded against my ribs, so urgent that I felt the vibration of my pulse in my fingertips. The mechanics of the gate made me start as they came to life—metal scraping against tarmac, jingling as it retracted to clear my way. I snatched the gloves from my hands and took a deep breath.

As I guided my car into a parking spot—moving at a crawl, not trusting my hands on the steering wheel—I tried to convince myself the nerves had hit me suddenly because I hadn't been at work for a few weeks, and because I'd moved somewhere new, and because the building had spooked me, nothing else. I was new to the area, new to the countryside, and felt like a fish out of water. Four weeks ago I'd still been living in an apartment in Hackney.

Almost another lifetime ago. Another life.

I turned the key in the ignition and pulled down the visor to check my hair in the mirror. Nurses don't do make-up or complicated hairstyles. They tie their hair away and wear nothing but moisturiser. Nevertheless, I didn't want to walk into my new job with hair poking out at all angles and cereal in my teeth. I had neither, thankfully, so I got out of the car and retrieved my sandwiches from the backseat. When I shut the door it seemed too loud in this quiet spot. I glanced at my watch: eight fifteen. I was a little early, but I knew it would take time for the staff to create my pass.

I locked the car and shoved the keys in my trouser pocket before making my way to the entrance of the ward. It wasn't the door with the pillars, but a smaller glass door with a pass scanner on the left side. I had pressed the buzzer and was waiting for someone to let me in when my attention was caught by a dark shape out of the corner of my eye. Then I heard a squawk from above, and I lifted my chin to see where it had come from. A large magpie stared down at me from the guttering on the roof, a thin twig hanging out of its beak.

"Good morning," I whispered, glancing behind me to check that no one had seen. It had slipped from my lips like a reflex. *Good morning, Mr. Magpie.* It was my father who'd always said it. Then he used to wave.

One for sorrow, two for joy, three for a girl, four for a boy.

I tried not to think about the rhyme. I tried not to think about my father and his superstitions, passed on to him from his superstitious mother, passed down from her own, even more superstitious mother.

A crackling voice said *hello*, breaking me free of the painful memories. I cleared my throat and explained for the third time that I was the new nurse on Morton Ward and that my name was Leah Smith. The door buzzed, and I pushed it open into the small reception area.

Ian was right—it was only a little warmer inside. Not that I minded. The nerves made my once-freezing blood run warm. I clenched and unclenched my fingers as I made my way to the reception, a long white desk at the back of the white room with green carpets and faded green sofas. The woman on the front desk wore her glasses down low on her nose, and while she talked me through my security pass, she never stopped moving. She rustled her way through two piles of documents as she took my photograph, with me standing awkwardly with a tense smile on my face. No one ever looks good on a webcam, do they? No doubt a pasty face and a frozen smile would be my best choice. A temporary visitor's pass was given to me in a plastic sleeve with a clip to attach it to my waistband.

"I'll try and get your proper pass done by the end of the day," she told me. "Then you can swipe in tomorrow morning."

"Thanks," I said, clipping the pass to the waistband of my trousers.

"I'm Sue," she said. "I work Mondays and Wednesdays, eight till six. Yousef works the other days. There's a lot of part-timers coming and going." When she smiled there was a faint residue of pink lipstick on her teeth. "Not to mention the turnover." She rolled her eyes. "I guess Crowmont isn't for everyone. Have you worked in a high-security hospital before?"

"Yeah, a couple of years in Whitmore."

"Oh." She leaned in slightly. "That's where *he* is, isn't it? The strangler." She mimed strangulation on herself, and I feigned a smile.

"Roger Cowell," I answered. Roger Cowell was a serial killer who hit infamy after murdering fifteen women in the seventies. I was used to the constant questions after working at Whitmore for a while. I'd learnt to recognise the little glint in the eyes of the more brazen and curious. Revealing where I worked was a good way of getting to know someone. The shy, polite types would nod, smile, open their mouths to speak, but then think better of it and move the conversation onto a different topic. The loud, brash ones would immediately start asking me about Roger Cowell.

Is he evil? Can you tell, when you look at him? I've heard he's lost weight and sits in his room all day staring at the walls. Does he sleep at night? Does he have nightmares? Did he tell you where the sixteenth body is?

"I didn't work on his ward," I replied. "So I never came into contact with him."

Sue smiled. She was obviously aware of what it was like to work in a notorious high-security hospital. Her smile turned into a knowing nod. "There are a few like that here. The questions get annoying after a while, don't they?"

I let out a nervous laugh. "Yes, they really do."

Sue directed me through to the metal detectors where a security guard told me to place my car keys into a plastic tray, along with the small amount of change I'd brought and my coat and other belongings. I stepped through the metal detector, still tense about my arrival at a new job, but calmed slightly by the no-nonsense but warm people around me. The third security guard was called Simon, and was slightly younger than Ian. He wasn't as chatty as the other two, probably because he had a more intense role in the security procedures.

After the scan, I was given back my belongings and told to put them away in a staff locker, aside from my lunch and my change for the tuck shop, which I was allowed to put in the fridge in the staff room. It was like being at a very strange, paranoid school where I was expected to be both pupil *and* teacher. Simon showed me to the office for the charge nurse who would give me instructions on my first day.

As I walked into the office to start my day, my palms began to sweat, and a sensation of walking to the head-teacher's office washed over me. I was sixteen years old again, with scuffed knees from a scrap with Rebecca Boyce on the tennis courts, waiting to receive the inevitable bollocking. Pushing away the memories, I knocked lightly on the open door and the man at the desk lifted his head.

"Leah?" he asked. Even though he was seated at a desk with a cup of tea, I could see he was short and stocky with powerful shoulders. He wore a black t-shirt and smart grey trousers.

"Yes."

He stood and crossed the room to shake my hand. "I'm Chioke Obi. Chi for short, if you like. Welcome to Crowmont. Would you like a cup of tea while we get down to it?"

"I'd love one, thanks."

"Then let's go into the staff room for a minute or two." Chi grinned and rubbed his hands together. I hoped that his eagerness was infectious enough to transfer onto me, seeing as I felt about as enthusiastic as a limp piece of lettuce that morning.

I followed Chi through the small network of staff rooms to the main area, with an oval table in the centre, a small kitchen area, and a couple of uncomfortable-looking chairs.

"Milk? Sugar?"

"Milk, no sugar," I replied.

Chi got to work with the kettle, all the time smiling, slowly putting me at ease despite my initial shakiness. After the first mouthful of soothing tea, and the first ten minutes where Chi told me more about the hospital and the ward I'd be working on, I began to relax, and the sweaty-palms sensation dissipated.

"The main thing you need to know is that you're the primary nurse for three patients," he said, with a hint of an African accent in his voice. "Tracy, Emily, and Isabel."

CHAPTER
2

The first thing you notice about a high-security hospital is that the patients are not as frightening as you think they're going to be. It's easy to conjure up images of serial killers standing in the shadows, their features obscured aside from a set of narrowed eyes. It's not *Silence of the Lambs*. I wasn't Clarice Starling walking past barred cells, dodging the semen of a psychotic killer. I'm Leah. I'm a nurse. I was there to help my patients.

In the past, when I'd been asked questions about Whitmore, I realised that people found it much harder to picture the average patient as someone who was unfortunate, someone who had been a victim for most of their life, who was never given the start in life that they needed. What they wanted to believe was that some people were born degenerates, or that they were evil to the core. That wasn't my experience.

In Whitmore I worked with many patients suffering from antisocial psychological disorder—or sociopaths, if you want to call them that—and discovered that most of the residents under my care had been abused by a significant person in their life, usually at a very young age. Children need love and care. They need to form an attachment. When a child fails to form an attachment with a caregiver, they fail to learn empathy.

That's how you build a sociopath.

I followed Chi through the corridors of Crowmont, still feeling the throb of my pulse in my fingertips. Despite my experience at Whitmore, I wasn't entirely sure what to expect. In some ways, Whitmore was more disturbing and more frightening because most of the patients were violent male offenders. But some were referred to us because they had self-harmed in prison, or because they had special needs. Not all were psychotic serial killers.

Crowmont was an all-female hospital. Many of these women had committed violent crimes, but the hospital was smaller than Whitmore. I knew that there were two main wings in Crowmont: One was for rehabilitation, where the patients were allowed more freedom to move around the hospital, and the other was the intensive care ward, where very sick patients struggled to socialise with each other. I was employed to work on the rehabilitation ward.

Chi had briefed me in his office. My main duties were to check in with the patients through the day. I would ensure they ate their food and took their medicine, and I would observe them quietly as they went about their day and help them if they were experiencing any difficulties.

I met Tracy first. She sat on the sofa in the communal area of the ward, with one leg elevated. Her arms were stretched above her head, showing the scars down her forearms. She had short hair and a snub nose. She was very overweight, verging on obese—patients often take comfort in food, especially when they're on medication that increases appetite—and in her late twenties. Chi introduced us and we shook hands.

I saw right away that Tracy was upset.

"I'm still a kitchen helper, aren't I?" she asked Chi. "They haven't taken that away, have they? I didn't mean it."

"It's all right. You can stay on in the kitchen. But Leah is here if you need her."

As we walked away, I asked. "What did she mean?"

Chi sighed. "There was an incident. It's nothing to worry about, but Tracy does occasionally need extra supervision."

I nodded my head. 'Extra supervision' usually meant suicide attempts.

Emily was a much smaller young woman with greasy hair to her shoulders. She was playing draughts with an older woman. She shook my hand as she fidgeted in her chair.

"Who's winning?" I asked.

"Debbie," Emily replied.

"I beat her every week," Debbie boasted.

Emily gave a shrug and scratched her shoulder. "Least I'm trying."

Chi clapped his hands together so loudly it made us all jump. "That's the spirit. People were designed to try. That's what we do." He grinned until Emily tentatively broke into a smile of her own.

"Maybe we can have a game or two," I suggested.

"You're on," Emily replied.

I got a good vibe from this hospital. No psychiatric nurse ever expects their job to be simple, but it was a relief to see patients smiling on my first day.

After a brief conversation about how I would be looking after Emily, and how if she had problems she should come to me, Chi led me away.

"Emily has come a long way," he said. "She was on the intensive care ward for so long I never thought she'd make it to rehabilitation."

"Was she a referral?" I asked, meaning someone who had come to the hospital through the legal system.

Chi pursed his lips, then glanced to the left and the right before he answered. "Yes. Emily is a convicted murderer. She killed her baby during postnatal depression. When she came to us she was on suicide watch for a month."

I took a second to let that all sink in. "If she ever leaves here, will she go straight to prison?"

"For at least another six years," he replied.

It was an unbearably sad case, but then many are in a place like Crowmont. The guilt that weighed down on her shoulders must have been a heavy burden to bear. Not to mention the judgment and the grief from the people in her life who were connected to her child and the crime she committed. The father. The grandparents. The uncles and aunties. An event like this would almost certainly tear the family apart.

Chi led me out of the communal area, using his swipe card to get through the door and into a corridor.

"This is where the patients' rooms are. They're all numbered so you can remember who goes in which room. On this ward, you need two keys to enter the room. So you would need to come and find me if you had a reason to go into the room outside the communal time. Right now, patients are free to keep their doors open, but at night they will be locked. Unless the patient is on twenty-four hour surveillance."

"Suicide watch?" I asked.

Chi nodded.

It was procedure that I was already accustomed to. At Whitmore, there were six-key rooms, where six nurses were required to be present when the door was opened. They worked as a team, ensuring that the patient was properly restrained, each entering or exiting the room one at a time, and each with a role to play in the restraint. At the end, when a patient was taken back to his room, he would be placed down on the bed, with each nurse leaving one at a time, from the nurse furthest away from the door to the nurse closest to the door. All outings for those patients were carefully scheduled with several members of staff, from the security team who monitored the CCTV cameras to the nurses on the ward, all designed to ensure the safety of staff and patients alike. Those patients were not allowed to leave those rooms whenever they liked.

But Morton Ward had a different atmosphere to Whitmore. Something about the long corridor of doors—almost all open, with music coming from some, the sound of chatting from others—reminded me of halls of residence at university. If not for the hospital-green walls and the heavy locks on the doors, I could have imagined I was about to go and greet a friend on my course.

Chi stopped outside the room furthest along the corridor, next to another locked door that led somewhere else deep inside the hospital. The door to this room was swung wide open so I could see the contents: a bed, a desk, a small closet to the right which led to a bathroom I couldn't actually see but presumed existed. It was a small room and would feel claustrophobic after an extended period of time, but one that you could probably grow accustomed to if forced. And, in this case, that sense of claustrophobia was exacerbated by the clutter, chaos, and covered walls. From ceiling to floor, every inch was plastered with drawings. Corners of A4 sheets of paper curled, and Blue Tack shone through the pearl of the paper like little blue beads. In the centre of every page was a bird illustration.

Magpies. Blue tits. Sparrows. Crows. Robins. Hawks. Eagles. Finches. Cranes. Flamingos. Black wings, yellow beaks, red breasts, iridescent blues, green feathers, brown eyes. The eyes were the most arresting and seemed to watch me as I followed Chi into the room.

"Isabel, how are you doing today? This is Leah. She is going to be your nurse from now on."

With all the birds on the walls I'd failed to notice the young woman bent over her desk. As she rose to greet me, I saw the charcoal stains on her fingers, and the fingernails bitten down to the skin beneath.

She was plump, with a soft, round face and a small belly protruding from her jogging bottoms and t-shirt. She was young, barely twenty years old, with brown eyes that twinkled beneath a fringe of medium-brown hair. Her hair was long and messy, as though she'd just rolled out of bed. But the most arresting feature was her easy smile, and the way she stood with one hand on her hip, relaxed. I wasn't used to seeing patients in high-security hospitals appearing so relaxed.

"Oh, what happened to Alesha?"

"She moved on," Chi said.

"But I never got to say goodbye." Isabel's eyebrows rose and her eyes seemed to grow larger with sadness. "Alesha was lovely. I hope she's okay."

"No need to worry, she's fine. She got another job, that's all."

But I knew it was strange for a nurse not to say goodbye to her long-term patients before she moved on to another job. Alesha must have left in a hurry. Unless she didn't want to upset Isabel before she left.

"So you're my new nurse." Isabel assessed me with eyes that trailed from my forehead to my toes. "Did you see the magpie outside?"

"Yes," I replied in surprise. Of all the first questions I was expecting, one about a magpie wasn't even in my top fifty.

"His name is Pepsi and I'm training him."

I almost laughed. "What are you training him to do?"

"Eat out of my hand," she replied eagerly, her words speeding up with excitement. "Fetch me twigs and worms. Squawk when I ask him to. Magpies are the cleverest birds, you know. They symbolise many things, too. Most people think they symbolise cunning and bad luck, but to me they're magic. And mystery. I'll show you Pepsi when we go on a walk into the garden."

"I can't wait," I replied. "But why is he called Pepsi?"

"I found him in the garden with his foot stuck in a Pepsi can. Chi helped me get him out of the can and nurse him back to health." Her eyes were glassy with excitement and she grinned from ear to ear. "Do you like birds?"

"They're beautiful creatures. I can see you like them very much." I gestured to the walls.

"I always wanted to be able to fly." She gazed at the walls. "Maybe one day." She came alive with movement so quickly that I took a step back, but she wasn't preoccupied with me, it was her art she was interested in. She began to search through a pile of papers on her desk, finally retrieving the item she sought, and passed it to me. "Here, take it."

I took the paper gently from her hands. It was a charcoal drawing of a magpie in flight with its wings outstretched, soaring through the sky. I had to admit that the artistry was excellent, and Isabel was an extremely talented girl. Looking at this bird gave me a sense of peace that I hadn't anticipated from my anxious morning. I was aware of the effect art had on people, though I'd never truly understood it, not even when my first boyfriend—an amateur graffiti artist—used to drag me to exhibitions, but there was an ethereal quality to this picture that gave me pause.

"Thank you," I replied, clearing my throat, suddenly self-conscious of my reaction to the gift.

"You're welcome," Isabel said, broadening her smile.

CHAPTER
3

I'd met my three patients, I'd taken a tour around Morton Ward, and I'd eaten lunch in the break room with the other nurses. It was a relatively quiet place, not as bustling with action as Whitmore was. Even the communal areas for the patients were calmer than Whitmore, with fewer residents and a more sedate atmosphere. I began to wonder why I'd been so nervous.

"What was Whitmore like?" asked a nurse called Tanya, leaning her elbows on her knees to get closer to me.

"The same, really, except they were all men," I replied.

"Smellier then?" she said with a laugh.

"At times, yeah." I tried not to think about the dirty protests or the patients who refused to shower for days at a time. "I was on rehabilitation like you are, though. I never saw the bad cases in intensive care."

Tanya's eyes widened. "I couldn't stand it on IC. Did for like three months and asked for a transfer. Most don't get it, but I was lucky. There's a biter, and she's a little shit. One of them scratched my arm from elbow to wrist with her fucking fingernails. I know they're ill, but it's bloody hard. I couldn't do it."

We've all been there. There's no way to work in psychiatric care without bites, scratches, punches, and kicks. I once spent New Year's Eve with a black eye courtesy of Bill Jones, a man with paranoid schizophrenia who thought I was there to stab him in the ribs.

"Who was your scariest patient?" she asked, sipping on her Cup-a-Soup. "Was it Cowell?"

"Probably," I admitted. "But I never saw him. The worst on our ward were from organised crime. Almost all of them were recruited as teenagers and turned into killers. They didn't stand a chance in the real world. It was pretty sad."

Tanya nodded. "It's a recurring theme."

"Do you have any high-profile cases here?" I asked. I couldn't help myself. As much as I'd told myself that I never gossiped and never thought of the patients as "infamous," there was a bubbling curiosity swelling inside and not a lot I could do about it. I was, and always will be, human.

"That's easy," Tanya said. "Isabel Fielding."

The name gave me a start. "Isabel? The girl with the birds?" Isabel was my ward, and even though it was my first day, I thought Chi would have mentioned if she was a special case. "But she's on the rehabilitation ward."

"Yeah, because if it turns out she's not crazy anymore, she'll go straight to prison. She gets reassessed in May. If she's fit to go, she gets transferred." Tanya set down her mug and eyed the door to the break room. "Chi doesn't like us talking about Isabel's case because it's so high profile. Do you remember the little girl found dead in a duck pond? She'd been murdered by a teenage girl."

I didn't respond right away because the blood was draining from my face, and I felt nauseated. Of course I remembered the story; it was all over the national newspapers. Three young children had been playing next to a pond. One of them had been murdered. One of them was found covered in the blood of the dead girl, who had either been struck by an object or beaten, I couldn't remember. What I did remember was the visceral thump of disgust at the thought of a child killing another child. I remembered the way my mind refused to accept that a child could be anything other than innocent, turning away from the story and pushing the paper across the table. And then, when my mind decided it wanted more, I pulled the paper back and devoured the story from beginning to end, needing all the gory details, searching online for as much as I could find before feeling sick again and forcing myself to stop.

"Yes," I finally replied. "I remember the story. So it was Isabel … ?"

"Yup. And since then, she's been in and out of juvenile centres, secure psychiatric wards, and now Crowmont. She's been here since she was sixteen. She started out in intensive care and then came to rehabilitation two years ago. If she does well in rehabilitation and they decide she isn't crazy, she goes straight to prison."

"She's my patient." My voice sounded squeaky. I wished she'd never told me. Maybe I could have continued my work without ever knowing. Of course I couldn't—the truth always comes out in the end—and I had no choice but to put my prejudices aside and continue caring for her as I would anyone else.

I was a professional.

Perhaps if I told myself that enough times I'd believe it.

"Look, you won't get any trouble from her. She's basically a kid, and besides, they say she's never admitted to it, and she reckons she can't even remember the event. Five years here and she's not once been violent. She does what she's told." Tanya shrugged and picked up her mug. "Make of that what you will."

The way Tanya stabbed the noodles in her soup made me think she believed Isabel was playing some sort of game. But I'd been a psychiatric nurse for long enough to know that patients could not keep up an act for extended periods of time. No one could.

"Anyway, I probably shouldn't have told you all that," Tanya admitted. "You'll have meetings about her every week so you'll find it all out eventually. The director monitors her pretty closely. She's by far our most high-profile patient."

After lunch, I spent my time in the Morton communal area, watching the patients. Tracy seemed to be a bit of a loner, choosing to spend her time on the sofas watching television. She only spoke to me when it was time for me to walk her to her therapy session. Emily was more of a social butterfly, talking with many of the patients and even chatting to me for a while. She was someone with a lot of nervous energy, wiry and lean, never still. We talked about me moving to Hutton and where I used to live in Hackney. Like I always do with the patients, I allowed myself to open up just enough without revealing too much information. I didn't tell her about Tom, and I didn't tell her about my parents.

But Isabel never left her room. Every so often I would have to go into the corridors to check that she was still okay. Every time I went to her room, I found her bent over on her desk working on another drawing. My main contact with her was when I walked her to art therapy.

Most nurses have a switch they can flip to deal with the stresses of the job. I'm no exception. Despite the jitters Tanya's revelation had given me, I managed to turn off the part of my brain longing to dwell on the murder of that poor child, and instead I saw Isabel as my patient, pure and simple. I was walking her to art therapy. That was my job.

"Will you keep the drawing I gave you?" Isabel asked.

"Of course," I said, though I'd completely forgotten about it. I'd placed the picture of the magpie in my locker before lunch, and now I didn't particularly want to dwell upon it at all. I didn't want to think about it because of my reaction, and because of the things I had thought about while looking at it.

What a waste of talent, I'd thought. *What a shame she's here and not out there in the world.*

Of course, now I knew what she'd done. I knew who she was.

"I'm glad," Isabel said. "As soon as you walked in the door I knew you were a symbol of magical new beginnings, just like Pepsi. I think we're going to get on, you and me."

"I'm glad," I replied.

Isabel stopped and looked at me with slightly narrowed eyes, and her head tilted to one side. "Oh, you've been told."

A flush of heat worked its way up my neck. "What do you mean by that, Isabel?"

"You've been told about what I did. I can tell by the expression on your face." She started walking again, slower this time. "I know you're trying not to think about it, and you're doing a pretty good job of it, but I can still tell. You've got the 'look.'"

I wasn't sure how to reply to that, so I didn't.

"It's all right. I know it must be hard to work with someone like me. I know what you must think of me."

"You're a patient here, Isabel. I want to make sure you're safe and well, that's all." I tried to give her a reassuring smile, but the smile was frozen, forced by unwilling muscles.

"It's not so bad here," she continued. "My brother comes to visit me. I get to do my art. It's better now I'm on the rehab ward. I didn't like the other one. This way."

I let her lead the way to the art room, where we said goodbye. I told her I would be back in an hour to walk her back to her room or the communal area.

She nodded and told me she would be ready, and then she leaned closer and whispered, "Want to know a secret? I never killed that little girl." And then she put her finger to her lips and breathed, "*Shhhhh.*"

TRUE CRIME JUNKIE

Did Isabel Fielding Kill Maisie Earnshaw?
by James Gorden

As you know, I'm personally invested in this crime which occurred in my town. Almost seven years on, I have gone through my shock and anger that such a heinous act was committed in the place I call home. But since then, I've grown suspicious, and I want to air those suspicions to you, my dear readers, because I need to talk about it. No one is talking about it anymore, and now it's time to open the conversation.

On 12th August 2010, six-year-old Maisie Earnshaw was found floating in a pond on the Fielding estate in Rotherham. Present at the scene of the crime was fourteen-year-old Isabel Fielding, and her brother, Owen Fielding, aged ten. Further away from the crime scene, but still on the estate, were David and Anna Fielding, and Jason and Riya Earnshaw, all drinking cocktails and telling bawdy jokes while their children played dangerously close to the pond.

Police had to rely on the eyewitness testimonies of the four adults and two children. David, Anna, Jason, and Riya all noted that the children went suddenly very quiet, but they had been making enough noise to drown out the sounds of the children playing. Nevertheless, when they noticed the change, they went to investigate. There, so they say, they found little Maisie dead in the centre of the pond, with Isabel covered in blood (famously, with it spread over her mouth like lipstick) and Owen splattered with blood.

What exactly happened?

Let's first look at Isabel. What do we know about this little girl? First and foremost, it's important to know that Isabel had shown no behavioural problems, and believe me, the media dug as far as they could into her past. There were no reports at school, no indication that she had a violent streak. She was a well-liked girl with a small group of friends. Her grades were above average but not outstanding. She was the kind of child that always remains in the middle, who is rarely singled out, the kind of student who needs little supervision because she can look after herself.

You could say to me: *But, James, these are exactly the kind of children who slip through the net! That's why this happened.*

But I don't think so. I think Isabel is a regular girl who has been stitched up by the real killer. She was quiet and co-operative at the crime scene. In the documentary *Maisie: The Angel in the Pond*, the interviewed police officers noted that Isabel showed signs of being in shock, and that she was confused as to what had happened. She showed no signs of the feral wild child you'd expect her to be after murdering a young girl in such a ritualistic manner.

Now, let's look at Owen Fielding. At eleven years old, Owen was barely considered a suspect. He was questioned by the police, but they decided he was telling the truth. He told them that Isabel took Maisie into the Scholes Woods, bludgeoned her with a rock, sliced unusual marks (the police never revealed what was carved) into Maisie's flesh, and then threw her into the pond. But why would a girl with an exemplary school record—who had no violent tendencies—do such a thing?

Owen, on the other hand, was considered top in all his classes. He was a gifted young boy and has grown up to be a gifted young man. He did have behavioural issues at school. He once stabbed a child with a pencil, and a few months ago was arrested and cautioned for assault outside a pub in Sheffield.

What if Owen was the mastermind of this entire murder?

What if Owen and Isabel murdered Maisie together?

What if someone else was involved?

It's all possible.

It might be difficult for people to believe that an eleven-year-old brother could set up a fourteen-year-old girl in such a horrific way, but stranger things have happened between family members. And, there's another factor... David Fielding could not account for twenty minutes in the timeline, and claimed he was "making drinks" in the kitchen. Could David Fielding have snuck around the side of the house and into the Scholes Woods? Could he have stolen little Maisie away, attacked her and thrown her into the pond, implicating his own daughter in the process?

Forensic evidence showed DNA for just Maisie on the stone that killed her. Most of the DNA on Maisie's body was washed away in the pond. The knife was clean of fingerprints. Could fourteen-year-old Isabel Fielding, average in every way, really have masterminded this crime?

I don't believe she could.

COMMENTS:

TrueCrimeLover: There are so many holes in the testimonies from the adults and the kids. I watched the documentary too, and you know what stood out to me? Owen Fielding never screamed. He, apparently, watched his sister kill a little girl and he NEVER screamed. Why?

JamesGorden: YES! It's so weird. You'd expect an eleven-year-old kid to scream his lungs out. I don't understand either. Something isn't right.

Bundy's Bitch: You're so getting killed by Owen or David, lol!

JamesGorden: Umm, why?

Bundy's Bitch: You just implicated them in a murder. If they're guilty, you're next, idiot!

Poe: I'm starting to think you're right. How could any of this happen with the parents so close to them?

IHeartHannibal: You realise if you're right it means someone smeared blood all over Isabel Fielding, don't you?

JamesGorden: Yes, I do.

IHeartHannibal: K... I just wanted to let that sink in for a minute.

CHAPTER
4

My first day working on Morton Ward was over, but I was still buzzing from new job excitement, no doubt ready to crash later as the spike in adrenaline dipped. As I turned out of the gates and onto the long country road, I waved goodbye to Ian and began my journey back towards Hutton village. It had an interesting history, Hutton, as you would imagine, being so close to a high-security hospital.

Crowmont had started out as an asylum in Victorian times, which added to its air of mystery now. On my way home, I couldn't help thinking of Crowmont as it might have been; conjuring images of Bedlam asylum in the 1930s, a patient escaped and killed newlyweds having a picnic near the tranquil river a few miles outside the village. I read the Wikipedia article about the killing. On a bright summer day this young couple was slaughtered by a paranoid and violent man. Following the attack, a siren was erected in the village, blaring out every day at 3pm to let the villagers know all the patients were safely behind their gates. But if the villagers heard the siren at any other time than 3pm, then that meant a patient had escaped from Crowmont Hospital.

No one had escaped since 1965.

I drove through the village with my fingerless gloves on, still cold despite the signs of spring emerging in the trumpet shape of happy daffodils. They filled the grass verges and the centre of the one tiny roundabout. It was a picturesque village, the kind you expect to have a pastry named after it, with shops built within old terraced houses and a neat park with swings and a slide. No graffiti in sight.

But I had to turn out of the village to get to my new home, Rose Cottage. Out along the back roads, alongside the farms and the dirty fields housing pigs, sheep, or cows, further out until the road became a track, and the drive was part of an old muddied field closed off by a steel gate. That was where my new home resided.

Before hitting the dirt track, I passed the chicken coops owned by the Braithwaites—the family of farmers I was renting the cottage from. A man raised his head above the coops, his movement disturbing fallen feathers that were whipped up from the wind. His face was impassive amongst the small cloud of beige feathers. When I lifted a hand to wave to him, he barely even nodded. I remembered him—Seb; one of the younger brothers who had been my main contact when arranging the rent for the cottage. He was a man of few words, but had remained transparent and forthright throughout the exchange, which I valued more highly than conversation, especially after the year I'd had.

The reason I had to drive along the back roads and through the farming country to get to my new home was simply because this house was cheap. Rose Cottage was not the quaint, idyllic little retreat you'd expect from the name. It was a leaning, run-down old building with an outside toilet and a feral cat that growled from the bushes every time I walked to the door. On the day we moved in, Seb advised me to "chuck the little shit some tuna every once in a while and it'll leave yer be," so that was what I'd done during my first few days at the house.

The lock on the front door was stiff, requiring me to jimmy it a few times before shouldering it to get into the house. I stumbled into the kitchen and almost fell on top of Tom as he stirred a pot on the stove.

"Smells nice." I closed the door after three attempts—finally slamming it shut with a scrape of wood against wood—and bent to remove my shoes.

"Pasta," he said with a shrug. "How was the first day?"

Exhausting. Nerve-wracking. "Fine. How was school?"

"The bus dropped me off outside the village on the way back," he said. "I had to walk for half an hour."

That wasn't good. I sighed. "The woman on the phone said the bus company came this way."

Tom shook his head. "Guess they made it up. I asked the bus driver and everything."

My heart clenched as I took a good look at my little brother. At seventeen years old, he deserved more than a run-down two-up-two-down home in the middle of nowhere with a sister who worked long hours and wouldn't be able to take care of him properly. But I didn't want him going into care, and I didn't want him living alone, so he ended up stuck with me.

He was a good kid to put tea on for both of us, but then he'd always been a good kid, even when things were bad at our last home... a place I'd rather forget, but as much a part of me as the veins running beneath my skin.

"But apart from the bus, what was the school like? A bit smaller than at Hackney, right? Were the teachers nice? The other kids?" I made my way around to the table and started grabbing cutlery from the drawers. We weren't completely unpacked yet but we'd made a good start. Of course, it's easier when you don't actually own a lot of stuff.

"Yeah, they were all right," he said. I couldn't help noticing that Tom didn't meet my gaze as he answered, which I was accustomed to, especially when he lied.

Are you being bullied, Tom? No. Stares at the floor.

Did Dad hit you? No, I fell. Stares at the wall.

He had eyes that roamed around a room, a body that squirmed under pressure. He had a way of hanging his head and bunching up his shoulders so that he looked bigger and smaller all at once. In short, Tom was a target and always had been, and no matter how much I tried to protect him, there was always someone to bully him. And there was always a reason why. Tom, my younger, innocent, sweet brother, was born with a birthmark that spread from his right temple down to his cheek. The discoloured, orange-red of it was particularly arresting at first glance, which often led to little children pointing in his direction, or them leaning across to their mum and saying in a hushed but audible voice: *Mummy, what's wrong with that boy?*

And Tom was gay, I was ninety percent sure of it, though I didn't know how sure Tom was himself. He was quiet, and he wasn't particularly flamboyant or camp; he had no dress sense—unless you counted black jeans and black hoodies as fashion—but when we'd watched *Twilight* together, he'd seemed far more interested in Jacob than Bella, and his band posters were never of the band, but the beautiful, androgynous lead singers.

I'd never spoken to Tom about his sexuality, not even after our parents passed away and I became his caregiver. Our alcoholic, alpha-male wanker of a father would never have accepted Tom for who he is, but Mum might have, eventually. I wanted Tom to feel like he could talk to me, but the wounds of our childhood were still too raw, and I knew he would need time.

But that didn't stop the bullies…

And along with the psychological pressure of being bullied at school came the stress eating and the weight gain. After our parents died, I tried to turn exercise and healthy eating into some sort of a game. We couldn't afford a fancy games console that could track our movements, and neither of us had a smart phone so Pokemon Go was out the window, but we could get off the bus a couple of stops early or find a random walker to follow for a while, making up silly stories about where they were going and what they were doing. But Tom was only interested for a few weeks before he started finding it lame. I was lame and old and no fun to hang out with anymore, but I couldn't blame him. He was seventeen and the hormones causing his oily skin were the same hormones driving him to push me away.

"It might take a little while to find your feet," I replied, keeping my voice as cheerful as I could.

"I told them where I was living and they all laughed. Said it was some old shack on a farm owned by a crazy family. They said people fuck pigs up here in the night."

I almost dropped a knife onto the table. "Tom! Don't talk like that."

He blushed, his left cheek matching the birthmark on his right.

"Besides, the Braithwaites are fine people. They rented this cottage to us for a steal, so I wouldn't complain if I were you." I straightened a fork. "I'm sure there's no pig… intercourse. Like eighty percent sure, anyway."

He laughed, and it was wonderful. I'd made Tom laugh. That was enough of a victory for today.

After dinner, Tom went upstairs to finish straightening his room while I unpacked a few extra boxes in the kitchen. As I pulled our toaster and kettle out of the box I realised how old and dirty they were. A new house meant new things, not toasters with rust spots and kettles with lime scale. I washed them as best I could, opened the cheap bottle of wine I'd bought to celebrate the new house, and took it outside with a threadbare throw and a chipped mug. There was a rusty garden chair outside the front of the house, a long-forgotten thing with tall grass growing over the legs, tangling nature and manufacturing together, rooting it in one spot.

I sipped on my wine, pulled the throw more tightly around my shoulders and watched the bats swoop and flutter in the twilight sky.

The worst was over. The worst had started with the funeral and ended when I arrived back to the cottage after my first day at Crowmont. It was over. I shed tension like a snake sheds its skin, drinking deeply, letting the wine warm my bones. This was where I was supposed to be, with my Tom, and my house. And without *him*.

When I heard the startling sound of an animal grunt from somewhere deep within the farm, I thought of the pig-fucking and giggled into my wine. Seb Braithwaite and his brothers might seem a little rough around the edges, but I couldn't imagine them doing anything so disgusting. Then again, I'd never lived in the countryside before. Who knew what these rural types were up to?

I drank my wine and leaned back into the uncomfortable lawn chair. It was after ten, and the sky was a clear, dark ink stain spotted with white pinpricks. I never used to see the stars in London, but here they were in abundance. All around, the bats swooped and fluttered, more than I'd ever seen before, as though they were hunting in a pack.

The movement was hypnotising, like a murmuration of swallows vibrating through the air. Soon my eyelids drooped, and I felt myself drift into a light slumber.

There were a few things I remembered about that night, but the rest was blurry, which was strange because I'd only had a couple of mugs of wine. Perhaps it was because of my long, stressful day at a new job and being worn out from moving house that week. Perhaps it was because I hadn't eaten enough. I'm not sure what it was, but I wasn't quite in my right mind. One of the things I remembered was clutching my mug as I slept, and waking with it still upright on my lap. I'd woken with a start, the imprint of a man's voice in my ears. The fat ginger cat that lived in our bushes was growling, and my arms were covered in goosebumps. My breathing was laboured, and there was sweat on my forehead despite the cold night air. I placed the mug down by my feet and must have drifted straight back to sleep, because the next thing I knew, I woke up at the kitchen table, having fallen asleep with my head on the table top. After retrieving my phone from my jeans pocket, I realised that it was 4am, and I was freezing cold because the kitchen door was wide open. After that, I went to bed and set my alarm for 6:30.

Why didn't I go to bed when I woke up in the first place? Did I sleepwalk into the kitchen? I hadn't done any sleepwalking since I was nine years old, but it was possible the stress of the last week mixed with the wine had messed up my sleep cycle. It still didn't feel like me, and I was more than a little perturbed by these things happening, but I had to sleep before work the next day, so I pushed it all out of my mind, and slept the remaining two hours of the night before I had to get up and do it all over again.

I still don't remember what I dreamt.

CHAPTER
5

The next day, Isabel took me out into the small, enclosed garden at Crowmont. There she introduced me to Pepsi.

He was a large magpie with a proud way of holding his head, beady little black eyes, and wings that shone electric blue in the sunlight. Chi stood by the door as I walked Isabel around the garden, her carrying her tame bird, and me walking alongside, not too close.

"Do you want to stroke his feathers?" she asked.

"That's all right," I replied, eyeing the large bird nervously.

"He's perfectly tame," she said. "He was a baby when I found him. Poor thing." She lowered her face to the bird and pursed her lips to make a kissing noise. "It was horrible seeing him like that. But when he was better I felt like one of those girls in a fairy tale about wolves or tigers with splinters in their paws." She laughed. "I guess it's a strange thing for a convicted criminal to do, especially one in a hospital like this."

"Not at all," I replied. "You're getting better and helping him get better at the same time. It makes a lot of sense."

"You're right, it does. At least, it does if I'm getting better."

"Don't you think you are?" I asked.

She shrugged. "I guess it depends what I've got to get better from." She angled her head away from me so that I couldn't see her expression.

"You don't agree with the doctors about your illness?"

"They tell me I have delusions, that I'm mentally ill. They've been telling me that for years. They give me pills, and apparently, it stops it all and makes me better. That's all I know."

I supposed it must have been hard for her to have been institutionalised for such a long time. She'd been fourteen years old, barely developed as a human being. Perhaps if I'd been given medication for a mental illness for so long I might begin to grow suspicious of my own sanity too.

"The doctors have trained for a long time, and they know what they're doing," I said. "It might feel strange to do everything they tell you to do, especially when you've been here for so long, but they are here to help you."

Isabel let out a laugh, a low, sad chuckle. "And it's more than I deserve, if I did what they say I did."

I decided not to continue the conversation. Yesterday, Isabel had told me she didn't kill Maisie Earnshaw, and I got the feeling she was hoping to bring up the crime in conversation again today. One thing I'd learned working with sociopaths was that they loved to talk about their crimes. Though I was curious—too curious—to know how Isabel felt about the crime for which she had been convicted, I didn't want to talk about it, not yet. I didn't want to be reminded, and it all felt too personal, too soon. The barrier between patient and nurse went up.

"You told me Pepsi brings you things. What does he bring you?" I asked.

As we'd been walking around the rather sad little garden at Crowmont, I'd noticed that most of Isabel's body language was particularly childlike. She played with her hair, tucking and untucking it from her ears; she walked in long, enthusiastic strides, sometimes bouncing on her toes; and she often licked her lips before she spoke. She did all three of these things before answering my question, excited to be talking about her bird.

"Sometimes worms. Sometimes silly things like bottle tops or crisp packets. Sometimes bits of grass or flower stems. I think birds have a different definition of things that are useful than people do. I'm not sure what I could do with a worm."

Chi knocked on the window separating the garden from the hospital and cheerfully pointed at his watch. Isabel sighed and launched Pepsi up into the air.

"See you soon," she said to the bird, watching as his wings unfurled against the cloudy sky.

We began a slow walk back to the hospital, with Isabel swinging her arms lightly against her body. She glanced across at me and then down at her belly, stretching her hoody against her body.

"Do you think I should lose weight?" she asked.

The question caught me off guard, but it wasn't the first time a patient in a psychiatric facility had asked me that question. Weight gain was a common issue, and it often made patients feel insecure or lacking in confidence.

"A healthy diet is definitely important," I said, choosing my words carefully.

Isabel smiled. "You're very polite, Leah, but I'll take that as a yes." Isabel opened the door into the hospital. "I'm going on a diet, Chi. I've become quite the podger, don't you think?"

Chi tutted at her. "Why be so mean to yourself? Isn't life hard enough already? But eating healthily is good."

Isabel tipped her head back as she laughed. "You nurses."

Chi lifted his shoulders. "What did I say?"

"I think Isabel thinks we're predictable. I said the same thing about healthy eating," I explained.

"I'm never predictable. Would a predictable nurse do this?" Chi dropped to the ground and leapt back up, spinning around in an elaborate dance move.

Isabel's laugh deepened, and she gave Chi a quiet round of applause. Though her laugh was quiet when she cracked up, it was still infectious, and I found myself joining in. Chi was unlike any charge nurse I'd ever worked with. He ran the ward in a relaxed way, always making sure the rules were adhered to, but never seeming stressed or overstretched. He made the organisational side of the ward extremely relaxed, and for that reason I had become comfortable almost immediately.

But it was perhaps that sense of ease that allowed me to forget where I was, because there came a time when I stopped thinking of Crowmont as a hospital, and that was how I made a terrible mistake.

It's the same old cliché, isn't it? Doctors and nurses never take their own advice, and they end up with unhealthy habits. Yes, I was a smoker, which meant I was allowed the occasional break outside the hospital in the smoking area. I'd taken that break alone on my first day, but this time there was someone else there already. A man leaned against the wall, staring contemplatively down at the cigarette between his fingers. He wore dark blue trousers and a light blue top with the NHS logo on it. He turned and nodded towards me as I approached.

"You're the new nurse on Morton," he said, straightening up

from the wall. He lifted his hand as though offering it to shake, then seemed to change his mind and saluted me like a soldier instead.

I noted the way his hair was styled in a slight quiff, with plenty of hair gel. It was an unusual style for a guy his age—which I put roughly at twenty-five—seeing as most young men were sporting a beard with a fifties-style cut. He leaned back against the wall and sucked on his cigarette, and as I watched him do it a jolt of familiarity hit me like an electric shock. Ignoring the strange sensation, I flipped open my packet and pulled out my own cigarette.

"Yeah, that's right. I'm Leah."

"Alfie," he replied. "I'm a porter here, and apparently, the only other bugger who smokes." When he talked he kept his head angled away from me, which gave me a reprieve from his piercing eyes. Perhaps it was because I hadn't had much contact with the opposite sex for a while, aside from my little brother Tom, or perhaps it was because he reminded me of someone—though I didn't know who— but his presence definitely had my nerves jangling.

I popped the cigarette between my lips and ignited my lighter.

"I've been here for years," Alfie continued. "Seen a lot of nurses come and go in that time, but I never seem to leave."

"I've heard there's a high turnover of staff." I pulled in a drag and sucked it into my lungs. Even after the exhale I felt anxious.

"Not from me. I guess I've got used to it." He brushed back his hair. "Weird thing to say, I know. It's a weird place to enjoy working at, but I do. Does that sound wrong? Sick?"

"No," I said, though I felt uncertain.

"It's got a deep history, this place," he said. "I've picked up a few stories working here, stuff that you'll find on the internet if you really want to know. I guess I have some sort of inquisitive mind, you might say." He turned to me and grinned, which made me shiver from head to toe. "Ever heard of the Peeler?"

I shook my head.

Alfie gestured to the wall of the hospital behind his head. "He was one of the patients here. Some sort of tortured artist, apparently. I think his name was William… William… O'Neil, that's the one. It was the 1920s, and he was a famous artist, like Picasso or any of them fancy artists who painted squares and shit and said it was a banana. Well, this William fella, he was a bit of a character, and he had a blinding temper. There were these two art critics who trashed one of his paintings in the newspaper, said that old Will didn't have any talent." Alfie flicked ash from his cigarette. "That didn't go down so well with Mr William O'Neil. Instead of drowning himself in whisky, like he probably should've done, old Will decides to travel down to London and find these two critics who said his painting was a heap of crap. He took the two of them to dinner and played all nicey-nicey with them until he invited them back to his hotel room. Then he offered them both a nightcap and a cigar, all the while acting like he was fine with the way they'd called him names in the paper, and, I mean, they were brutal. They said he was talentless, a hack, an ape with a paintbrush—nasty, nasty stuff. Now, that's pretty difficult to get over, I'm sure you can agree." As Alfie took a drag, I rubbed my arms for warmth, that chilly March breeze easily penetrating my cotton shirt. "Old Will slipped them both a sleeping pill. There was no way he was letting those insults slide. After the two critics had fallen asleep, O'Neil strung them both up, tying them to the beams in the room. He stripped them naked, gagged them, and slowly, agonisingly slowly, began to peel the skin from their bodies with a sharp knife, like peeling the skin from a grape."

My lunch churned in my stomach as I took another drag of my cigarette, sickened by the story, the way Alfie had told it, and the ashy taste of smoke in my mouth. I brushed the hair back from my face and struggled to find a response.

But Alfie laughed. "Sorry, love. I forget that not everyone is as morbid as I am."

"No, it's okay. It was interesting."

"There's a whole lot of interesting in these walls," he said with a wink. "Trust me."

CHAPTER
6

I fell into a routine more quickly than I imagined I would. Even the craggy moors and shadowed forests felt like home after a few journeys to and from Crowmont Hospital. Tom carried on at school, walking the thirty minutes from the bus stop every day without a single complaint. The exercise would at least do him some good. After work I sat out on the lawn chair and watched the bats. At the weekend I battled with the ant problem in our kitchen, putting down poison for them and staying up to make sure they didn't escape.

On Sunday, when I was clearing away empty cardboard boxes, I found the magpie illustration from Isabel. Pepsi stared at me with black beady eyes, and it felt as though the bird was in the room with me, waiting, watching. I snatched the paper and considered throwing it into the bin, but instead I tucked it into a desk drawer and left it there.

We lived on threadbare carpets, with curtains that needed a good wash and chairs that creaked when you sat on them. We were more

SARAH A. DENZIL

solitary than we should've been. Tom always disappeared into his room in the evening, playing his loud bands, tapping out essays on the ancient laptop we couldn't afford to replace. I was painfully aware of the other teenagers on their iPads, Surfaces and Mac laptops, top of the range and brand new. But my Tom would be studying for his A-levels on a laptop that took five minutes to boot, with a webcam that hadn't worked for years.

But we were together, and that was what mattered. At least, I told myself that as I sipped wine and listened to the pigs grunting in the nearby fields.

We never talked about our parents. Sometimes I wanted to, but my own fears held me back.

Our parents were the reason we'd moved to Hutton. Tom and I had been living with them at the time; in fact, we'd lived with them most of our lives, as children tend to do. I'd even moved back after a disastrous three-year relationship with a man who made a full-time job out of finding ways to avoid an actual job. The day it happened was a day I would never forget. It was the reason I sat and watched the bats swooping through the air, sipping on wine, letting my eyes droop every night. It was the reason I woke in the morning, bleary-eyed, with a stomach churning with anxiety. It was the reason I continued to drive to work with my pulse too quick, the wine from the night before sour on my tongue.

Perhaps it was the reason I was so anxious on my first day at Crowmont. Perhaps what happened to my parents was the reason for everything that happened to me after moving to Hutton. But all I could focus on at that time was the fact that my parents were dead and I needed to look after my little brother.

At least the job seemed to be going well. Tracy took a few days to warm up to me, but before long I was supervising her as she assisted the kitchen staff, and chatting to her and Emily in the communal

44

area. Isabel was much quieter, requiring me to go to her room most days. We mostly talked about birds as we walked together to her art therapy sessions. She would tell me all about the omens different birds brought.

On Monday, she handed me a pencil sketch of a white dove.

"Purity," she said. "Innocence."

"Doves are beautiful, aren't they?" I replied. "Thank you for this."

"I saw a dove once. Dad took me to a rich girl's birthday party once. They had a magician there performing all kinds of card tricks. But he had this one trick where she had to go up and open a box. It was empty. Then, a few seconds later, he told her to open the box again, but this time a white bird came out and flew up into the sky. Everyone was clapping and cheering as the dove flew away, but all I could think about was that bird stuck in a box, waiting for it to be opened. How long had the bird been in there, waiting?"

"Did you think it was cruel for the bird to be stuck in the box?" I asked.

"Of course. Who wouldn't?" she replied.

She seemed agitated as I took her to her art therapy lesson, and I couldn't help wondering if something was bothering her today. It was later in the afternoon when I realised what it was. She had a visitor, her brother Owen. Chi told me as I ate my sandwich at lunchtime.

"You don't need to do much," he said. "Just hang back and make sure neither of them exchange anything. All gifts go through security, but Owen knows that. They can hug but not for too long."

"How long is too long?" I asked.

"Until you start to feel uncomfortable," Chi said with a smile.

The visitor's area was a glass-panelled room with tables and chairs set out in rows. The chairs were fabric armchairs, not the rigid school chairs you see in TV dramas set in prisons. I walked Isabel to the room, noting the way she fumbled with the sleeve of her hoody, visibly nervous about the visit. Her face was paler than usual, but she had made more of an effort, washing and drying her hair, and wearing a blue-coloured top that suited her much better than the grey outfits she usually wore.

"Since he turned eighteen he's come every week," she said. "But Mum and Dad stopped coming a long while ago."

I didn't reply. It wasn't my place to comment on her family dynamic. If we'd had more time I might have asked her if that was upsetting, or if she was okay with it, but we were close to the room, and, anyway, I wasn't her psychologist.

There were a few visitors in the room that day, but Owen sat closest to the door, with shirt sleeves rolled up, and his elbows on his knees. The fact that he was one year older than Tom gave me a jolt when I saw him. He was a boy, and I hadn't prepared myself for that. Isabel was three years older than the boy sitting on a green fabric armchair in a high-security hospital, and Maisie Earnshaw had been six years old when she was murdered.

To my surprise, Owen stood and shook my hand.

"You must be Leah," he said.

I was taken aback, but I smiled and said, "It's nice to meet you, Owen."

"If you're confused, Isabel and I talk on the phone every Thursday. She mentioned that she had a new nurse."

"Oh," I said. "Well, I hope Isabel has told you nice things."

"Of course," Isabel said. "She's my dove. And for you, little brother, a magpie." Isabel handed him the black and white watercolour.

"Unpredictable and deceitful. Are you trying to tell me something, big sis?"

"They're survivors," Isabel said. "Just like you."

I took Chi's advice and stayed at the back of the room during the visit, watching as Isabel leaned towards her brother, talking quietly.

I'd witnessed a few visitations at Whitmore, and they were usually either uninteresting or heart-breaking. The family visitations were the worst, when you saw young children acclimatised to visiting high-security buildings, whether in a hospital or a prison. Some patients often flit between the two, staying in the hospital for a few years, then going into prison for a while, and coming back when they decided to hurt themselves in prison. On and on went the cycle, and all the while their sons and daughters were growing up around it all.

But I tried not to judge. I tried.

As I leaned against the wall, I heard very little of their conversation. Isabel asked about their parents and Owen answered but changed the subject quickly. He told her about his nights out, about drinking too much and suffering hangovers. He was rarely animated or showed much emotion, whereas Isabel was the one leaning in, touching him on the arm or hand, smiling warmly. Owen almost seemed disinterested.

For a brief moment I closed my eyes, and a headline popped into my head: *Child Killer Covered in Blood as Young Brother Watched.* What must Owen have been through that day? Had he forgiven his sister? Why did he visit her? Out of duty, or another reason? I closed my mind to the thoughts rattling through it. It wouldn't do anyone any good to dwell on them. But I was sure I wasn't the first of Isabel's nurses to think the very same thing.

At the end of the day, it wasn't my business. I was there to monitor, nothing else.

As the visit was wrapping up, I gave the security guard Isabel's watercolour of the magpie so that he could return it to Owen after it had been checked. There's not much you can hide in a piece of paper with a bird painted on it, but Chi had told me to put it through security, and I knew how important these rules were. As he was leaving, Owen gave Isabel a brief hug before saying goodbye to me and walking out. He had a stiff gait with a straight back, not at all like the slouching way Tom walked around. Owen was the antithesis of Tom: tall, slim, handsome, and confident. All the things I would wish for my little brother. But I would not have Tom change places with Owen Fielding, not for anything.

After the visit I ducked outside for a quick cigarette break, only to be joined by Alfie again. He leaned casually against the bricks with one foot on the wall, smoking his cigarette with his hand cupped, as though ready to hide his habit should he need to. I'd noticed many men over the age of fifty smoking in the same way, influenced by the way James Dean and Marlon Brando would sneak a cigarette around the disapproving older generation in their coming-of-age films. Alfie had that air to him, as though he was from a different time. I was beginning to find his presence a comfort, even though his stories about Crowmont left me reeling.

"Here's another one—the Monster of York. Ever heard of him?"

I shook my head.

"It was 1892 when it started. There was a workhouse in York full of little orphan kids with no home or money, living hand to hand and plate to plate. No one noticed when they started to go missing, but one day, a little boy from a wealthy family was taken and the police started a search. What they found was a foot. And later on, they found a finger. Then they started finding more body parts, all of them small, all of them from children. All of them from *different* children."

I felt a tingle of nerves work its way down my arms, anticipating the horror that would unfurl during the story. I sucked on my cigarette to calm myself, wondering whether to ask him to stop telling me these tales of murder. Then I realised I didn't want to tell him to stop. I wanted to know more.

"It was a butcher's son," Alfie continued. "Twenty, he was. The boy wasn't of sound mind, but his father had always thought he was a gentle simpleton. I guess you could say he was the village idiot in them days—not PC to say it now, though, is it? The police found him leaning over a teddy bear he'd taken from one of the children, whispering how God had made him do it. The children were unworthy and had to be a sacrifice. Unworthy children, can you imagine?"

I shook my head, shivering, skin prickling.

"What I want to know is: Who was God in this sorry tale? That boy had a father, right? What if God wasn't God, what if it was his father?" Alfie grinned.

I'd had enough for the day. I ground my cigarette into the wall and went back to work.

TRUE CRIME JUNKIE

Who is Owen Fielding?
by James Gorden

A few weeks ago I wrote a blog post about Isabel Fielding and whether she really did murder Maisie Earnshaw. It got more hits than all of my other posts put together. Some of you even left some insightful comments. Some of you left some frankly disturbing comments, but let's pretend that didn't happen, shall we? I know I will.

Owen Fielding is now eighteen years old and still lives with his parents. He is studying his A-levels at Sheffield College, apparently. According to my sources he's studying business studies, maths, and French. Sounds like he's being prepped to take over Daddy's business.

Now, in my last blog post I mentioned that Owen Fielding was a gifted young lad who stood out among his peers. Well, these days I have a secret source, someone close to Owen who shall remain nameless. This person tells me that Owen isn't acing his A-levels. Not even close. He's getting Cs and Ds. That's not what we expect from a child genius, is it? Could it be the trauma of watching his sister kill a kid without even shouting out for help? Or could it be another reason? Maybe Owen doesn't want to be the best in the school anymore. Maybe he wants to be middle-of-the-road like his darling sister. One thing we do know is that Owen visits Isabel in Crowmont Hospital regularly. Isn't that an odd thing to do? She is a convicted murderer, after all.

Either Owen is a pretty forgiving fella, or he doesn't care about what Isabel did when she was fourteen. Perhaps he's a young lad falling apart at the seams, going out drinking instead of studying, self-medicating his guilt away. Perhaps there's something more to all this. Perhaps he idolises his sister for what she did. Perhaps... Perhaps...

COMMENTS:

TrueCrimeLover: You're bang on, James. Owen is suspicious AF. Why didn't he scream? Why didn't he stop his sister? Why was there blood on his clothes? He's not the innocent little kid people think he is.

OhioMom: James Gorden you should be ashamed. Leave the boy alone.

James Gorden: What do you even care? This didn't happen in America. It happened here.

OhioMom: We heard about the case here too. It's horrible what you're doing.

James Gorden: What? Trying to uncover the truth?

RedRose: It's a conspiracy. All the adults were in on it. Don't you know about the paedophile ring the Fieldings were running? Check the missing person's reports. They have a satanic basement for ritual killings, I guarantee it. The Fieldings were playing a sick game getting the children to commit murder. They framed their own kids!!

CHAPTER
7

Outside of work, my focus was on the new house. At the weekend, Tom and I went into Hutton and bought a couple of cans of white paint. We painted over some of the dark mould that had crept around the windows in my room. We bought a cheap clothes rail and hung our belongings on it, pretending we were cool and arty, not poor. It was Scandi-chic and minimalist, not because we couldn't afford wardrobes. I made batches of chili con carne to heat up in the week, and a large pasta bake to get us through to Monday. We weeded some of the garden, and I untangled the lawn chair from the weeds so I could move it around at night. I stocked up on tins in the kitchen and bought a cheap box of wine for the week.

We were almost out of the meagre amount of money our parents had left us. But I had a couple of weeks until my first month's pay at Crowmont, and I knew we could make it last as long as we were sensible.

Tom only ever asked me about work when I asked him about

school. I think it was to prove a point. He was as terse as ever when it came to opening up about school, and I wasn't much better about my job. I would often come home exhausted, especially if I'd been asked to help with a difficult patient. There were times when I was needed to help restrain someone, and that was never easy.

My little brother was withdrawn and quiet, even more than usual. Weekday evenings were mostly spent apart, with him disappearing into his room, and me occasionally attempting to bribe him with cups of tea to get him to let me in. Every now and then he did, and I sat on the edge of his bed with my tea, dunking a chocolate digestive into the light brown liquid as I watched him play some online game about orcs and elves.

I'd been a teenager once, not all that long ago, and yet I failed to find the words to reach him. At least during the weekends he was more open. We painted the walls together, we weeded together, we walked the farm fields together, and went to the Braithwaite's farm-shop to buy fresh eggs and milk. All the time I found myself growing accustomed to this new rural life. There was air here, and it fed the soul. There was space, an abundance of space, that made me feel insignificant, and yet larger somehow. Even after a mere few weeks I felt more strength in my arms and legs than I had for a while. All the weeding, walking, and painting had paid off, and I was leaner and happier than I had been for a while.

But there was an itch deep down that I couldn't scratch with long walks in the countryside, or fresh air, or time with my little brother. It festered deep within my intestines, like a tapeworm, nibbling at my insides. I wanted to scratch it so bad, and I had hoped with all my heart that this change of location would have dealt with this pesky sense of unease. But the feeling persisted, despite my attempts to ignore it.

The temperature dropped again that weekend, and the heating in the house gave up. While we were waiting for one of the Braithwaites to come and fix the problem, we had a couple of cold nights in the cottage. I wore long johns and long-sleeved t-shirts to bed, but I found myself awake at night, listening to the owls. Later in the night, the owl calls gave out to the slow patter of rain on the window, leaving tracks down the dirty pane of glass. I turned on my lamp and watched the tracks as they travelled down the panelled windows. As I watched, my eyes began to droop, and I thought for a moment that the rain was running up the window instead of down. I blinked, and it went away.

And then I fell asleep.

I woke up to Tom placing a mug next to my head.

"You're going to be late," he remarked.

When I opened my eyes, I realised I wasn't in my bedroom because the sunlight was coming from the wrong direction. My face was resting on a hard surface—the kitchen table—which I was slumped over as though I'd passed out. My laptop was a few inches away from my head, still open but now sleeping. I lifted my body and wiggled my finger across the mousepad to wake it and check the time. It was almost seven.

"How did I end up down here?" I mumbled, my mouth dry and my jaw stiff from the long sleep on such a hard surface.

"God knows. Were you drinking wine again?"

I didn't remember drinking any wine.

"What were you researching? The Monster of York? Sounds, well, creepy."

I barely glanced at the screen before closing down the laptop and getting to my feet. "I need to shower."

"Take your tea," Tom called after me.

I spun back and picked it up.

On the way to Crowmont I couldn't stop thinking about my strange night-time behaviour. This was the second time I'd woken up on the kitchen table instead of where I'd drifted to sleep. Was there something wrong with me? Why would I start sleepwalking now of all times?

I remained distracted as Ian let me through the gates and into the compound of the hospital. I parked up, grabbed my pass, and let myself into Morton Ward. With my phone and other items dumped into my locker, I started my shift.

There was group therapy on throughout the day, so I ended up spending a lot of time watching Isabel as she worked on her art in her room. We'd talked a little over the last week, mainly about Pepsi and how he was learning to "talk" on command, and how she could call his name from the door leading into the garden and he'd swoop over to find her shoulder. We'd talked a little about how her visits from her brother brightened her week, but we'd not mentioned her parents. Today we discussed her art therapy sessions and about the other patients. I had a headache, and I was quieter than usual, which Isabel noticed immediately.

"You didn't sleep," she said. I found it odd that she came out with a statement rather than a question. Most people would ask if I hadn't slept, but not Isabel. She knew. She paused, looked up from her art, and smiled. "Don't look so surprised. Of all the people you know in this world, am I not the most likely to have sleepless nights?"

It was the first time she'd referenced her crime, however abstractly, since we'd walked in the garden and she'd showed me Pepsi for the first time.

"Is there something wrong?" she asked.

"No, not at all. I'm adjusting to a new place and a new house, that's all it is." I ignored the persistent itch that said otherwise.

"Your eyes can't stay still," she remarked. "It's very peculiar."

I hadn't realised I was letting my gaze roam around the room. Perhaps it was because my mind felt fractured, or maybe I was drawn to the vibrant colours. "Your art can be quite distracting sometimes."

"I find it distracting," she said. "It's a distraction from being in here. Give me another distraction. Tell me about your new house."

"Well," I said, proceeding with caution. "It's an old cottage that needs a bit of love and care. We… I recently repainted some of the rooms to get rid of the mould—"

"We? You live with a boyfriend?"

"No."

Isabel placed her pencil down on the desk and straightened her spine. "You have a housemate?"

"Yes."

There was a moment of silence as the lie hung in the air. Isabel's gaze never moved from mine. Could she tell that I was lying? Was she sitting there wondering why I was lying to her? I couldn't be sure, but she seemed to let the subject drop.

"Do you have a garden?"

"Yes, but it's very overgrown with weeds. I've been weeding it recently, trying to get it in order, but the grass is very high and there's a feral cat living in the bush—"

Her eyes lit up. "A cat, how exciting! I asked Chi for a kitten once, but he said no. In fact, I think he said 'Hell, no!'" She pouted in a comical fashion before picking up her pencil. "What have you called the cat?"

"Nothing yet. He's wild, so…"

"Call him…" She lifted her chin as though contemplating names. "Pye. P-Y-E."

"Where did you come up with that?"

"It's another name for a magpie. That way we both have a pet magpie."

"All right then, the feral cat shall now be known as Pye."

She nodded and returned to her work. "And there you are, living in your cottage with your housemate and Pye the cat. What could be more wonderful?"

I nodded in agreement, feeling much better, with my headache finally beginning to fade.

But then I heard her say, "And here I am trapped like a bug under a jam jar, a human being treated like an animal in the zoo, dosed up on drugs and isolated from the world. They should kill me. They should put me out of my misery."

"Isabel, don't say that!"

Her head jerked up. "Say what? That your life is wonderful? I think it is."

"No, the rest of what you said … about being an animal in the zoo."

She frowned at me, confused. "I never said anything like that. I was drawing this jackdaw, see?" She held up the illustration for me to look at.

My headache returned almost instantaneously. I could have sworn I'd heard her speak, but it hadn't sounded exactly like her—the voice had been raspier, harsher. I rubbed the back of my neck and tried to make sense of it. She had said it, I was sure. Why would I imagine such a thing? I needed to keep a closer eye on Isabel. She wasn't as stable as she'd first seemed.

CHAPTER
8

What goes into making a sociopath? Was the Monster of York born that way, or was he created? And if he actually believed his delusions, at what point did his mind break? I'm no psychologist, but I've been around many. Work Christmas parties are pretty interesting when you're sitting around a table with a bunch of psychologists talking shop. The human mind is fragile, built upon tiny impulses of electricity sending signals to the rest of the body. Our thoughts, our feelings, our language, it all comes from the brain, so when one of those little electric impulses goes haywire, we follow suit.

But that's the point where you need to be a psychologist to understand it all. Studying to be a nurse hadn't equipped me for understanding every part of the human mind, especially not fully understanding a sociopath. Yet, even though I knew I couldn't comprehend every part of this complex phenomenon, I couldn't stop thinking about what it took to break a mind.

The next day I encouraged Isabel to spend more time outside her room, deciding to use the same tricks I used to try on Tom before he got bored of it. I convinced her that there was more to drawing than just birds. That she should try drawing people.

"In that case, I'll draw you," she announced.

It was agreed that I would be brought out into the communal area and placed on a stool next to an open window. The April sunlight warmed my skin as I sat there, self-conscious and on display, but at least Isabel was out of her room and around others.

It was the first time I'd seen the way other patients reacted to Isabel's presence. Of course, the vast majority were aware of the crime Isabel had been convicted of, and child murderers were viewed with contempt and suspicion. The room carried on around us—Emily and Debbie played draughts, Tracy spread out across the sofa watching one of her soaps, some of the others sipped tea and coffee, pretending to have a conversation—but all the while they kept one eye on Isabel. A couple of the less aware simply sat and gawked at her. One of the tougher girls said, loud enough to hear: "The child killer's out."

I immediately felt ashamed for forcing Isabel to come into the communal room, but she somehow managed to block out everything around her, slowly placing her pencils down on the table in front of her, and spreading out a large sheet of paper. She began to work, moving methodically, barely speaking, except to tell me to keep still, or to ask me to lift my chin, uncross my legs, stare out of the window. I felt like an exhibit at the zoo, sitting there with so many eyes watching me. In a way, it bonded us, going through the same experience, each being stared at as though we were in a fish tank.

A few of the other nurses broke the tension by coming over and making conversation, asking Isabel about her drawing, and praising the likeness. Most of the nurses were shy of Isabel, aware of her past and unwilling to get too close to her. They treated me in a similar manner in the break room, never asking me direct questions about Isabel, skirting around the Isabel-shaped elephant in the room. Some even considered me with some sort of awe, telling me over and over again that they couldn't do my particular job. They avoided Isabel because they didn't feel they could be around her. One even said the words "as a mother," as if those without children might find the crime less abhorrent.

After what felt like hours, Isabel finally allowed me to see the finished piece.

"Wait, stay there," she said, as I was about to get up and go to her. "I want you to see it in the sunshine."

Isabel lifted her drawing and walked across to me, staring all the while at the paper between her fingers. She hesitated before handing it to me.

"It's still a little rough," she said. "I might work on it some more later."

"I'm sure it's wonderful." I held out my hands to receive the drawing, my insides twisting with nerves and butterflies fluttering in my stomach. A convicted murder was offering me a portrait of myself. Sometimes my job was bizarre.

I gently lifted the paper from her hands, forcing myself to remember that I was a nurse, and this was helping Isabel improve as a patient. I smiled at her before daring to view the drawing.

The surprise, no doubt, registered on my face. She hadn't drawn a true likeness of me seated on the stool; instead she had drawn me out in a flourishing garden, standing and looking up at a sky filled with sunshine. All around me there were small garden birds, sparrows and tits and robins, all fluttering their wings, some on my shoulder or my outstretched hand. In Isabel's eyes I was some sort of Disney princess, an ethereal member of the animal kingdom.

"Well, do you like it?" she asked.

A few of the other patients began to crowd around the chair where Isabel sat. Some leaned closer in to get a peek of the portrait. Others merely glanced in our direction.

Emily was one of the first to get a good look. "It looks like you," she remarked. "Got your hair just right."

I lifted my hand to my face, feeling the tight bun at the back of my head and the fringe across my forehead.

"Yes, you have captured me, I think," I said. And I wasn't lying, because although the experience of looking at myself on paper was odd, almost disconcerting, I felt as though Isabel had captured some sort of essence of me. No, I don't think I'm a Disney princess, but what she'd drawn had my features, had the way I believed I looked in the mirror, and felt very true to the way I thought of myself.

"But do you like it?" she asked.

"I like it very much," I said. "It's a beautiful drawing." I went to hand it back to Isabel, but she refused to take it from me.

"It's yours," she said. "Hang it on the wall of your crumbling cottage that needs cheering up. I can't stand white walls, and I can't stand the thought of you staring at white walls. You need colour, Leah. A lovely nurse like you should always be in colour."

I looked down at my black blouse in dismay. Perhaps she was right.

After assessing my lack of fashion sense, I attempted to give her the drawing. "No, take it. You're going to need your best work to enter when I put you up for the Koestler Award."

The Koestler Award is run by the Koestler Trust, set up for prison and high-security hospital inmates. Any incarcerated person can enter with their original art, and cash prizes are awarded to some of the participants. I'd helped a few patients apply in the past, most notably an ex-gang member who loved to paint delicate portraits of Disney princesses lost within long stretches of enchanted forests. He would stand proudly behind his portraits of dainty Cinderellas and

SARAH A. DENZIL

Snow Whites, with his pot belly poking the back of the canvas, his large sausage-like fingers gripping the borders of the painting, and his shaved head bent solemnly over his work. I thought Isabel could benefit from the potential art sales that often came with entering the award. It was a good way for people who were incarcerated to earn some honest money.

Isabel's eyes widened. She pulled her knees up onto the chair seat. "No."

For once, Isabel stopped smiling. She gripped her knees tightly, slumping down into the chair and withdrawing into the folds of her top.

"But…" My mouth gaped open in surprise. "I thought you would be pleased."

Sensing the change in tone, some of the others slipped away, giving us room. Isabel shook her head before staring out the window into the garden.

"I don't want people to see them."

"But it's a great way to earn some income. People buy pieces. It's a good, honest way to make money while you're here at Crowmont." I placed the drawing down on the table between us.

"I don't want people to know I've drawn them. I don't want sickos collecting my art because…" She angled her chin down and her voice fell to a whisper. "Because of what happened."

"Isabel, it's all right. It's all anonymous. People don't know whose work they're purchasing. All they know is that it's someone from a high-security hospital or a prison."

"Really?" she asked.

"Yes, so keep hold of this so you can apply."

I had to admit that watching Isabel's face brighten made me smile, and I was smiling for the rest of the day, even as I walked a tearful Tracy back from her therapy session, and even as Pye the cat hissed and scratched my ankles as I walked back up the drive to the rundown cottage.

Isabel was right about the white walls of the cottage, and she was right about colour. The first thing I did when I got home was run upstairs, change out of that boring black shirt and put on a bright red t-shirt with yellow flowers on the sleeves. I even thought about applying lipstick, but was too hungry to wait for tea. My change of outfit earned the barest eyebrow rise from my little brother, but I didn't care because I felt brighter.

As I set the kitchen table for that night's feast of tuna pasta bake, I wondered if a sociopath could have the empathic abilities of an artist. Could someone truly capture a subject's inner beauty if they themselves were a true sociopath? Was Isabel even capable of murder?

TRUE CRIME JUNKIE

Who is David Fielding?
by James Gorden

Can we all agree on one thing? Yes, I know we'll get into it in the comments, insults will be thrown around and someone will ultimately be called Hitler, but let's pretend this isn't the internet and agree on one thing: The person who murdered Maisie Earnshaw is a deranged psychopath. But I'm not convinced that the right psychopath is currently behind bars, or in a straitjacket, or whatever happens within the walls of Crowmont Hospital.

So, let's take a moment and look into another potential suspect: Isabel's father, David Fielding. A self-made millionaire with a property business that erects tower blocks and apartments in Sheffield, Leeds, and the surrounding areas. He has his hands in many pies, from restaurants to private gyms, but it's his property business that he's most well-known for.

How did David become the richest man in Rotherham? Well, there's a good story involved, of course. I decided to contact David's old business partner and university housemate, Lee Brown. Both being northern lads, David and Lee hit it off at Leeds University, both studying business degrees. In their second year they moved into a shared house together and first started up the company Field-Brown (see what they did there?). Lee and David were best mates. They worked hard and played hard. They saved money to fund their business and even managed to snag some outside investment. They were motivated young men who were going places together.

But where is Lee Brown? And why is David Fielding's business now called Fielding Enterprises?

Let me tell you, it took a while to loosen Lee Brown's tongue. It certainly took more than a few Peronis when we met up in Leeds for a conversation. But once the sun went down, he began to spill the beans.

Lee told me that David was his best friend and the person he trusted most in the world. Lee thought they were brothers in business and in friendship, but it soon became clear David didn't feel the same way. There was a risky business venture the two of them decided to invest in. Lee tells me it was a mutual decision to invest, but David was the driving force behind the investment and the one who suggested it. Lee was busy with another project, but he signed everything David put in front of him, distracted and not particularly bothered about checking through the contracts.

"I trusted him completely," Lee said. "Why would I need to read through every insignificant piece of paperwork? I was an idiot, basically. The company was up and coming. They were building apartments in and around Leeds and wanted investors from the ground up. None of those apartments even got made. The housing market imploded, the company went bust, and that was the moment I realised David had put everything in my name, not the company's name, and not his own. He bankrupted me within months, cut me out of the business and carried on without me. I was so shocked and so hurt that I never even sued. I went home and I drank, and I never spoke to him again."

Lee has since picked himself up again and owns his own restaurant in Wakefield. I'm glad for him, but I wanted to know more about David.

"Do you think he's a sociopath?" I asked. We were into our fourth round by now, and I may have slurred a bit at this point, but don't worry, the recorder was on, everything was captured. I'm not pulling this from hazy drunken memories.

Lee ran a finger around the rim of his pint glass and stared down at the table. "I'm no psychologist, so I dunno what he is, but I do know he didn't care about me one iota. He's all for himself and always has been. I just didn't see it. I thought it was all bravado, you know? I thought he put on a show, but it was real."

"What was real?"

"The women," he went on, "the girls. He liked them a lot, and he was engaged at the time so it wasn't right. I thought it was all exaggeration, but now I'm not sure. I think he was sticking it in whatever he could find."

"Can I quote you on that?"

Lee looked up at me sharply. "I dunno, mate. Maybe I should go."

I tried to persuade Lee to have another drink. I offered him a bourbon, and he agreed to stay for a while, but he barely spoke any more about David Fielding. Then, when he left, he didn't let me walk him to the door. That was the moment when I realised Lee Brown was afraid of his own business partner.

He left me at the bar with half a glass of bourbon left, thinking about David Fielding and his past antics. Were they the antics of an arrogant young man believing the world was at his feet and all he had to do was take it? Had he subscribed to the method of business that involves survival at any cost?

Or was his ruthlessness in business indicative of a deeper flaw, one that went past the womanising and the screwing over of his friends, and cut down deep to a rotten core?

Was David a sociopath?

And if he was, did he have the opportunity to murder Maisie Earnshaw and frame his own daughter in the process?

COMMENTS:

REDROSE: How can we believe anything the adults say? They could all be lying. Even the Earnshaws.

JAMES GORDEN: Why would the Earnshaws be lying?

REDROSE: Because they're sick fucks.

IHEARTHANNIBAL: RedRose, you're the sick fuck.

TRUECRIMELOVER: David went into the kitchen for twenty minutes, right? Is that long enough to kill a little girl? According to the police reports and the building plan, he could've gone out the front door, round the front of the house and down the hill.

JAMES GORDEN: I think so too. Time is tight, though.

TRUECRIMELOVER: He's a fit man though, right? Used to run the Great North Run. Don't see why he couldn't sprint there and back, wash his bloody hands in the sink and serve up a mojito.

JAMES GORDEN: But why wouldn't Isabel say something about her dad?

TRUECRIMELOVER: She's too afraid. She's safe inside Crowmont. If she ever got out, she could be his next victim.

JAMES GORDEN: Which begs the question, if David Fielding did it, why aren't there any more victims?

CHAPTER
9

I mentioned to Isabel one day that I woke to the sound of blackbirds outside my bedroom every morning, and the next day she told me she was going to draw me a picture of them singing to me. She got me to sit just outside her room and give her extra details so she could picture the image in her mind.

"Describe your cottage to me," she said.

"It's an old farm outbuilding, very small, red brick, old," I replied. It suited me to sit outside the room, because I liked to give her space. The tiny room felt claustrophobic enough without my presence in there as well. "Probably once a house for a gamekeeper or tenant farmer, I guess." I shrugged, not exactly an expert on rural matters.

"Is it next to other houses?"

"No, it's on its own, surrounded by fields."

She bent over her notepad and went to work. Her brother Owen had brought her some new art supplies to use during his last visit.

Isabel had been through a rough patch, so I was spending a little more time with her than usual. After her few hours in the communal area with the other patients, her presence had whipped everyone into frenetic excitement, and Isabel found herself targeted by bullies. I hadn't realised, but Chi had previously been through a similar situation after encouraging Isabel to socialise more. Isabel was more than willing to leave her room, but the other patients were never happy to see her. Since she had drawn me in the communal area, the patients had been whispering behind her back, talking about the fact she'd been there with them. They wrote unpleasant messages and slipped them under her door. There was an incident where an egg was thrown into her room, ruining some of her favourite artworks.

I'd come to work to find Isabel even quieter than usual. She'd handed me her morning picture, which had been a pigeon that day.

"They're gossips," she'd said, about the pigeon. "Mean little gossips." Then she turned her head away so that I wouldn't see the red around her eyes.

"Have you been crying, Isabel?" I'd asked.

"At least it got Katy moved back to Grafton Ward." She'd tugged at her sleeve as though hiding her hands from me.

"What is it? Did someone hurt you?"

It took a while, but I'd finally managed to get her to tell me about how Katy, one of the older and larger patients, in Crowmont for violence against others as well as learning difficulties, had grabbed her by the wrists, spat in her face, and called her a kiddie killer.

Because it'd been my idea for Isabel to socialise, I couldn't help but feel responsible for everything that had happened since then. Perhaps it was my guilt that caused me to relax a little and reveal more about myself than I usually would.

"So you live on a farm?" she asked. "With your housemate?"

"On the edge of a farm. It's a rental."

"Sounds lovely." Isabel bent her head and continued on with her drawing.

The corridor was quiet today, as the sun was shining and most of the patients were by the windows that looked out into the gardens. Watching Isabel work in the silence that followed her questions put me into something of a trance, and the last fortnight of interrupted sleep began to catch up with me as I felt my eyelids droop. I inhaled sharply through my nose, forcing myself to stay awake. Despite the welcome warmth and the fact that I was tired, I still had a job to do. I still had to supervise my patient.

When I forced myself awake, I took in the sight of Isabel bent over her desk. Warm brown hair spilled over her notepad. She was dressed in her usual jogging bottoms and sweatshirt. Blue today. All of the patients wore the same comfortable clothing. There were strict rules about what could be worn. Nothing that could be used as a weapon. No belts. No drawstrings. Even buttons could cause some damage.

"You know, I still can't remember the day Maisie died," Isabel said, her voice far away and dreamy. "But I meant what I said the first day I met you. I didn't kill that little girl. I don't think I could. I don't have it in me."

"If you can't remember," I replied gently, "how do you know?"

But Isabel didn't reply. She sighed heavily and slumped closer to the desk instead. She sounded exhausted.

As I sat and studied my patient, I noticed a couple of woodlice crawling around the carpet towards her feet. I wasn't sure if Isabel was afraid of bugs, so I didn't want to frighten her.

I rose slowly from my char. "Isabel, I don't want to alarm you, but there are two large woodlice crawling towards you."

She lifted her head and regarded me with interest before dropping her gaze to the carpet. Then she lifted her head and looked at me again. There was a brief pause as she glanced from me to the woodlice and back to me again. "It's okay, Leah. I get woodlice in my room every so often, but I leave them be. I can't bring myself to kill them."

"What about putting them outside?"

But she shook her head. "My room is plenty big enough for a few bugs." She grinned, and every part of that smile seemed genuine to me. Her eyes slightly crinkled. Her slightly crooked teeth were charming between her soft lips. She was pure, childlike innocence.

Let me tell you a secret. I never killed that little girl. Shhhhh.

That moment remained as clear as the sound of a bell in my mind, but I'd always assumed that her words were Isabel's way of playing with me. Because she said them on my first day, I'd presumed she was testing me, like a person with sociopathic tendencies would. But Isabel didn't display *any* sociopathic traits. She wasn't narcissistic. She didn't talk about herself or her crimes. She wasn't violent. She was often nervous or insecure about her art, and she didn't have the superficial charm most sociopaths used to their own advantage.

And then I realised that I believed her. It hit me hard, sending shockwaves down my limbs and spine. My back shot up straight in my chair, and my jaw dropped. My heart beat a little faster, and I sat there wondering what I was going to do about the girl in front of me, quietly drawing my home, young and vulnerable and locked away from society. In little over a month, she was about to be reassessed, and in that assessment, she would be found fit to go into prison rather than stay in Crowmont. I knew she would. Isabel was the patient with the best track record, who built a rapport with staff members and remained polite, mild-mannered, and obedient at all times.

But even worse...

"The killer is still out there."

Isabel sat up and turned to me, tucking a strand of hair behind her ear. "What? Did you say something?"

I'd spoken out loud without even meaning to. I wiped my

forehead with the back of my hand and shook my head. "I was just mumbling to myself about tonight's tea."

She nodded. "You know, I find it kind of fascinating listening to people talk about their boring chores. Alesha used to tell me about how she had to pick up her kids from school, then go food shopping, then take them home and cook for her husband every night. He worked later, so she took on more of the duties at home. I don't suppose I'll ever have a husband to cook for."

"You don't know that," I replied. "You might leave one day."

"And go to prison," she said. "Big-girl prison this time, filled with women, not the kids I was with in the juvenile detention centre."

"But you could still be released from prison one day. Can't you?"

"Yes," she said. "But not for a long time. Not that it matters. Here, I've finished your picture. Do you like it?"

She held up the pencil drawing so that I could see it. There I was, standing in front of my panelled windows watching the blackbirds cluster around. One sat on the windowsill, another hovered in the air. Three were perched on the branch of a nearby tree. They all had their beaks open, releasing song into the air. I looked at her picture, and I could hear the sound of birdsong, calling to me, speaking to me.

"Blackbirds are good omens," Isabel said. "They represent shyness or insecurity. The colour black is supposed to represent the supernatural. Do you believe in the supernatural?"

Her words brought back a recent memory that I had been trying hard to shut away. At first I wanted to ignore it, but then I decided not to do that.

"At my parents' funeral I felt a strong presence."

Isabel placed the drawing back down on her desk. "I'm so sorry. When did it happen?"

"Six months ago. They... it isn't a happy story. My father was an alcoholic, and he killed my mum before killing himself. That's why we moved to Hutton. I was working in a different high-security hospital at the time, and I knew there was one here. I figured I'd be able to get a job here, so we moved." It was only after I stopped talking that I realised I was gripping the sleeves of my blouse and pulling them down as though trying to hide my hands beneath the fabric.

"You felt the presence of your parents at their funeral?"

"Just my father," I said.

"I'm so sorry," she replied.

I smiled slightly. That was a phrase I had grown accustomed to when I was still back in Hackney. The parents of the children at school with Tom said it frequently when I went to collect him from school. My neighbours called round with casseroles and a weak smile, the same words on their lips. Everyone liked my father. They couldn't believe what he'd done. But the person behind closed doors is not always the person out in the world.

"So who did you move here with?"

The words pulled me from my thoughts and thrust me back into the corridor at Crowmont.

"What?"

"You said 'we moved here.' Who did you move with? A boyfriend?"

I was still distracted by thoughts of my father on that rain-soaked afternoon in the cemetery when I'd heard his voice call my name. Wet dirt landing on wood. The musty smell of my one good black dress that I'd pulled out from the attic storage. My mother's perfume sprayed on my wrists.

"With my brother," I replied. "Tom. My little brother."

CHAPTER
10

When I left work that day I felt ashamed of myself for the way I'd opened up to Isabel. After working as a nurse for several years, it was disappointing to see how easily my guard could come crumbling down. In any other hospital, telling a patient about your private life is no big deal, but in a high-security hospital with patients suffering from illnesses such as antisocial personality disorder, those private details could be used against you.

But at the same time, I felt deeply connected to Isabel after our long conversation. I couldn't deny that each day Isabel became more to me than a disturbed patient with a terrible crime in her past; she was a talented artist who could be sweet and considerate. Her morning drawings were often the highlight of my day, and the way we talked, you would think we were friends, or niece and aunt, or sisters. With the date of her reassessment looming over me, I felt sick at the thought of her being transferred to a maximum security prison.

No, I told myself, I was experiencing dangerous thoughts. I unlocked my Punto and speedily reversed out of the parking space, barely noticing Ian as he waved goodbye to me through the gates. I was too close to Isabel now. I'd already begun down a perilous road of believing she might be innocent. In fact, I was sure of it. There was no part of the girl sitting in her room looking at me with wide, childlike eyes that married with the thought of a murderous teenager bludgeoning a child to death before mutilating her corpse and smearing the blood across her mouth like lipstick.

The two together did not make sense.

I cooked for Tom that night, and in my distracted state I let the potatoes boil over and burned the chicken. Tom was far too polite to say anything, but I could tell by the way he chewed and swallowed quickly that he wasn't impressed.

"How's school going?" I asked, hopeful of directing my thoughts away from Isabel.

"Fine."

"It's been a few weeks now. Are the other students okay?"

"Yeah."

"You've not shown me any essays for a while. Can I read some?"

"Maybe."

I was about to give up when I noticed Tom pull down the sleeve of his shirt for the third or fourth time. I'd seen that same movement when my patients were hiding a self-inflicted wound. I reached across the table, but he pulled his arm away from me.

"What are you doing?"

"I just want to look," I said. "Show me."

"No, leave it alone."

But before Tom could get up from the table I managed to get hold of his shirt and pull it back. Underneath his beaded bracelet there was a bruise about the size of a thumb.

"What's that? Has someone hurt you?"

"It's nothing," he said, snatching his arm away. "I banged it on the door, that's all." But I knew he was lying because of the way his eyes roamed all over the walls.

"Tom…" But I didn't know what to say. I felt rage bubbling up from my abdomen at the thought that someone would hurt my gentle brother, but at the same time I felt a deep sense of impotence, because even if I did try to step in, it could make things worse for him. When I'd first realised Tom was being bullied I'd researched as much as I could on the internet, and what I found from desperate parents' first accounts was that the school had done little to nothing, and the bullying had escalated after they'd intervened.

"There's nothing you can do," he snapped.

"I can listen!" I had to raise my voice as he stormed out of the kitchen, slamming the door behind him.

Throwing my fork down onto my plate, I stood, making the chair screech against the old kitchen tiles. As I began furiously scraping leftover burnt chicken into the kitchen bin, there was a knock at the door. I opened it, already knowing it would be Seb Braithwaite here to fix the sticky kitchen door. The handle required some yanking before it opened to reveal Seb standing there, his light blue eyes flicking from me to the half-cleared kitchen table.

"Bad time?" he asked.

"No, come in."

"Brought my tools." He lifted his toolbox as evidence. "Thought I'd take a look at the door for you."

"Thanks, I appreciate it."

His laconic nature was fine by me, and I set about tidying the kitchen, working quickly, still fuelled by my anger about Tom's bruise. Those uptight village kids needed to be taught a lesson. Elbow deep in washing-up suds, I resolved to speak to the school, and if necessary, the parents of the kids involved. Meddling caregiver be damned, I couldn't sit back and see my brother miserable at the end of every day.

"That'll do it." Seb stood up, his height almost blocking the doorway. His broad, farm-built shoulders filled the narrow space. He demonstrated the door, pushing it back and forth so I could see that there was no more sticking. It opened and closed perfectly.

"That was fast," I said. "I didn't even get to make you a cuppa."

"No worries," he said. "Need any milk and eggs?"

I checked the fridge. "A pint would be good, and maybe half a dozen."

He nodded. "I'll stop by in the morning."

"Thanks. How much do I owe you for the eggs from last week?"

"Nowt. They're on me."

I was so relieved that for one embarrassing moment I felt my chin wobble and a surge of emotion stung my eyes. The tear was swiftly wiped away with the back of my hand, and I cleared my throat.

"Thank you. I really appreciate it."

"No problem."

Just as he was about to duck through the door I caught him on the shoulder to stop him. The kitchen was tiny enough that I barely needed to reach out. He turned back slowly, with an impassive expression on his face. For a moment I wondered whether I'd annoyed him by stopping him from leaving, and considered abandoning the thought that had popped into my mind.

"Can I ask you something?" I said, tentatively, regretting the decision already.

He merely nodded.

I took a step closer, and he inched back away from me. "You can say no if you want. It's a big favour to ask and… well, you've done a lot for me already. But it's Tom. The kids at school are bullying him." I paused to glance over my shoulder, afraid he might have wandered into the room at the wrong moment. "At first I thought it was just name-calling and usual teenage crap, but now he has a bruise on his arm and I'm worried. Your family are respected in the village." It was more like an apprehensive fear, but I remained tactful. "Would you... Could you... maybe take him to school once or twice? It might act as a warning. Show the bastards that someone else is on his side."

Seb exhaled through his nose and half of his mouth lifted in a slight smile. "Sure. I'll pick him up tomorrow morning. Is that it?"

"That's everything, yes. Thank you so much."

As I watched him walk down the driveway, Pye leapt out from the hedgerow and Seb stumbled as he sidestepped out of the feral cat's way. I couldn't help but giggle as the burly farmer continued down the path to his Land Rover, swearing as he went. When he got in the cab, he turned to me and waved, and I saw that his face was red with embarrassment.

"He fancies you."

I spun on my heel, clutching at my chest. "Tom! I didn't hear you come down the stairs. What are you, a mouse?"

"Vole, actually. They're smaller than mice." He flicked on the switch to turn the kettle on. "He fancies you, though."

"Does not."

Tom raised his eyebrows. "Does too."

"I'm sorry about grabbing your arm like that."

He fiddled with the sleeves of his shirt. "It's okay. I'm sorry I didn't tell you."

I stepped across the room and pulled gently at a strand of Tom's dyed-black hair. "What can I do about it? Want me to go into school? Want me to beat them up? I can, you know. Hey, just tell them your big sis beats up serial killers for a living, that'll scare 'em."

"Nah," he said, staring intently at the kettle. "None of that works."

A tear dropped onto the kitchen counter, and as I watched another fall, I felt a tug come deep down in my stomach. He was in pain, and it ached to watch.

"Come on, kiddo." I pulled him into a hug and held him close, thinking about our parents' funeral, with the two graves and Tom's hand in mine. I thought about the moment I'd heard my father's voice, clear as day. I thought about the hole their deaths had created, even my father's, deep inside me, and the perpetual itch of grief.

Father. The word choked me.

There was a time when he had been a good dad to me, but those memories were fading, and now I couldn't remember him as anything but the bully he'd turned into.

I'd stopped thinking of him as a dad after what he did. Some fathers didn't deserve the title of 'dad,' and he was one of them. Yet everyone else had loved him so much. *That* was what got to me the most when I thought about him. They'd never seen him destructive and dangerous, with a belly full of Scotch and a self-loathing so deep it spilled into his fists. We were his property. What happens when property misbehaves? It gets hit. But never the face, because then our outward image of perfection would crack and everyone else would see.

The first thing Tom did after our father died was dye his hair black. I already knew he was sneaking Goth jewellery in his pockets to wear outside the house. He used to wear as much black clothing as he could get away with without Father making unpleasant comments. But if Tom dared to show any kind of "alternative" personality... *bam.* Hit. And the dress code hadn't stopped at Tom: My skirts were measured; my tops were shapeless and high-collared. No daughter of his would look like a slut.

His.

Property.

But here we stood. Together. Stronger. Alive. And there *he* was, in the ground gathering worms.

But Mum. Oh, I missed her. I missed the stories she told me at night when she tucked me in, and I missed the way she stroked back my hair as her eyes were tearing up. She cried a lot when she said good night to me—a whisper of a cry, with silent tears running down her face. I missed the sound of her voice, and the pretty dresses she wore around the house. I missed listening to her hum as she made apple crumble, and the bread she used to bake for us every weekend. I missed her so much that not even holding Tom tight could erase the hole her death had left when my father snapped and took her away from us.

After a mug of hot chocolate, Tom went to bed and I turned on my laptop, intending to do some more research into the bullying. But after reading the same stories over and over again, I decided to type another topic into the search engine: the murder of Maisie Earnshaw.

Of course I'd already done this once when I first started at Crowmont. But I'd stopped after reading the Wikipedia page, not wanting to go down that dark rabbit hole. This time I wanted to delve even further into the gory details.

There were BBC news articles about the case and the trial. There were *Guardian* articles criticising the press for the coverage of the case. Some thought the coverage had been racist because of Maisie's Indian ancestry. There were opinion pieces written about Isabel and what her punishment should be, ranging from hanging to rehabilitation.

And then I found other opinion pieces. These weren't news articles, they were blog posts about the murder and what followed Maisie's death. Many of these were about how they believed Isabel Fielding was innocent.

I sucked in a breath and leaned away from my laptop, needing to take a moment. It was after eleven, and I should be about to go to bed, but there was a fire inside me now and it wouldn't go out until I'd read more. I went to the fridge, poured a glass of wine, and continued reading.

For some reason, some of the blog post links were already

purple, showing that I'd clicked on them before. But as I read them, the information seemed fresh. Had Tom been using my computer? Or perhaps I'd been reading this stuff when I'd sleepwalked down to the kitchen table. I glanced at the glass of wine in my hand. How much had I been drinking recently?

Sipping slowly on my wine and determined to keep a clear head, I read some of the blog posts by a guy called James Gorden. All of them suggested that Isabel was either innocent, or that she'd been goaded by her brother, father, or both, and once I'd started reading them, I couldn't stop. I devoured all the blog posts and the comments, and felt drunk by the time I came to the end. Drunk on wine, and drunk on the information I'd just read.

CHAPTER
11

Isabel considered the entry form with suspicion, turning it one way and then the other as if she was going to find new information on the back, despite it being blank. Her brow furrowed as she handed it back to me, now slightly crumpled.

"It's not very long," she remarked.

"It's very easy to enter. Have you chosen which pieces you're going to send?"

She handed me the illustration I had posed for in the common room and a watercolour of a crow perched on the edge of its nest. "I feel bad for not sending in a drawing of Pepsi."

"Oh, I'm sure he'd understand."

We spent most of the morning packaging up her art and taking it to the post-room. I wrote the address for the Koestler Trust on the front of the envelope and put it in the outgoing pile ready for collection. I'd previously signed the form for Isabel so she could enter.

And now I felt good. At least this way she was actively improving her situation rather than sitting back, taking her medication, and waiting for her life to pass her by.

After finishing Isabel's entry, I went outside for my cigarette break and stood with Alfie for a short time. He seemed tired and out of sorts, with circles of purple around his eyes. He didn't speak for a while, but then he told me a new story.

"The Angel of Death," he said. "Otherwise known as Alice Stone. She was a young, aspiring starlet in the 1920s, living the highlife in London. When she was sixteen years old she gave birth to a child. But Alice was poor and living with an abusive father. She smothered the baby in its sleep and her father buried it somewhere. Don't think they ever found it. Alice was a pretty little thing who turned the heads of a few casting directors in London. One of them went missing shortly after Alice went for an audition for the West End. A week later, Alice found her actor boyfriend in bed with his lover. In a fit of rage she stabbed them over and over with a kitchen knife. When the coppers found her, she was sitting out in the back garden staring at two shallow graves. They couldn't get any sense out of her. She sat there, rocking back and forth on her heels in some sort of catatonic state. The bodies were still in the bedroom."

Alfie never failed to give me the shivers. "Did she kill the casting director too?"

"They found his body half-undressed near his abandoned car out in the forest. They reckon he tried to rape her and she fought back, killing him in self-defence."

"The Angel of Death," I whispered. "What chance did she have? Destitute, abused by her own father, and pregnant at sixteen."

"Yeah, but no one made her kill those people," Alfie said. "That was her choice."

But was it? Did any of us have much choice in life, or were we all marching to the beat of our own circumstances? Once she killed that child she became traumatised and troubled. Then she was corrupted again by the casting directors, used and spat out, given a stomach full of empty promises. Finally, the one person she thought she loved betrayed her in one of the worst possible ways. She'd given him her body. She thought he'd given her his. But then she realised he was giving his body to another, and she couldn't stand it. She couldn't bear it.

"You're rather sympathetic to murderers." Alfie exhaled smoke and grinned at me.

"Murderers are created," I said. "There's always a reason for what they do, if you look hard enough, if you dig deep enough."

Alfie turned towards me, leaning his shoulder against the wall. There was a curious smile on his face. "Is that true of all bad deeds?"

"Like what?"

"Like stealing, or lying, or hitting your partner in a fit of rage."

I didn't like it. Did he know about my father? No, he couldn't know. I was being too sensitive. "I suppose so." But that didn't mean I had to forgive my father for what he had done. I never would, and I would always cling to that.

"Interesting. I do so love our chats." Alfie stubbed out the cigarette and walked away.

Later that afternoon, Isabel stepped triumphantly from the scales after weighing herself.

"Five pounds down so far," she said. "My joggers feel a bit looser already. And my skin is clearing up. I'm so glad I decided to do this."

Chi, who was walking by, stopped to give Isabel a high five. "Keep up the good work."

"I intend to," she said with a grin.

"Lasagne and chips, or pasta salad for dinner later, what do you reckon?" he asked.

"You should have a word with the cafeteria, Chi. We get way too many carbs here. I was watching a cooking show on the television yesterday and they talked for ages about carbs and how bad they are."

Chi looked at me in surprise and jabbed a thumb at Isabel. "Check out this girl, here. Watching cookery programmes, getting in shape. Where has the old Isabel gone?"

"It's Leah," Isabel said with her smile broadening. "She's helped me a lot. I'm so glad you hired her."

"Well, I do make the best decisions," he said. "Now, Ms Smith, with me, please. We're having a staff meeting."

"All right then. See you later, Isabel."

She waved us off as we made our way down the corridor.

"She certainly seems to be improving," Chi said. "I mean, we've never had much trouble with her, but recently she's been coming out of her room more and even watching what she eats. It's setting a good example to the other patients."

"They aren't very kind to her. I doubt they pay much attention to what she does."

"Oh, they do," Chi said. "They pay a lot of attention to everything she does. A young girl like that, from a good home and everything else, doesn't get accused of murder every day. I know they give her some issues but they're also in awe of her, you know?"

I followed Chi into his office, surprised that we weren't meeting in the staff room or one of the small meeting rooms usually reserved for patients when they met with their psychologist.

"Everything all right?" I settled into the chair opposite his desk, suddenly concerned.

"Yes," he said. "And no."

"Okay."

"First things first, you're a good nurse, Leah. I've been working here for a while. I see good and bad nurses step through those doors. You're a good nurse. You care about the patients. You're able to see around their past crimes or their difficult upbringings, and you talk to them like they're human beings."

"Well, they are," I replied, wondering what was coming next.

"Quite right." Chi tapped the surface of his desk. I didn't like it. He was nervous and that wasn't like Chi. "But there are some issues."

"Okay." I leaned back, bracing myself.

"You've been late a couple of times. It's not that bad… a few minutes here and there. Usually I wouldn't be too concerned, but you also spend a little too long on those cigarette breaks of yours."

"I can fix that. It isn't an issue," I said. "I'm sorry I've been late. With the move and getting my little brother settled into a school I haven't been sleeping well. But things will be less stressful soon and I'm sure I'll get back to normal."

"That's good. I'm glad." He tapped a finger on his chin while thinking, and then met my gaze directly. "The other issue is that you're spending a good deal more time with Isabel than you are with your other patients. That needs to change."

"I have? I didn't realise." The revelation was a shock to me. I had spent time sitting for her so she could draw me, but I didn't know I was with her longer than the others. Now that I thought about it, I could see that Chi was right. I had been dedicating more time to Isabel than Tracy or Emily. "She's been a bit vulnerable recently. Some of the other patients called her names in the communal area and it was my fault. I encouraged her to go out there."

"Which was good. Isabel needs to spend more time with other people, and I'm glad you've given her the confidence to do that. But don't you see that you could give Tracy and Emily confidence too?

You need to spread yourself out a little more. I want to see Tracy and Emily improving over the next few weeks."

"Sorry… I… I didn't realise I was doing that. I don't have favourites. I mean, at least I try not to."

Chi started to get up from his chair. "We all have favourites, Leah. Come on, let's get back to work." He glanced at his watch. "Oh holy Mary, I'm late for a meeting with the governor." He rushed towards the door and swung it wide open. "Now, remember what I said. Just because Isabel is innocent doesn't mean you get to prioritise her. Treat the others the same." He hurried off down the corridor away from me.

It was only when I started making my way towards the patients' communal area that I realised what he'd said: *Just because Isabel is innocent.*

Innocent.

CHAPTER
12

Chi's words reverberated around my mind as I drove back to Rose Cottage. I hadn't had a chance to ask him about why he thought Isabel was innocent. Had it been a slip? Did he mean what he said? Did everyone at the hospital think she was innocent? The nurses certainly seemed to be warming up to her. They even made jokes with Isabel now that she was spending more time outside her room.

But on the other hand, I was mortified to realise that I'd been putting Isabel ahead of the other two women I cared for. Chi was right—why hadn't I applied the same enthusiasm to my work with Tracy and Emily? Why was I so drawn to Isabel?

Tom had left me a note on the fridge door. *After school dissertation meeting*. I knew he was nervous about his English dissertation so my stomach sank when I realised I'd forgotten. I sent him a quick text with some love hearts added on the end and glanced at my watch.

I wondered how it had gone with Seb. The sight of one of the Braithwaites with him might frighten the little bullies enough to make them stop.

I had a couple of hours before I needed to pick Tom up. A couple of hours alone to read more of the blog posts by James Gorden. Surely, if so many people were suspicious about the day Maisie Earnshaw died that must mean it was worth investigating.

A blur of movement caught my eye, lifting the fine hairs on the back of my neck. A skinny line of ants crawled in procession up the kitchen counter, bold as brass despite the many methods I'd tried to kill the little buggers. I snatched open the kitchen cupboard to find the ant killer, spraying some in the air around them, watching them struggle against the toxic gas. The dry, acidic fumes hit the back of my throat and elicited a coughing fit. I backed away, staring at the wriggling ants.

"Isabel would never kill an ant," I whispered to myself. "She wouldn't harm a fly." And yet here I was, reaching for the ant killer like it meant nothing.

Feeling woozy, I sat down at the table and wiped my forehead with the back of my hand. The thought of Isabel being innocent had got to me, so much so that I was tense from head to toe. Perhaps it was the amalgamation of everything: the slow-burn build-up of everyday stresses. Tom's bullying, moving across half the country, living in a rundown house, a new job, Isabel's innocence… There it all was chipping away at my sanity like a woodpecker on a tree. *Chip. Chip. Chip.* And *itch, itch, itch* went my past at the same time.

What happens when we're being slowly chipped away? All I could think about at that time was carrying on. I stood up, cleaned down the kitchen side, and sat back down to do my internet research, keeping one eye on the time. I had James Gorden's site bookmarked and opened it immediately. There wasn't much time, so I quickly browsed his blog for his contact details and sent him an email.

Dear James,

My name is Leah and I am a nurse at Crowmont Hospital. I would love to meet for a coffee to talk about your blog.

How about Costa Coffee in Hutton, Saturday 11am?

Best Wishes,
Leah

When I clicked send, my pulse began to race. A headache formed across my forehead from temple to temple, throbbing, foggy, intoxicating. What had I done? The number one rule of working in a high-security hospital was not to discuss the patients. Confidentiality was the big one. Talk to the press and you're fired. Yet here I was, emailing a conspiracy theorist blogger about the most famous child killer in Britain. I felt sick. I tried to get the email back, but it was too late. I poured myself a glass of water, hoping to make the sickness go away, but I gagged on it. There were nurses who didn't take this kind of stuff seriously. Some nurses joked about the most shocking things they'd seen in A&E or told their friends about the time someone famous came in with an overdose, but not me. I'd always taken my job seriously because it had always been the one part of my life that I could control—that I could make mine. And now I'd gone against everything I believed in.

But deep down I knew I had to. If there was an innocent young woman incarcerated for a crime she didn't commit, didn't I have a duty to at least look into it? If that girl was facing a transfer into a dangerous prison, shouldn't I help her? There was nothing to stop me meeting James, asking him questions and telling him nothing in return.

I moved strands of sweaty hair out of my eyes and took a deep breath. There, now I had a plan. It was time to pick up Tom, so I grabbed my car keys and made my way to the kitchen door. With my hand on the doorknob, movement caught my eye in my peripheral vision on the right. Another ant was crawling its way up my wall. I ignored it and went out.

The next day at work I took the time to play draughts with Emily for an hour, talking to her about how she was feeling and how things were going at the hospital. Chi's warning had resonated with me, and I wanted to do right by all my patients.

"You're not as good as Debbie," Emily said. "I might beat you."

"I'm pretty rusty," I admitted.

"Why do you spend so much time with the child murderer?" Her eyes rose to meet mine and the challenge in them was clear. She was angry—furious, even—that I showed such sympathy to Isabel.

"She's a patient here too," I replied, careful not to say the wrong thing.

Emily shrugged. "When I realised I'd killed my own baby I wanted to die. I've spent years wanting to die." She rolled up a sleeve for proof and a kick of disgust hit me in the stomach. Ugly red lines would later plague my nightmares. "But I was ill when it happened. I had no idea what I was doing, except that I thought it was the best for her." She pulled the sleeves down with such force that I feared she'd hurt herself. "But that cunt knew exactly what she was doing when she *murdered* a little girl."

"Emily," I warned. "Everyone in here is a patient. That means they're here to get better. Isabel is ill and she takes medication like you do. She deserves to be treated like everyone else."

Emily rested her elbows on her knees and moved her face closer to mine. "They say she worships Satan. They say she carved a pentagram on the little girl's back and bathed her in sheep's blood.

Isabel was making a sacrifice to the devil."

"That's nothing more than malicious gossip, Emily. We weren't there so we can't make judgments about an event we didn't witness. Aren't you glad that you've been given a second chance and treated kindly?"

"Yes," she said. "But I was ill."

"So is Isabel," I reminded her.

"That was a different kind of ill," she replied. "Sick. Isabel is sick."

I sighed. "I understand that the crime was devastating and that it makes people feel very strongly, but don't you have any compassion for Isabel? If she did it, it's because she was very ill."

Emily frowned. "'If she did it'? If? You think she's innocent!"

"That's not what I meant. I… I just meant that the only people who know what happened were Maisie, Isabel, and her brother Owen."

"Her brother told the police she did it!" Emily said. "Everyone knows she did it."

"Not everyone."

Emily created a king out of her draughts, clacking the two pieces together. She made a disgusted noise with her throat.

"Maybe we should talk about something else. Did you go to the tuck shop today?"

She nodded, and we began to chitchat about nothing. After the game was over I came away feeling shaken. So much for me inspiring Emily in the same way I inspired Isabel. All I'd managed to do was drive her even further away. I should have known the conversation was getting out of hand and needed to be directed away from the subject of Isabel. Why had I let it continue until we were both frustrated? Perhaps the lack of sleep was impairing my judgment.

I had wanted to talk to Chi about what he'd said about Isabel being innocent, but he was working on the intensive care ward as a new patient had been admitted. He was going to be gone for most of the week, according to the bank nurse who'd been put in charge.

We'd also had some changes with the security staff, and the woman on reception had quit for a job at a GP surgery. I'd now officially been at Crowmont long enough to see the high turnover of staff in action.

After taking a quiet and subdued Isabel to her art therapy, I had a quick cigarette break. For once, Alfie wasn't there so I could lean against the wall and contemplate my time at Crowmont alone. Emily had been right to question my motives, because even though I had my doubts about Isabel's guilt, I shouldn't be letting those feelings show in front of the other patients. But still, my mind drifted to the watercolour of a mockingbird Isabel had passed me that morning.

"Imitation," she'd said. "That's what mockingbirds do. They don't have a personality of their own so they take on the cadence of other birds. Some can imitate ringtones or people's voices. Or a baby's cry. I read about a mother who lost her way in the woods and froze to death because she thought she heard a baby crying. It was a mockingbird."

The painting was in my locker now, waiting to be taken home and added to the collection of birds to go up on my wall. I had an illustration of Pepsi—who now took grain from my hand as well as Isabel's—a portrait of me surrounded by doves, a pigeon, my window surrounded by blackbirds, a mockingbird, and a sparrow. My room was filled with colour.

"Afternoon."

The sound of Alfie's voice pulled me from my thoughts with a start.

"Afternoon," I replied, surprised that I hadn't heard the door open. I'd been so lost in my own thoughts that I'd blocked the world out again.

"Everything all right?" he asked.

"Fine."

Alfie exhaled through his nose, as though he didn't believe me for an instant. "All right then."

He sucked on his cigarette and stood next to me in silence. Even though we'd spent many cigarette breaks together, we'd never talked much about ourselves, which was a relief for me. I hated trying to fend away personal questions from the other nurses: *Do you have a boyfriend? Any family? What's your little brother like? Losing your parents must have been so hard.*

"The patio murders." Alfie broke the silence with puff of smoke. "It was 1998. Liverpool. A man reported witnessing his neighbour digging up his patio tiles at 3am. He thought it was suspicious so he phoned the police. The police dug up the patio and found five bodies, all prostitutes from the area. But the sixth body was a baby."

"A baby?"

Alfie nodded. "Gary Hoskins' wife, Lily, had a baby. Lily smothered the baby and they buried her under the patio with the prostitutes."

I shook my head, disgusted.

"Gary and Lily Hoskins had five other children. *Alive* children."

I took a drag of my cigarette, not enjoying this story. "That's horrible."

"It is," Alfie admitted. "The five children were interviewed by the police. Three of them had witnessed their parents murdering women in the cellar. Two admitted to helping them."

"Fuck." I rubbed my tired eyes and wished I hadn't come out for my break.

"Lily came to Crowmont shortly after she was sentenced. They thought she was a psychopath. Don't think they called it antisocial personality disorder in those days. She was mentally challenged, too."

Goosebumps prickled up and down my arms. "Is she still here?"

Alfie shook his head. "No, she died last year. Breast cancer."

"Did you ever see her?" I asked.

"No," Alfie replied. "And I'm glad I never did."

CHAPTER
13

'd never been particularly comfortable with parallel parking, making Hutton village my nightmare come alive. As March had slowly transitioned into April, it'd brought the first wave of tourists to the area. Hutton was a pretty spot in the middle of moorland, which made it perfect for walkers. That meant the Saturday I met James Gorden was busier than usual, and parking spaces were few and far between.

Ten minutes late due to a stressful attempt to squeeze my Punto between a Range Rover and a transit van, I hurried towards Costa sweating through my clothes. I'd misjudged the weather, wearing a thick cardigan and jeans when it was perfect t-shirt weather. I still struggled to get used to the changeable temperatures in the north. One minute there was a wintry breeze, but the next moment brought bright spring sunshine to warm up my skin.

In a room filled with middle-class parents and hikers, James

Gorden was a scruffy anomaly and not difficult to spot. Despite the fact that the photograph he used on his blog had been taken from an optimistically flattering angle, I knew it was him by the faded black t-shirt and overgrown beard. A cup of coffee and a brownie sat on the table before him.

"I'm sorry I'm late," I said, placing my bag down on the table and reaching in for my purse. "Parking was a nightmare."

"So, you're Leah." He looked me up and down as if I were a lab specimen, and the right side of his mouth twitched. "Not what I expected."

His greeting wasn't exactly what I'd expected, but I decided to ignore it and move on.

"I'll go get a drink." I walked away wondering if I'd made the right decision by meeting this man. Apart from the blog, I knew nothing about him. He could be a rude, arrogant prick, and certainly his first comment to me suggested that was quite likely. Then again, he could give me some important information about Isabel, and didn't I have a duty to at least listen to his ideas?

Returning to the table with a latte, I told myself to give James the benefit of the doubt. Maybe the guy didn't get out much and had no idea how to talk to people. Sometimes it's easier to be an internet persona than it is to be a real-life person. I'd spent my fair share of time on forums, enough to make me cringe at the thought of my posts and unfortunate selfie avatars. A sip of my latte helped deal with my jitters, but there was one thing I wanted to make clear before my anxiety went away.

"I can't tell you anything about the patients or the security at the hospital. I can't tell you anything about Crowmont."

"Then why am I here?" James snapped. "I've come from Rotherham, you know."

I could hear the South Yorkshire in his voice, elongating the vowels.

"I'm sorry," I said. "But I have a genuine reason for meeting you.

I want to hear what you think about Isabel Fielding. Do you honestly believe she's innocent?"

He had oddly sensual, full lips that were almost lost within his tangle of a beard. At that moment, his lips spread slowly into a knowing smile. "You work with her. You know her. You see her every day and you think she's innocent." He rocked forwards in his chair excitedly. "I fucking knew it! I know she's innocent. I just know it."

"But how is it possible? Who else could have done it? You don't actually think it was her father, do you? How would he have had time?" Despite my fears, I had to admit it was a relief to talk to someone about all the questions that had been building in my mind since I'd begun working at Crowmont.

James lifted his hands excitedly and leaned closer. "This is confidential, Leah. All right? It's important you don't tell anyone about our conversation. I've tested out a few theories about David Fielding. I trespassed on the Fielding estate while they were away on holiday. I walked the distance from the kitchen door to the pond. It took less than five minutes." He held up five fingers. "Three minutes fifty-seven seconds. How long does it take a grown man to bludgeon a little girl to death? One blow and…" James shrugged to represent the death of Maisie Earnshaw. His eyes were alive in a way that disturbed me.

"But the other children—why didn't they scream? Why didn't they call for help? Why would they let their father kill Maisie? And didn't she have carvings on her back? Who did that? Everything makes more sense if it was Isabel and she frightened her little brother so much that he froze up." I'd been wondering about all this for so long that my questions fell out of my mouth without much thought. These doubts were the main reason I kept going back and forth about her innocence. Deep down I felt like I knew her, like I could never imagine her committing a crime—but could I trust myself? Could I trust my feelings? Were my thoughts and feelings worth anything when it came to the hard facts?

"Occam's Razor." James sipped his coffee. "The most logical conclusion is generally the right one. But not always. Look, I'm not saying there isn't anything wrong with that family. I'm not saying that at all. There is something rotten at the core of the Fielding family, but I don't think it's Isabel." He bit into his brownie and grinned.

"Okay, so let's imagine that Isabel is innocent and it was her father who killed the little girl. Isabel has been incarcerated for years, right? Murderers who kill for fun generally end up doing it again. Why hasn't David Fielding killed more kids?"

James smirked and lifted a finger. "Ah, but how do we know he hasn't murdered anyone else? What if David or Owen, or both of them, are clever enough to cover their tracks? What if they've been getting away with it all this time? Here." James grabbed his phone and pulled up a website. "Missing persons reports from the last few years. All in the South Yorkshire area."

He flicked through some, but I didn't understand the relevance. These missing persons reports were for adults, not children.

"The victims don't have to be children." He answered my unspoken question. "Think about it. What happens when a child goes missing? The media goes into meltdown mode. Every major newspaper jumps on the story. What happens if some loser goes out for a packet of cigarettes and never comes back? Most of the time no one cares because they assume they overdosed in a squat somewhere or jumped into a river."

"You think the real murderer could be choosing victims who wouldn't be missed? Like prostitutes or homeless people?"

"Exactly."

James sipped his coffee while I let his words sink in. The problem was, there were too many possible explanations for both Maisie's murder and the missing persons reports. All his theories were based on shaky foundations and speculation.

"Have you been to the police?" I asked.

"Yes," James replied. "They still believe they have the right person and they say there's no evidence that David Fielding is a murderer, or that the missing people have been killed. Apparently, there's nothing they can do without bodies." James took a gulp of his coffee and shook his head. "I'd love to break into their house and search the place top to bottom. I know David Fielding is connected to this entire thing, but I can't figure it all out on my own."

I was beginning to get the feeling that James had created a conspiracy theory out of little to no evidence and I felt my resolve slip away. And… yet… there was also a possibility he was right. I squirmed against the itch in my stomach as my heart swung one way and my mind another. I thought of myself at the funeral again, with the whisper of my father's voice in my ear. *Leah.* Perhaps I couldn't trust either my heart or my head.

"I'm losing you," he said. "You're starting to think I'm obsessed, that I'm too close to all this. But you have to admit that it's a lot more complicated than Isabel Fielding being a child psychopath. Why would a young girl from a good background murder a child? Psychos like John Wayne Gacy or Fred West are made from their childhoods. They aren't born like it. You're a psychiatric nurse. You understand that too, right? You're a sensible woman, from the look of it. You know there's more to all this. You know there's something wrong with that family, not just Isabel. And you want to help, don't you? You want to help Isabel."

"I don't know. I just don't know what to do. She… she's not like…" I stopped myself before I blurted out personal information. "I should go."

"Wait." He reached across the table as though to grab my hand, but stopped before his fingers touched mine. "Wait a minute. Let me show you something." James pulled a messenger bag out from underneath the table and opened the flap to reach inside. He pulled out an A4 sized folder. "These are the letters Isabel has sent me over the years. Read some of them and see for yourself."

I stared at him, aghast. "You're in contact with her? How is this possible?"

"I've been writing to her for two years now. There's nothing strange about it. Isabel is allowed to have mail, and she's allowed to send me letters. I'm aware that the letters are screened in and out of the hospital, but I wanted to talk to her." He shrugged as though none of it was a big deal and pushed the manila folder across to me.

I sighed and opened it, pulling out the first sheet of paper. It was written longhand on a small jotter page. Seeing her handwriting reminded me of how we'd completed the form for the Koestler Award together, and how proud I'd been of her for entering. Now I wasn't sure what to think or what I would read.

1st June 2015

Dear James,

Thank you so much for the letter. Yours is in fact the first letter I have received in several months and it made me smile to know you are thinking of me. I shall keep it safe in my desk where I draw my birds. For you I've enclosed a little pencil drawing of a bluebird. They are good omens. They represent spiritual joy and a general contentedness, which I wish upon you, friend, as well as myself.

The truth is that I am not content at the moment but one day I hope to be. Please don't read this and think: well maybe she is crazy then! Her mind is warped and insane! That isn't at all what I mean. All I think is that I can improve on my mental health. We should all be improving. All striving to be better.

Better than what? Is that the burning question and the one you long to ask? Better than a murderer?

But I cannot answer your unspoken question because the truth is I don't remember what happened before the police came that day. I've said this every time I was asked. I still don't remember what happened, and I'm not sure I ever want to remember. Maybe one day I will. The psychologists certainly want me to remember.

I thank you for your letter, and I thank you for expressing your belief that I am not the cold-hearted killer the rest of the world believes me to be. Perhaps I am, perhaps I'm not. I guess I'll be the last to know!

Happiness to you, James!
Isabel

It sounded like her, that much I couldn't deny. The paper exuded brightness to the point where I had to put it down and close my eyes for a moment.

"She doesn't sound like a killer, does she?" James said.

"That means nothing. Some people with mental health issues disassociate from their violent tendencies."

"And has Isabel ever been violent in Crowmont?"

I didn't answer that. Instead I picked up another sheet of jotter paper.

30th July 2015

Dear James,

I'm so glad you enjoyed the bluebird! I had a feeling you would. Today I have painted you a little owl. They represent what you would imagine they would: wise, contemplative, and enlightened, which is what I assume you to be.

Thank you for creating a blog about my innocence, but I am afraid that it will draw too much attention to the case. It has been a long time now and I'm not sure I still want to be talked about. What's done is done! I'm treated well, I have medication that stops me from being a danger to myself or anyone else, and I have a pet magpie. His name is Pepsi, and I rescued him when I found him with his foot stuck in a tin can.

I'm sorry to disappoint you, but I had a lovely childhood. Owen could be a pest, but he was my brother, and I loved him. We played like normal children, building dens, sharing toys. If you are insinuating that you think Owen killed little Maisie, I don't believe it at all. He was only eleven, and he was a normal little boy. I miss him! I hope he comes to visit me when he's eighteen.

My parents don't visit me anymore. They tried for a while, but it was too much for them. They supported me during the police interviews and the trial, but they've decided I'm no longer their daughter. Don't judge them too harshly, they've done what they believe is right. What would you do if your child killed another child?

Honestly, I've come to terms with it. I don't remember the event, but I'm pretty sure I must have done it in some strange trance. It's the one thing that makes sense, right? Unless I was possessed by a demon or controlled by an alien. Believe me, I've looked at every possible explanation to how this could have happened!

Maybe one day I'll be able to forgive myself, but right now all I can think about is Maisie's family. My heart aches for them.

Wishing you the best,
Isabel

I read through more, but they were all very similar. In every letter Isabel expressed remorse and took responsibility for what happened the day Maisie Earnshaw died. But she never once admitted to killing Maisie, remaining adamant that she couldn't remember anything about the day Maisie died.

"None of these prove anything," I said. "Except that she can't remember."

"Don't you think it sounds like she's covering up for someone?" James said, jabbing his finger at the last letter.

All I can tell you, James, is that I can't remember, and at this point, I'm not sure I ever will.

Those were her last words to him before communication stopped.

"Maybe," I finally agreed.

CHAPTER
14

Pye the cat swiped at my ankles as I rummaged through my bag for the door keys. At the same time I almost tripped over the dozen eggs left on the doorstep with a note from Seb: *We had extra*. I laughed and shook my head at the terse note. Tucking the cartoon of eggs under my arm, I entered the tiny kitchen and locked the door behind me. The sounds of Tom's metal-pop music filtered down the stairs of the narrow cottage, filling every corner with the sound of guitars. But I didn't mind because it brought the place to life. I left the eggs on the worktop and hurried upstairs.

Tom's pale face was almost luminescent from the draining light of the laptop screen. "Hey—" he started.

But I didn't let him finish. Instead, I crossed the length of the room in two strides and pulled him into a tight bear hug before he even knew what was going on.

"What the—what's going on? Are you dying?"

I held his face in my hands and planted a kiss on his forehead. "I'm just glad we're out of that house in Hackney."

There was nothing else that needed to be said. We both knew what it was like living with our parents. We were two out of the three people on this planet who had seen my father's rages first-hand. My mother, resting in peace, was the one who had known them best.

"Me too." Tom closed his laptop and put it to one side. "Thanks." His face flushed with embarrassment.

"For what?"

"For not leaving me in foster care or whatever." He shrugged his shoulders as if nonchalant about the whole thing, but I could tell by the way his cheeks turned scarlet that it meant a lot, and that he was fighting through teenage embarrassment to tell me how much it meant.

A tear sprang into my eye but I ignored it and said, "It smells like teenage boy in here. I'm getting you some Febreze."

"Fine." He shrugged and reached for his laptop.

"So… did you get a lift with Seb?"

Tom nodded.

"And?"

He shrugged.

I sighed. "Are they leaving you alone, Tom?"

"Yes," he said. I wasn't convinced but I decided not to press the issue any further.

And with that, we were back to normal. We were back to lame sister and hormonal teenager, but at the same time I felt a little lighter. All the way home from the café I'd been thinking about the Fieldings and the eerie patio murders Alfie had told me about at the hospital. I had first-hand experience of the rotten core within a family. For us, it was my dad. The man all the neighbours came to when they had a problem. He was the one who would jump-start their car, or help put up a shed, or go drinking with them down the pub. And for a while he was that for me, too—a superhero dad with an easy smile and a funny joke on his lips. Sometimes I think that was all he wanted to be. But he didn't have it in him, sadly, and one day, everything changed forever. I closed my eyes and blocked out the thoughts.

"You look weird."

I opened my eyes to find Tom staring at me with an expression somewhere between exasperation and concern.

"Thanks." I rolled my eyes to express the sarcasm.

"Everything all right?"

"Yeah, just a lot on at work. What are you doing tonight? I got paid so we can afford things now. Want to go to the cinema in Hutton? They've made it all fancy with comfy seats and a café, apparently."

"I need to finish my dissertation essay," he said. "Maybe next weekend."

"Okay, but don't stay in your room all day. At least nip out for a walk at some point. You do know we live in an area of outstanding beauty, don't you? There's no overnight street vomit or corner condoms here."

He shook his head but cracked a smile. "All right, whatever stops you nagging." But I knew he didn't mean it. *Too late, Tommy-boy, I already know you love your lame sister.*

After leaving Tom to the fluorescent glow of his laptop screen, I decided to follow my own advice and go for a walk. At the end of our drive you could join a separate dirt track leading back to the Braithwaites' farm, or continue on in the opposite direction out onto the moorland that spread out into the National Trust's North York Moor. It was a popular spot for hikers, but we rarely saw them past the cottage. They usually made their way onto the moor via the public footpaths that began at the village and wound up through the hills onto the flatter moors that overlooked Hutton and its surrounding areas.

One of the first things I'd done after moving into the cottage was

buy a map of the moorland around the house. I didn't trust myself not to get lost. Here I was, a city rat let loose in the countryside, with no idea how to orient myself should I get lost. As I slipped on my trainers and tucked the map into the pocket of my jeans, I thought of myself as a fish flapping uselessly outside of its water tank. I finally understood the old cliché, but I was determined to change my circumstances. I would fit in around here. Tom would make friends. I would find peace away from the relentless bustle of London, and I would finally move on after my parents' deaths. I would scratch that itch of grief that never gave up, not even for an instant, and I would catch every broken piece that fell from my mind and put them all back together.

I would heal.

But for now, as I walked out of the cottage and onto the deserted part of the moors, I decided to think about Isabel Fielding and her family. James Gorden was a little eccentric and possibly not the best at social interactions, but some of the things he said actually made sense. It *was* bizarre that Owen never called for help, and it *was* strange that David Fielding had disappeared a few minutes before Maisie was found. Isabel had insisted for seven years that she couldn't remember what happened that day. I wasn't an expert on memory loss, but without head trauma that seemed unlikely. Either she was lying, or she had suffered some sort of emotional break to cause her to forget what happened to Maisie.

Did a lie about what had happened that day mean she was capable of murder? Did it mean she was capable of lying about who she was for all these years?

A rugged landscape lay before me with jagged rocks pushing out of the dark, mossy earth, and all I could see was murder. The murder of my mother. The murder of Maisie Earnshaw. Where was the justice for Maisie if Isabel was innocent? What was wrong with this world if the guilty were never punished for their crimes? My father was never punished. He took his own life before anyone could force him to stand trial. I hated the thought of him at peace and longed for hell to exist, solely to punish him for what he had done.

The spring breeze turned cool against my skin before I realised I was crying. I'd made a decision, and there was no turning back now.

It was the following Saturday and dark clouds mottled the sky above the M1. Twice I'd had to put on my wipers when drizzle hit the windshield, and each time my breath caught in my throat when the water smeared across the glass, impairing my vision. I needed new wipers.

I'd never been to Rotherham before. When I reached the town, it appeared to me as grey as the cloudy sky, lined with identical houses on identical streets. But my destination wasn't in Rotherham itself; it was out on the outskirts, near a long stretch of green by the golf club. I turned onto a private driveway that was flanked by a sparse wood. The drive led up to a modern mansion of a home, with a long front lawn, white walls, and large glass windows. A fountain stood erect in the centre of a circular carpark. When I saw the place, I swallowed nervously, aware how out of place my old Fiat Punto in bile-yellow appeared in this grand place. Even at the gate I'd felt ridiculous speaking into a buzzer about why I was here. I'd lied and said I was a friend of Owen's, hoping that the lie would at least get me in the front door.

My hand trembled as I lifted it to rap the door knocker. What was I doing here? *Getting answers.* Helping Isabel. Uncovering the root of the evil within the Fielding household. Well, here I was, a few feet away from the location of Maisie's Earnshaw's brutal murder. If I looked to the right I could see the woods where she had been bludgeoned to death. Over that grassy knoll was the duck pond where her body had been found, dark brown curls submerged in water spreading out around her.

The door opened.

"Leah?" Owen's brown eyes widened, and for the first time I saw Isabel in them. Whenever Owen visited Crowmont I usually remarked on how different their features were. Owen's face was narrow with a pointed chin whereas Isabel had more of a heart-shaped face, rounded rather than pointed. "Is everything all right with Isabel?"

"Yes. Sorry to turn up like this, but I hoped… wanted… to speak to you and perhaps your parents."

"Okay," he said. He didn't seem to question the ethicality of the situation, which was good. "Come in. I'll ask Irina to get you a coffee. We have a new machine that makes cappuccinos and macchiatos. What do you fancy?"

"Americano is fine." As I followed Owen into the Fielding's beautiful home, I noticed for the first time that he was unkempt and scruffy, with unwashed hair and a baggy t-shirt. He rubbed his eyes and walked with sagging shoulders—all the tell-tale signs of an awful hangover. "Were you out last night?"

"Went to a casino in Leeds. Think I might have got home around three, maybe four." He shrugged. "But on the plus side, I did win a few hundred playing poker. Dad's pretty pissed off about the whole thing, though. IRINA!"

His booming voice made me flinch back from him, surprising me with its sheer volume. Owen was a slender man but when he shouted, it was as though a 6'5" boxer had stepped into the room.

He led me through a long, open lounge that overlooked the back of the estate and the sweeping lawns leading down to the woods. My eyes locked onto the patio area where the four parents had sat drinking cocktails while Isabel had supposedly murdered six-year-old Maisie.

I was vaguely aware of Owen calling my name, but the words barely made it through the sound of blood rushing through my ears. A wave of dizziness almost knocked me sideways.

"Ah, so you're here for that."

Pulling myself out of the dizzy spell, I turned to face Owen, who frowned at me with a look of resignation. "What do you mean?"

He pointed out the French doors to the patio. "You're here for that. You want to know more about that day. It's generally why people come here."

"I'm sorry… I…" I trailed off, not sure what I could say to make the situation any better.

"IRINA!" Owen yelled, causing me to take a step away from him.

A blonde-haired maid came scurrying in from another room. The expression directed at Owen was one of murderous contempt. "Yes."

"Americano for Leah and espresso for me."

Irina placed both hands on her hips and spoke in a thick Eastern European accent. "Fetching and carrying isn't in my job description, sir."

"Oh, go on. I'm hungover as hell, and besides, if you don't, I'll tell Father that it was you who smashed his paperweight, not the dog."

The murderous expression on Irina's face turned to fear. Without another word she spun stiffly on her heel and left the room.

"Sit down." Owen waved a hand over the sofas arranged in a square next to the doors.

I sat sideways from the window so that I didn't have to face the patio. I couldn't look at the spot where, all those years ago, David and Anna Fielding had sat with the Earnshaws and decided to let their children play out of sight. Was it strange that the Fieldings had never moved away from this property? I couldn't imagine ever remaining in the same house where a young child was murdered. But perhaps that was the reason *why* they were still here. Who would buy this house knowing its history?

Owen placed himself on a white leather sofa opposite me, crossing one leg over the other, leaning back until he almost sank into the leather. Though his posture was almost completely relaxed, there appeared to be some underlying tension, as his foot swung up and down in a frantic manner.

"Are you going to spit it out, Leah?" he said, his small brown eyes meeting mine with intense ferocity. "You drove all the way down here from Hutton for a reason, didn't you? What is it? What do you need to know?"

Irina walked into the lounge carrying two cups while my mouth flopped open in shock. Owen had every right to challenge me. I'd barged into his home without any notice, for the primary reason of dragging up a painful memory from seven years ago. I had no right to be here. I was Isabel's nurse; my duty was to care for Isabel and nothing else. But for some reason I didn't move. Instead, I took the cup of Americano offered to me by the Fieldings' housekeeper.

"I'm sorry," I said, eventually. "I didn't mean to intrude, though I know that's exactly what I'm doing. It must be a shock to see me here in your house, given what I do for a living and where I work." I sipped on my coffee and tried to check whether Irina had left the kitchen and was out of earshot.

"I didn't mean to snap," Owen said. "You've done a lot for Isabel and for that I'm… we're… grateful. Mum and Dad might not visit, but I know they still care about her well-being, and you're part of that, so thank you for that. But you're right. It is rather jarring to see my mentally ill sister's psychiatric nurse on the doorstep."

I put down my coffee cup and tried to compose myself so I could explain myself better. "I know what Isabel was convicted of doing all those years ago, but despite that, I've grown to care for her. She's demonstrated herself to be sensitive and talented. I don't know whether what she did was done in some sort of fit where she wasn't herself, or whether I'm wrong, or whether there's another explanation. But I feel like I owe it to the Isabel I've come to know to find out more about what happened that day. I know you must have been through all of this before with police and psychologists, and I know I'm not exactly qualified to investigate this. I'd probably lose my job if my boss knew I was here, and God knows I need that job, but something compelled me to come, and I feel like I need to see it through." When I'd finished speaking, I nervously rubbed my palms against my jeans and waited for Owen to react.

Owen sighed. "All right." He flashed me a megawatt smile. "You're too sweet a person, do you know that? You've won me over." He paused and ran a hand through his dishevelled hair. Owen seemed older than his years and had far more confidence than I was used to seeing from a teenager. James Gorden's insights into Owen came back to me. He'd seen Owen as some sort of child genius. Would arrogance come from knowing you were incredibly smart? Was that what I was seeing in Owen? Or was I overthinking his behaviour? "What do you want to know about that day?"

"Did you see Isabel kill Maisie?" I asked, my voice far quieter than I would have liked. Despite me having the advantage in age, Owen had the advantage in confidence and it was turning me into a meek little mouse.

"Yes," he said. But he paused and his foot went still. He reached into the pocket of his pyjamas and pulled out a packet of cigarettes and a lighter. "Want one?"

I reached across the space between us and took one. After our cigarettes were lit, we each leaned back against our seats.

"Like I told the police, I watched her kill that kid."

The statement hung there for at least two drags of my cigarette. It was so matter of fact, so final. Not what I expected at all. Did I believe him?

"But you were young. And traumatised."

He shrugged. "But this. But that. Isabel apologists always find some way to explain it all away. I saw her kill that kid."

"There's a condition called False Memory Syndrome—"

"I know. I've seen psychologists. Many of them. Some figured I was right, others figured the false memory nonsense could be true. I don't believe it at all. I saw Isabel kill that kid and that's that. I love my sister and I'm sorry for her, and little Maisie, but Isabel belongs in the mental institution. I'm sure that's not what you want to hear, but it's what I know, so." He shrugged again. His demeanour was nonchalant and his voice was flat, as though we were talking about the weather or where we were going on holiday that year.

As I was about to ask Owen more questions, the front door of the house opened and two sets of footsteps made their way in. I heard a large, booming laugh echo through the open rooms, then a man as large as his laugh entered the room.

"Hello," he said, looking down at me. "I take it you're the owner of the yellow Punto outside the house? Well, I am relieved. I thought Owen had his drug dealer round again."

"Fuck off, Dad." Owen rolled his eyes and flicked ash into his cup.

I stood slowly, unable to force my gaze away from the man in front of me. From his eyes to the slightly rounded shape of his face to the colour of his hair, the likeness to Isabel verged on disturbing. Next to him was a short, slender woman dressed all in white, but I barely noticed her.

"I'm David," he said. "And you are?"

"Leah," I replied. "I'm Isabel's psychiatric nurse."

CHAPTER
15

could've concocted a lie about being a friend of Owen's and scarpered out of that house as quick as my legs could carry me, but I didn't. Owen's response to my questions hadn't sated my interest into what happened the day Maisie died, it had served to generate an even deeper hunger for the truth because Owen could easily be lying. Why was he so unemotional about the day his sister murdered a child before his eyes? I couldn't understand his cool, matter-of-fact approach to what must surely be the darkest day of his existence.

But it wasn't just Owen. As soon as David Fielding walked through the door I felt a strange pull towards him that almost knocked me off my feet. He was attractive, that was evident, but what I felt wasn't any kind of sexual attraction or chemistry, it was deeper than that. David Fielding possessed what can only be described as magnetism. Before meeting him, I considered a magnetic charisma to be part of the fantasy world of Hollywood, amongst film stars with white teeth and sharp cheekbones, but instead, a man walked into a house in Rotherham and captivated me with the same eyes he shared with his daughter.

Anna Fielding stepped forwards and held out her hand. "Nice to meet you, Leah. I'm Anna."

I took her tiny, cold hand and shook it gently, afraid I might break her. Anna Fielding was as insignificant as her husband's presence was commanding. With her white jeans and white linen shirt she was little more than a furnishing inside their home, blending into the carpet.

She smiled weakly and let my hand go, barely registering what I'd said. In contrast, David continued to assess me with inquisitive eyes. All the while, his expression remained blank, hiding whatever he was thinking. As a heavy silence fell over the Fielding house, I wondered if it was too late to rush out of their home and make my way back to Hutton without looking back. If I was right about Isabel, one or more of these people could be a murderer. The Americano churned in my stomach, and the air went very still. I realised I wasn't breathing.

"Is Isabel okay?" David asked. He glanced quickly at his wife and then back to me. Anna Fielding wandered away from us, choosing to sit down on one of the sofas and open a magazine. I was sure she hadn't registered what I'd said to her at all.

"Isabel is fine," I replied. "I'm not sure how to explain why I'm here. I..."

"She's here for answers," Owen said, exhaling smoke into the room. "Like they all are."

For the first time I realised I was smoking in David Fielding's house. I turned quickly and dropped the cigarette into my coffee.

"I don't mind you smoking," he said with a low chuckle. "Anna, what are our plans for dinner tonight?"

When his wife didn't answer, David lifted his hand and clicked his fingers. "Anna."

"Yes?" She set the magazine down on her knee and finally looked up.
"What are our plans for dinner?"

The tiny woman shrugged. "Whatever Irina wants to make."

"Why don't you join us?" David turned to me and raised his eyebrows in an exaggerated 'why not, it could be fun' expression.

Before I knew it, I was nodding in agreement. Behind me, I heard Owen begin to laugh. His low chuckle rumbled through the room before he broke into a cough.

"Good," David said. "I'll talk to Irina and check we have enough food in. Is there anything you don't like or are allergic to?"

"No," I said.

As David left, I turned to face Owen, who was grinning from ear to ear.

"Don't feel bad," Owen said. "No one can say no to Daddy."

The longer I spent in the Fielding house, the more I felt like an outsider in this perfect family home, so perfect that it sparkled bright white. I couldn't help thinking that the Fieldings wanted guests to know they were *clean*. White was such a domineering colour when it was used in abundance. What did it say about them? What was it manufactured to say? 'We're innocent'? I stalked the corridors looking at family photos, noticing the absence of Isabel in every single frame, and I scoured every wall, every mantelpiece, and every bookshelf. Anna's bony hips led me through each room while I listened politely as her slurring voice told me all about the house. David had built it especially for them to start a family. They were going to live for the rest of their lives in this magical spot with the sparse woods behind them, away from the town, away from other people. This was their haven.

She didn't put it exactly like that, but that was the gist of her words as she flicked her hair between her fingers and scratched nervously at her wrist. Anna Fielding was a strange woman, there was no doubt about that. Her sharp edges poked out of her expensive clothing, her arms never rested by her side, but instead her fingers twitched to life at every moment, and her eyes tended to roll around as she talked. If I wasn't in such an extravagant setting, I would have taken her for a heroin addict. The slurring of her words certainly made me wonder if she took too many prescription drugs, and it was clear that she felt incredibly anxious having me around. But at the same time, she hadn't even reacted when I mentioned that I was Isabel's nurse. It was as though it hadn't even registered in her mind.

It was a relief to come down the stairs and back into the lounge. The tour had at least taken up some time before dinner, and now David was leaning against the kitchen island with a glass of red wine in his hand. He smiled as I entered the open-plan room and walked towards me with a second glass.

"I can't, I'm driving—"

"Oh, come on, you can take a little sip. You have to try this merlot. It's exquisite."

Before I knew it, the wine glass was in my hand and I had raised it to my lips for the barest of sips. It was gorgeous and full-bodied, exactly how I'd imagined it would be. Nothing like the cheap swill I drank from a box at home.

"It's lovely," I said.

"It should be." David laughed. "Cost me a fortune."

I gazed down at the wine with dismay. I couldn't let it go to waste if it was expensive, and I didn't want to insult my host after intruding on his home. But it was a large glass of wine and I had a long drive. I had to pace myself.

But then David said. "A toast, to my daughter, Isabel." He raised his glass and took a long drink of the merlot.

"To Isabel," I whispered, sipping the heavenly liquid.

Anna called from the dining room to ask for David's help with setting the table, leaving me alone in the kitchen with the wine. It was an odd thing to do, toasting to Isabel. Why would he do that? He hadn't visited her for years, according to Isabel. I certainly hadn't seen him visit in the weeks I'd been working at Crowmont. Perhaps he wanted to put me at ease. Or perhaps he'd merely found the perfect excuse to get me to drink the wine.

"Feeling a little out of place, are we?"

I turned to find Owen standing behind me with a sardonic grin plastered across his face. He had what appeared to be a tumbler of whiskey over ice in his right hand, and he slowly rattled the ice against the glass. He'd changed for dinner into a black turtleneck top and grey skinny jeans. His hair was slicked back with hair gel.

"Feeling like you shouldn't be here?" He raised his eyebrows and lifted his glass. "Perhaps you shouldn't. Maybe you should get out while you can." He sipped his whiskey and smiled.

"Do you want me to go?" I asked, desperately longing to down the glass of wine in my hand.

He shrugged. "I don't care either way. It might be more entertaining if you stay, however."

"Entertaining? In what way?"

He smiled broadly before waving me into the dining room. I followed him, feeling even more puzzled about the Fieldings. I'd clearly stumbled into a bizarre family dynamic. But what else would I expect from a family who had been through the things the Fieldings had endured? Perhaps it was James Gorden and his conspiracy theories getting to me, but I kept looking for ways to attribute their strange behaviour to evidence that one of them was guilty of the murder of Maisie Earnshaw.

The dining room had been arranged as though they'd invited me over as a guest. There was even a pretty centrepiece of candles and a vase of roses.

"This room is beautiful," I remarked, genuinely surprised by the decor. Unlike the rest of the house, which was predominantly white and airy, the dining room was narrow and painted a deep maroon, not unlike the Merlot in my wine glass. There was just one window that looked over the gardens, framed by curtains in a dark chocolate brown, the same brown as the table. The red theme paired with the candlelight made it feel as though you'd stepped into a room from a different era. As flickering shadows bounced across the faces of the Fieldings, I almost felt that this room was too intimate for me to share with them.

"The dining room is my domain," Anna said, tapping her fingers on the back of one of the leather-coated chairs. "David had full reign of the rest of the house, but I wanted the dining room."

"That's why it's so dingy," David said. "Anna always did like the dark."

"Oh, I don't think it's dark," I said, allowing my eyes to trail over the coving and the luxurious curtains. "It's actually very cosy."

"That's exactly what I said." Anna seemed more relaxed in this room, though she still moved in quick, jerking motions, like a startled kitten at times. "Please, sit down."

I took my seat and placed the glass down on one of the pretty silver coasters. I wasn't in the slightest bit hungry; instead, my stomach had so many butterflies I was concerned that I wouldn't be able to eat a single bite.

Irina hurried through carrying plates of what looked to be a small portion of pate with melba toast. At least there was a small morsel I could nibble on and make it seem as though I was eating without being rude.

"Where are you from, Leah?" David asked. "It sounds like you have a London accent."

"I'm from Hackney," I replied.

"That's East London, isn't it?" David slowly spread his pate onto the toast, all the while keeping his eyes fixed on me.

"It is."

"An Eastender!"

"Sort of," I admitted, cringing slightly. When I picked up my knife to cut the pate, my fingers began to tremble. David caught my eye for half a heartbeat before directing his attention to the food on his plate. "It's more northeast than the east end."

He'd seen the way my hands were shaking; of course he had. He was a man who noticed everything. I thought back to James Gorden's blog post about how David had screwed over his best friend and realised I was completely out of my depth with David around. He was going to outsmart me and there was nothing I could do about it.

"Do you live in Rotherham?" he asked.

"No, I live in Hutton. It's close to the hospital."

"Yes, I know it is," he said.

"Which hospital?" Anna's wide eyes regarded me, and for a moment there was a shine to them like she'd come out of a stupor.

"It doesn't matter," David said sharply, without looking at his wife.

I thought about answering her question, but I didn't want to rock this unsteady armistice we'd created. It was clear that the reason David had invited me to stay for dinner was so he could get the measure of me. I forced a small piece of pate on toast into my mouth and chewed.

Owen suddenly burst into a fit of laughter. "What hospital? Oh, Mother, you are a hoot."

"Shut up, Owen," David snapped. The sudden rise in the volume of his voice almost made me drop my knife, and it did cause Anna to drop hers. David's face reddened, and he brushed a stray hair back into place. "I do apologise for my family. We don't have guests for dinner very often, as I'm sure you can tell."

"Your hospitality has been very welcoming," I replied, taking a sip of my wine to steady my nerves.

"Thank you." David's smile brought the first flash of white into the room, before he turned back to his plate and devoured the last of his starter.

The main course turned out to be roast beef with a rich gravy and sautéed vegetables. Irina was an excellent cook. So good that I forgot all about the butterflies in my stomach and ate almost all of the food on my plate. Perhaps I'd been eating cheap pasta bakes for so long that the first sight of real food was enough to override my own fears. The talk through the main course remained friendly, staying firmly on safe ground with neutral topics like the spring weather, the food, Anna's charity work, and David's business. I was probed further about my background at Whitmore hospital, as well as my new home in Hutton and my brother, Tom. I managed to avoid telling them about my parents, but David was clearly attempting to probe further before any discussion about Isabel would begin. I was sure that Isabel would come up soon, but I wasn't sure when, and I was nervous to be the one to bring up such a touchy subject.

During the main course Irina topped up my wine glass twice, despite me objecting. It seemed that Irina couldn't understand English at the most convenient moments, leaving me pondering whether David had asked her to top up my wine whenever I reached halfway down my glass.

Owen and Anna were both like church mice during the main course, though Owen finished his whiskey before I'd finished even half of my wine, and proceeded to push his beef around the plate without eating it. His expression remained thunderous even as Irina came back to collect the plates.

"That was lovely, Irina, thank you," I muttered, not exactly comfortable with a paid housekeeper serving me food in someone else's home. I wasn't used to the way the Fieldings lived.

I glanced at the time on my phone. Eight-thirty. There was a text from Tom asking when I'd be home. I'd already texted him to say I wouldn't be back for dinner, but without a proper excuse I could only imagine what he was thinking. The problem was, I couldn't think of anything to tell him. I hadn't been gone long enough for a full shift, and where else would I go except for work?

Irina brought a tray with four dessert glasses and placed them carefully in front of us all in turn. I poked at the meringue, cream, and raspberries of the Eton Mess and tried not to think about where I was and why.

"So, Leah," David said. "What is it like working at Crowmont?"

I glanced guiltily across at Anna, but the woman seemed oblivious as always.

"I enjoy it. It's not an easy job, but all the patients are there to get better and I like to help them."

"Even if they've killed someone?" Owen asked, his eyes sparkling.

"Yes, even if they've killed someone. Especially then. Taking a life is psychologically demanding."

He snorted. "I bet."

"It's a truly horrible situation. There aren't any winners when someone is murdered," I said. "Many of the patients I worked with in Whitmore had been involved in organised crime from a very young age. They saw violence right from being a child and grew up thinking that violence was a normal way to live. When they took their first life they saw it as a rite of passage. And many of them experienced nervous breakdowns because of what they'd done. Many couldn't cope with prison and would harm themselves or others. At Whitmore I saw a change in them. They found some peace, I think."

"That sounds very noble," David remarked. "And how is our Isabel doing?"

Anna did look up that time. Her confused gaze moved from David before reaching me. "Isabel?"

"It's all right, love. Eat your pudding."

Anna obeyed her husband and her doe eyes dropped to the table. But I sensed that she was listening.

"Isabel is doing really well." I hesitated. It felt wrong to talk about my patient. "I… I'm sorry for coming here. I shouldn't have. I'd be fired if the hospital knew." Whether or not my eyes pleaded to David Fielding I don't know, but I think my heart did.

"Why did you come here?" He leaned across the table towards me and the candlelight turned his eyes into two orange flames. I automatically shrank away from him.

"Honestly, I'm not sure."

"She thinks Isabel is innocent," Owen said, raising his eyebrows.

"Which means you think one of us is guilty," David said with a smile.

Owen let out another humourless laugh. "I need more whiskey."

"No, that's not… I just wanted to meet you all in case you could shed more light on what happened that day. You don't see Isabel everyday like I do. She's a sweet girl who is extremely talented. I don't know if she is guilty or not because I wasn't there. All I know is what I see when I work with her." Without thinking, I reached for my wine and took two big gulps, almost finishing the glass. There was heat spreading up my collarbone, and I didn't need a mirror to know my neck was being decorated by unattractive red blotches. The wine had gone to my head, just as I had worried it would.

David's eyes lingered on my wine glass. "Leah, why don't you help me clear these plates into the kitchen. I'm sure Irina would be grateful for a few moments of rest."

I followed his lead by rising from my chair, collecting the dessert glasses and carrying them into the kitchen. Alcohol and adrenaline coursed through my veins; hot blood pounded in my ears. The atmosphere in the house was heady with wine and tension, which made me long to leave as soon as I could. Finally, I realised that there were no gratifying conclusions to be found here, only more questions that I couldn't ask, and answers I couldn't trust.

David stood by the sink rinsing the dessert glasses. With his shirt sleeves rolled up I caught a glimpse of his powerful arms and the tattoo on the inside of his left forearm. I was surprised to see the wings of a bird stretching out in mid-flight. Isabel would know which bird it was in an instant, but though recognised it as a bird of prey, I didn't know the exact breed.

"You like birds, too," I noted. "Isabel draws me a bird every morning and tells me their significance in folk tales."

"Isabel is a sick young woman," David said. He lifted his hands out of the sink, shook them, and dried them on a towel. Then he rolled his sleeves back down and crossed the space between us, pushing me back against the kitchen cabinets.

With his face a mere inch from mine, he lifted his hand and wrapped it gently around my neck, squeezing very slightly.

"You're not the first moron to think Isabel is innocent. Do you think I haven't had psychologists, police, doctors, nurses, all kinds turn up at my door with conspiracy theories about how I'm the real murderer and I should be in prison? Do you think I haven't heard it all?" He squeezed tighter, his thumb beginning to dig into my windpipe. "Don't presume I'm an idiot, and never presume you can walk into my house and play pals with my son. Don't ever come here again, and keep your nose out of my family's business."

David let me go and stepped back, leaving me standing there with sweat sticking my top to my shoulder blades, and tears in my eyes. I don't know whether I mumbled an apology, or whether I let out anything more than a whimper from my sore throat, because leaving that house is still a blur.

CHAPTER
16

One thing I do remember from that night is that I'd had at least two very large glasses of wine. I was over the limit, but I couldn't stay in that house, and I couldn't leave my car there, either. My stiff, trembling fingers dropped my keys twice before I managed to get into the Punto, and then I almost backed into a plant pot while turning around in the driveway. When I had to stop to allow the gates to open, I stalled the car, which I hadn't done for over a year.

I was too wound up to sort out the sat-nav app on my phone, so I drove until I realised I didn't know where I was, and then I searched for street signs until I managed to find my way out of Rotherham towards the north. My throat ached, but I didn't think David had applied enough pressure to leave a bruise. He'd made his threat with just enough force to leave me trembling and sweaty. The man was not someone to cross, that was for sure.

It was after nine pm and the roads were dark. My pathetic headlights didn't make visibility much better and I was too afraid to drive on the motorway after drinking wine. When I found a quiet road, I decided to pull over and finally sort out the sat-nav so I could find my way home, as well as taking a moment to pull myself together. The temperature had dropped, but I was still sweating through my clothes, only now the air was sour from the alcohol making its way out of my pores. My upper body was shaking from the chill, the alcohol in my system, and fear of David Fielding.

A few moments later I set off down a road without street lamps, at least now with a better idea of how to get back to Hutton. Forced to drive hunched over the steering wheel so I could see where I was going in the dark, even with full beam on, I reduced my speed and hoped to come to a brighter road soon. And then it started to rain. My windscreen wipers smeared water across the glass, blurring the darkness, reducing the amount I could see to a small rectangular section of my windshield.

When I missed the sharp left turn up ahead, instead of continuing on, my wine-addled brain decided to still try to make the turning, overshooting it by a few feet and ploughing into a tall, looming tree by the side of the road. There was no airbag in my old car, so I plunged towards the windscreen and back, whipping my head back and forth. My forehead almost hit the steering wheel, but I was saved by the constricting seat belt in the nick of time. I turned off the engine and climbed out of the car to see what the damage was, using the torch app on my phone so I could see in the dark.

Shit. The bumper was completely hanging off. My bonnet was bunched up and bent in the centre. There was no way I could drive this car back to Hutton village as it was, but I also couldn't call any roadside assistance or the emergency services—I was *drunk*. I gazed down at my phone. There were no best friends or reliable family members. Tom didn't even have his learner's license yet. What was I going to do? Stay there and get murdered in the dark by an opportunist? Or worse, David Fielding back to silence me for good.

But there was one phone number I could try, and I had to hope he was in a good mood.

I travelled back to Hutton in the cab of Seb's tractor with my Punto dragging along behind us. It was a quiet journey, with Seb only talking to ask if I was hurt, and to inform me that my car would have to go to the garage in the morning. If he knew I'd been drinking, he didn't say a word. Of course he knew; anyone with eyes could have seen I'd been drinking. I was such a bleary-eyed sweaty mess it was a miracle I'd managed to get as far out of Rotherham as I had.

By the time I got back to the cottage, pulled off my shoes, and made it into our tiny lounge, it was midnight and Tom was sitting up watching *Nightmare on Elm Street*, our joint favourite movie, along with *Die Hard* and *Hellraiser*.

"What the hell happened to you?" he said. "I called you."

"I know. I'm sorry. I crashed my car and Seb had to pick me up."

"What? But… where were you? How did you crash the car?"

I collapsed onto the sofa and pulled a cushion onto my lap. "It's a long story."

"You smell like fags and booze. Were you drinking?" Tom jumped to his feet, anger flashing in his eyes. "I can't believe this."

"Tom, don't—"

"You're just like Dad."

It was like a stab to the gut to hear him compare me to our father. I threw the cushion down and stood to face him. My little brother stood opposite me defiantly, with his arms folded across his chest, eyes glazed with angry tears. "That was uncalled for. Take it back."

"No, I won't. Not until you stop drinking. I'm sick of finding you in the kitchen passed out. I'm sick of you sitting out in the garden drinking wine. It's weird, Leah. You're fucking weird."

Before I could even open my mouth he was already heading out of the room. I cringed as the door slammed behind him. Stomping footsteps made it up the stairs before his music began to blare out of his room. I couldn't even yell at him to turn it down for the neighbours, because we didn't have any. Instead, I curled up on the sofa and fell asleep to Freddy Krueger slashing his way through dozens of school kids.

The horror of the movie seeped into my subconscious, infecting my feverish dreams. David Fielding chased me down a dark road, his hand outstretched to catch me. Breathlessly, I took a left turn, and then a right, desperately trying to get rid of him. When I thought I had finally lost him, he came flying overhead on wide eagle wings, swooping down to grab me. He was monstrous—part bird, part man. He had a beak for a nose and claws for fingers. I screamed and screamed before running away, throwing my body down a pitch-black road.

But then the streetlights turned on one by one, beginning at the end of the street until the light closest illuminated a figure standing in the middle of the road, right in front of me. It was the first time I'd seen his face in months: my father, standing there, holding my mother in his arms as she bled from an ugly red slash across her neck. He was crying, and for some reason that made everything worse.

I woke, covered in sweat, to a banging on the door.

Freddy Krueger was no longer terrorising school children; the television had turned itself off some time in the night. My phone was out of battery and I'd pawned my watch some months ago, so I had no idea what the time was, only that it was early morning judging by the light filtering in through the windows. I dragged my fingers through my hair and made my way into the kitchen, still worried that I'd open the door to find David Fielding standing on my doorstep with a bloodied knife in his hand.

But it was just Seb.

"Hi," I said. "Thanks again for last night. What do I owe you for the tow?"

He shrugged his heavy shoulders and squinted beneath bushy eyebrows. "I know a mechanic who can fix that for you if you take it in on Monday. Won't be cheap, but he won't rip you off, neither. Thought you might want this."

I realised then that he was holding a flask. He passed it to me along with the business card for his mechanic friend.

"Thought you might need some strong coffee. Why don't you go for a walk after you've had that?"

"Thanks. I… I will."

"All right, then." Seb turned around and walked down the path to his tractor, leaving me standing in the doorway holding a thermos flask of coffee.

I went back inside and sipped on the coffee. It was rich, delicious, and piping hot. I decided to pour Tom a cup and take it up to him. Perhaps he would forgive me quickly enough to agree to a walk through the moors after we were dressed. But he was still fast asleep with the covers pulled over his head. I placed the coffee on his bedside table and left him be.

As I ate breakfast and contemplated the night before, I came to a decision. It was time to put an end to my obsession with Isabel's innocence. Enough was enough. It wasn't my place to *save* her or whatever it was I was trying to do. Her reassessment was coming up, that I couldn't deny, and there was perhaps one last thing I could do to try and help, but I'd seen first-hand that David Fielding was a bully and that his wife was afraid of him. I'd also seen the odd way Owen behaved at dinner, which made it clear that neither of David's children was particularly well-adjusted. James Gorden had been right that there was a rotten core at the heart of the Fielding family, and it was David, plain as day. Innocent men did not put their hands around the throats of women.

I finished the coffee and placed my breakfast dishes in the sink. There was no way I could say for certain that David Fielding killed Maisie Earnshaw seven years ago. I was no expert. Why did I think I could get to the bottom of this mystery? It was time to collect everything I'd learned over the last few weeks and send it all to someone who could solve the mystery. It was time to hand it all over.

After the breakfast dishes were cleaned, I typed up an email including everything I knew about the Fieldings. At first I'd decided not to mention my trip to their home, but then I realised I had to include it. Without mentioning David losing his temper, there wasn't any point to any of this. I included links to the missing people James had noticed and then I sent it to the local police. The message was clear: *I believe Isabel Fielding is innocent of killing Maisie Earnshaw.*

Tom seemed determined to ignore me that morning, so I left without him, heading out onto the moors through the farm fields. This time I continued up a steep hill that overlooked Hutton and the surrounding areas, and I found a small abandoned farmhouse nestled within a valley. The walls were crumbling, but an old door remained. It took a few jerks to come loose, but I managed to prise it open and headed into the interior of the dingy building.

There were still a few cabinets from an old kitchen and a bathroom with a green toilet covered in dust, the bowl filled with old cigarette butts. What furniture had been left was long rotted away, and the old wallpaper sagged at the corners, but it was clear that this house had once been a home. Someone had lived in this beautiful spot, and perhaps they'd been happy. I wandered around the room, letting my fingers trail through the dust, smiling at the thought of the family who might've once lived there. This family would've been nothing like the one I was born into. This pretend family loved one another, not hurt each other.

When I realised that the house reminded me of the one I grew up in, the walls seemed to close in on me and the dust clogged my throat. I had to get out of there.

CHAPTER
17

had no choice but to take a few days off work so I could take the Punto into the garage to get it fixed, relying on Seb once again to tow the vehicle with his tractor. On the way to the mechanic in Hutton, I spotted three magpies clustered together on a dry stone wall and couldn't stop myself from waving. Seb noticed and smiled, which was perhaps the first time I'd ever seen him smile.

"Didn't take you for superstitious," he said. "You look too smart for that."

"Well, looks can be deceiving." I thought about leaving the conversation there, but Seb was so quiet that I ended up chattering on. "My da—father had Irish parents who were very superstitious. He would always leave out of the same door he came in, always salute magpies, especially if there's just one of them, and he used to tell me to put my tooth on the windowsill after it'd fallen out."

"Did it work?"

"What, the tooth thing? I dunno."

"Was he lucky then?"

I stared out at the moorland as I thought about it. Streaks of fluffy white clouds stretched across the pastel sky. "He was. But he never knew he was lucky, and then he pissed it all away."

The thing I liked about Seb was that he didn't probe at all. In fact, conversations with Seb were pretty sparse, but he was always there when I needed someone. I'll take deeds over words anytime. The rest of the journey into Hutton was silent, but when we reached the garage he stayed and did the talking for me, haggling the mechanic down to a reasonable price, then took me straight back to the cottage. I'd persuaded Tom to stay off school, so for the rest of the afternoon we watched eighties horror films and laughed at the terrible special effects.

I didn't once think about the email I'd sent to the police, and I barely gave Isabel a passing thought. For once I felt happy and contented. At least, I thought I did.

On Thursday evening I collected the Punto with its brand new bumper and bonnet. I'd been lucky to not have damaged the suspension, so it hadn't taken too long to fix. I'd also taken the cheapest possible outcome and not bothered with getting the front bumper and bonnet painted, leaving me with a yellow car with a green bonnet and bumper. The kind of car a kid would create out of building blocks. On the way back to the farm I kept my head down and avoided eye contact with the pedestrians pointing and laughing, while trying to ignore the hot prickle of shame working its way up my neck. When you're poor, shame comes as naturally as breathing, but unlike breathing, you never get used to it. I needed the car to get to work, and I needed money from work to pay the bills and feed Tom. That was all that mattered.

Tom cooked spaghetti for tea while I prepared a dessert of bread and butter pudding, one of Mum's specialities, as well as a good way to use up stale bread. We caught up with our soaps, ate second helpings of dessert with instant custard, and Tom went upstairs to finish up his homework, leaving me alone in the kitchen. For the first time, I thought about Isabel and her family. My fingers traced the area on my neck where David Fielding had pinned me against his kitchen cabinets, his face so close to mine that I could smell the expensive red wine on his breath. I hadn't heard from Chi at work, so at least David hadn't gone straight to the hospital to complain about me turning up at his house. While I'd been concentrating on fixing my car and making sure my relationship with Tom was back on track, I hadn't had time to think about what it would be like going back to the hospital and facing Isabel again.

I reached for the wine—just one glass to ease off the nerves and help me sleep. I was edgy enough to believe that I'd have unwanted nightmares. The problem was, I had the kind of brain that enjoyed reaching into the depths and revealing my worst fears to me on a regular basis. If you ever find yourself sitting alone with your mind on a loop of all the worst things that have ever happened to you, then you'll know exactly what I mean, and the only thing that turns it off is alcohol.

I'd been right about the nightmare. My mind slipped easily into the same dream I'd experienced a few nights ago, which ended with my father cradling my poor dying mum in the middle of that dark street where I'd crashed the car. But this time, instead of waking, I ran towards them, pushing my father away from Mum. I was crying so hard I could barely breathe, but despite the fat tears running down my cheeks, I continued to push down on her wounds, desperately trying to stop the bleeding. As Mum's last breath rattled through her chest, I lifted my hands to see that they were covered in blood. Slowly, I rose to my feet, the lights from the car almost blinding me. Just as I realised I was waking, Isabel's face flashed up.

My hands were not covered in blood when I woke—they were covered in dust. My hair was tangled with broken stones, and my back was sore. I'd sleepwalked to the abandoned house.

Wincing at the stiffness in my limbs, I hurried out of the building as quickly as I could, emerging out into the early dawn as I brushed cobwebs away from my clothes. I checked my pockets to find my phone. Thankfully, it was there, and I checked the time: 5:35am. No missed calls from Tom, and I still had time to run home, shower, and leave for work.

But what the hell had happened? My sleepwalking was escalating, and now it was clear that it was linked to alcohol. My head was fuzzy from the wine, but I didn't feel sick or shaky. Was I an alcoholic like my father? The thought that Tom might be right was almost too much to bear. Drink drove my father to violence and murder. If I really was like him, was I capable of the same?

Forty-five minutes later I was on the road making my way to Crowmont. Thanks to the world's shortest shower, I was still on time, but I had to hurry. The Punto struggled its way along the narrow, uneven roads as I tapped my fingers against the steering wheel and wished it would go faster. Chi had already given me a warning about being late to work, and I didn't want to let him down again. Ian and Brian waved as I made my way into the carpark. I almost tripped and fell as I climbed out of the car, but managed to keep my balance at the last moment, saving myself from a faceplant against the hard tarmac. When I reached my locker, I practically threw my belongings in and attached my pass to my shirt at the same time.

It was one minute past 8:30 as I walked onto the ward. Not too bad. "Leah, can I have a word?"

My heart sank to my knees. I'd been so close.

"Sure." I spun around and walked back the way I came, towards Chi's office.

As he shut the door behind me, I examined his face to work out whether he was angry or annoyed, or whether this was a regular meeting about hospital matters. It was no good—Chi appeared as cheerful as ever, which could mean anything. The man was unflappable.

"How's the car?" he asked.

"Fixed, thank God."

"I saw the bonnet in the carpark. It's like the Noddy car. My daughter loves that book." He grinned at me, his eyes twinkling.

It couldn't be too bad. Could it?

"It gets from A to B. Well, just about. It's a bit slower than pretty much every car out there. I'm sorry I was a bit late this morning, I'm trying to sleep better, but it's a bit of a process—"

He shook his head. "It's not about that. Leah, since you've been off there've been some developments with Isabel. Or, rather, some setbacks. There was an altercation in the communal area which has unfortunately had an unsettling effect on her. She's been in some distress for a while. She hurt herself quite badly as well."

I took a step towards Chi, surprised and upset by his news. "What did she do?"

"She stole a plastic fork from the kitchen, sharpened it, and cut her arms. She's going to be fine. She's had a few stitches. Luckily the plastic wasn't sharp enough to do too much damage, but she's still very depressed, and the event caused the other patients some stress. She did it in front of everyone in the communal area."

That didn't sound much like Isabel to me. She wasn't someone who ever seemed to crave attention. Chi must have noticed my frown, as he echoed my thoughts.

"It seems out of character for Isabel to behave in such a shocking way, but I've spoken to her psychologist in depth and we both agree that this was a cry for help. There's going to be a more formal meeting later today, but it's clear that Isabel will need to be on suicide watch for the next few days."

"Well, I'm here to help, Chi. You know that."

He nodded. "I appreciate that. We're going to need your help for this, definitely."

CHAPTER 18

There was an empty room around me, transformed from the colourful, lively place I'd once known. The walls were blank. The desk was empty. The floor was clear. It was a sterile room where it was difficult to imagine laughing, crying, or even breathing, and it was Isabel's room.

She entered slowly, dragging her plimsolls across the carpet. Her head was bent low, but I dipped my eyes so I could get a good look at her. Though it had been less than a week since I'd last seen her, it was like she was a different person. Isabel had been slowly losing weight over the weeks, and now I noticed how the loss of weight had sharpened her features, almost to the point where her cheeks were sunken and gaunt. Her hair hung over her face in a different style. I saw that she'd trimmed her fringe, and was it my imagination, or was her hair a slightly darker shade? There was a hairdresser who came to the ward every once in a while, so perhaps Isabel had requested this new look. Whatever she'd done, it made her seem more sallow, less healthy, more tired.

"How was art therapy today?" I asked, moving out of her way so she could go sit on her bed and I could sit on the chair outside the door, which was open, as always. I would never be in the room alone with her and the door closed.

Isabel slumped her body down onto the bed. "Okay, I guess."

"What kind of bird did you draw today?"

"I didn't draw anything."

"You haven't given me a sketch today, have you? What are you going to draw for me today?"

She rested her elbows on her knees and placed her head in her hands.

"Isabel?"

But she didn't respond. It wasn't the first time I'd seen a patient unresponsive to my questions, but I was surprised to see Isabel like this.

"What happened to your art? The room seems bare without it, doesn't it?"

I sat patiently as Isabel remained quiet. After speaking with Chi, I'd attended a meeting with Isabel's psychologist to discuss moving forwards with her care. It was concluded that she required 24/7 surveillance until she improved again, and if she didn't improve it was suggested that she move to the intensive care ward for a short period of time. In the intensive care ward, Isabel would not be able to use the communal area, and instead, would be supervised when she was let out of her room. I didn't want that to happen for her.

The meeting had been short and sweet, with Isabel's psychologist explaining that her actions had appeared to be a cry for help, and perhaps attention, too. But Isabel had never struck me as an attention seeker.

"When I was at Brookhill, the youth offender institution they put me in shortly after... the crime, I learned pretty quickly that I was never going to have a normal life ever again. Learning curves tend

139

to stick when you're being punched in the face by a fourteen-stone inner-city girl-gang member. Everyone already assumed I was guilty, and why wouldn't they? The jury thought I was guilty. Everyone did—even I did at times, though I wish I could be sure." Isabel rolled up the sleeves of her jumper so I could see the bindings from where her cuts had been dressed I winced, but forced myself not to look away. Then she pulled the jumper down past her collarbone so I could see the faint lines of old scars. "They liked to sharpen their fingernails and drag them down my chest. They each took turns."

"That must have been hard," I said.

She sighed, tipping her head back until it rested against the wall of the room. "Of course it was." She tapped the fingers of her left hand on her knee and regarded me with sleepy eyes. "You're here late tonight. Did you take on the night shift?"

I nodded. "I did."

"Need the money?" She half smirked.

Though it was a little cutting—and true; I'd even taken a nap in the break room and eaten vending machine food for dinner so I could continue on for the day—I was relieved to see a slight smile on her lips. It was better than the impassive expression with which she'd entered the room.

"I'm here to look after you, as you know. Some of the other nurses have families, whereas it's easier for me to work later."

"You have a brother, though, don't you? I miss my brother sometimes. Do you miss yours when you're working here?" she asked.

"Honestly, I'm so busy here that I don't get the chance to think about it much. But I do think of funny things to tell him when I get home, so, yes, I miss him."

"It must be nice to see your brother every day."

"Do you wish you saw more of your family?" I asked.

"Some of them."

"You look tired, Isabel. Maybe you should have some rest," I suggested. "It's getting late."

Isabel placed a finger on her lips. "Shh, lights out. People are trying to sleep around here." It reminded me of my first day when Isabel had told me a secret. *I didn't kill that girl.* I still believed her, but the issue was bigger than I could manage alone. Part of me felt like I'd let her down.

I'd done everything I could, I reminded myself. It was up to the police now.

"You look tired, too," Isabel said. "You don't sleep very well, do you?"

I paused, wondering whether I should change the subject from me to a less personal topic. But then I changed my mind. "No, I don't."

"Why is that?"

"I have nightmares," I said.

Isabel leaned away from the wall. "You do? Are they bad ones?"

I thought of my father standing in the middle of the road holding the dying body of my mother. There was the blood dripping down from her fingers, pooling on the cold tarmac. There was the nightgown blowing in the breeze. And then, I thought about the phone call from the hospital and the long talk I'd had with both doctors and police officers, informing me that my father had killed my mother and then himself. Here I was in the hospital, sitting on a chair watching a girl to make sure she didn't hurt herself, but maybe Isabel wasn't the only one who needed surveillance.

"Yes, they're bad dreams."

"I have nightmares too," she replied. "But I like the dreams where I become a bird and I fly away from the hospital. Sometimes I'm flying alongside Pepsi. Sometimes I'm on my own. Other times I walk out of here with Owen because I'm finally free. All the nurses line the corridors clapping as I'm released. You give me a big hug."

"And the nightmares?" I asked.

"I don't want to talk about those."

As much as I wanted to, I didn't press. A niggling part of me wondered whether Isabel's nightmares could unlock some secret that would resolve the murder of Maisie. But it wouldn't. That was wishful thinking, not based on reality.

"I've been sleepwalking," I said. The words were out of my mouth before I even thought.

"You have?" Isabel's eyes widened. There was a slight pink flush to her cheeks, which was good to see after her pale appearance when I'd first arrived.

"Yes. It started when I moved here."

"Why?" she asked. When I hesitated, she added, "You don't have to tell me if you don't want. I know I'm nothing but a patient. You don't have to tell me your life story."

"It's okay. Perhaps I need to talk about it," I said. "Maybe you deserve to know that even people outside Crowmont have a difficult time."

"It would help," she said. "Sometimes all I can think about is how lucky everyone else is. It's like my mind is stuck on a loop and I can't turn it off, and all I imagine is people eating ice cream in the sunshine, laughing and joking and holding hands with each other. But it's not always like that, is it?"

"No," I agreed. "It isn't. It never has been for me. My dad had an accident at work when I was six, and it meant he was unemployed for a while. He started drinking to fill the gaps in his days, and he never stopped, even after he found a new job. The drinking made him violent, but for a long time he managed to keep it under control, at least outside the house. I moved out as soon as I was sixteen and went to live with some boyfriend who smoked weed and wrote poetry. He was a university student until he dropped out in the second year. I left my brother at home and I'll never forgive myself for that.

"I got a job, I saved up, went to college and took my A-levels through evening classes, and then I trained to be a nurse. Whitmore was the first place to give me a job, and that's how I became a psychiatric nurse." I picked at the sleeve of my blouse before continuing. "But no one ever becomes a nurse to be rich. After a bad break-up with a different boyfriend, I moved back in with my parents. I didn't want to, but Mum insisted that my father was getting better. He wasn't. Now, when I look back at everything that happened, I think she wanted me there because she hoped I'd help. At least I could protect Tom at last.

"I took my brother, Tom, out for the day to get away from our father. Mum was supposed to come with us, but she didn't feel well. He'd hit her hard in the ribs the day before. One was fractured, though I didn't know that at the time. Mum never complained. I wish she had.

"Tom was sixteen and should've been hanging out with his friends rather than his uncool older sister, but Tom didn't have that many friends, so he didn't mind going to the zoo together. We spent most of the day watching the monkeys in the enclosure, and we ate chips with gravy at the café." I exhaled deeply through my nose. "I dropped Tom off at home because I needed to go to my ex's place to pick up some belongings. If I could change that moment I would."

"What happened?" Isabel's voice was gentle, encouraging.

"Tom found my parents dead in the upstairs bedroom. My father had slashed Mum's throat before stabbing himself in the neck. The arterial spray had soaked the curtains in blood." I allowed myself to look up from my blouse sleeve so I could watch Isabel's reaction. Her eyes were wide and her mouth was twisted in horror.

"I don't know what to say," she replied. Slowly, she stood up from the bed, walked across the room and took my hand, squeezing it gently. Her hands were warm and soft. Her grip was gentle.

Tentatively, I patted her hand before easing it away. "It's okay. It was a difficult time for us both, but we got through it."

"Not unscathed," Isabel said as she settled back onto the bed. "No one walks this earth without scars; your nightmares and sleepwalking, for instance."

"Yes, they started after we moved to Hutton. I'd wake up and find myself at the kitchen table, often collapsed in front of the laptop. The other morning I woke up in an abandoned farmhouse on the moors near the cottage I live in." I laughed. "I had to run home, shower, and come straight to work."

Isabel settled herself down on the bed, lifting her knees into a more comfortable position. "You poor thing, Leah." She placed her hands under her head and closed her eyes. "In the morning, do you think you could help me put my pictures back on the wall?"

I couldn't help but smile. "Of course I can."

CHAPTER
19

There was no reply to the email I'd sent to the police, but I did have several messages from James Gorden asking me if I had any further information about Isabel and her family. I chose not to tell him about my adventure to the Fieldings' house. He hadn't updated the crime blog for a while—perhaps he was waiting for me to get in touch—but I didn't want to talk to him. I wanted to forget all about David Fielding's hands across my throat. I even wanted to forget about Isabel's hand on mine as she comforted me about my parents' deaths. Even now, after swearing to stop obsessing about the murder of Maisie Earnshaw, I was allowing myself to get too close to Isabel.

It was the second night of Isabel's suicide watch. With the change in my shifts, I'd slept through most of the day, missing Tom as he went to school, and Seb as he left milk on our doorstep. The cat didn't bother to attack me as I walked out of the cottage and made my way to the Punto. Maybe the little shit was becoming domesticated.

Even though I'd actually slept well for once, I felt on edge. The night before, when I'd spilled my guts to Isabel, I'd thought for a moment that telling someone what I'd been through was going to help me, but there was still a niggling itch inside me that said otherwise. Since my father had killed my mother, grief had worked its way over my body like a cheese grater to my skin. I ate, I slept, I breathed, I drove to work, I talked to others, and I maintained a job, but it was all hanging by a thread. If I was honest with myself, I'd have to admit that I'd been hanging on by a thread since they died.

Tom was at an afterschool study group, but I'd arranged for Seb to collect him later. Not in his tractor this time. As far as I knew, the bullying had calmed down since Tom had Seb looking out for him. It was a small village and many of the parents of the kids at school knew the Braithwaites by reputation. Rumours spread quickly in a small village; the gossip machine had most likely already noted that Tom had the Braithwaites on his side, and I was sure that not even spotty teenage boys were stupid enough to cross a family primarily made up of strapping farmers.

I was early for my shift, so I decided to smoke a cigarette before starting. To my surprise, Alfie showed up at my regular smoking spot. He nodded and smiled.

"Not seen you for a while."

"I took a bit of time off to sort out my car," I replied. "Got any more stories for me?"

"Let's see." He leaned against the wall of Crowmont Hospital, his ashen-brown hair picking up brick dust. "Yeah, there was another famous patient at Crowmont. I think it was the late fifties. She was from London, this girl. Her name was Laura something. Laura Simpson. She wasn't much of a murderer, in fact she killed only one man: her father."

My skin turned cold. "What happened?"

"The father was an abusive piece of shit. He kept her locked up in the cellar for long periods of time, beat his wife, drank. One day, Laura snapped and killed him. She stabbed him seventy-five times, all over his torso. When the police arrested her she was having hallucinations, saying ants were all over her body. She'd dug little holes into her arms with the same knife."

"These stories you tell me," I said, shaking my head. "I need to stop listening to them."

"The real world is disturbing," Alfie replied.

"Do you think Laura deserved to be punished for killing her abusive father?" I asked.

He took a drag and stared up at the sky above the metal frames of the gates around Crowmont. "I'm not the law, am I?" He hesitated. "But I wouldn't punish her. There was a case once, another one at Crowmont. Graham Edwards was found guilty of killing Susan Brown. This was before fingerprints and forensics. Edwards was brought here, when Crowmont was still an asylum, because he had an IQ of fifty-one and wouldn't survive in prison. He died here fifteen years later. Thirty years after that, forensics reassessed the evidence and realised that it was Susan Brown's husband who raped and killed her, not Graham Edwards. He died in this place and he didn't do anything wrong." He shrugged his shoulders. "Not very fair, is it?"

"No," I agreed.

He turned and looked me directly in the eye. "But what can you do?" As he flicked his cigarette onto the ground, a magpie flew in front of us and landed on the lawn to the left of the carpark. Was it Pepsi? I wasn't sure.

"Good morning, Mr. Magpie," said Alfie as he turned and walked away.

Isabel was at her desk this time. She was drawing again, which I took to be a good sign.

"How are you feeling today?" I asked, pulling up a chair and placing it by the open door of her room. It was late evening and outside I knew the sun was setting—not that you could tell while inside the hospital. Such institutions always blocked out the outside world, merely leaving you a glimpse. Hospitals reminded me of schools, where you could watch thunderstorms from the window, clustered with your class, bonded together as one for an afternoon. It felt like the storm would never touch you if you were in class with the teacher. Perhaps it was because in school, or hospital, or prison, you hand over the control of your life to someone better: a teacher, a doctor, a guard, a boss.

"Like I slept for a week," she said, smiling. "What about you? Any sleepwalking?"

"None."

"Nightmares?"

"None."

Her smile widened. "You're healing, Leah."

"I hope you are too."

"It's too late for me," she said sadly. She turned back to her desk, pencil in hand.

"What are you drawing today?" I asked.

"Pepsi," she replied. "I haven't seen him for a few days and I miss him."

"I think I saw him outside," I said.

"While you were having a cigarette break?" She lifted her gaze from the paper and flashed me half a smile. "I can smell it."

"Sorry."

"It's okay. I like the smells of the outside world. Sometimes you smell a little bit like alcohol, too."

I was shocked. I'd never come to work drunk. "I… Isabel, that can't be right."

"It is," she said. "Only a little bit. You try to cover it up with chewing gum and body spray, but I can smell it a bit. Do you drink at night?"

There was nothing I could say. I glanced anxiously in both directions along the corridor. It was possible that there'd been a few days where I'd been hungover, but I would never have been over the limit when driving. But what if it'd been more than I thought? What if Chi had noticed the smell?

"It's okay," Isabel said. "I would never tell anyone. You're my favourite nurse, you know. You're the kindest nurse I've ever had. You helped me apply for the Koestler Award, you let me draw you, and you tell me all about yourself. You even care about my reassessment and the fact that I might go to big-girl prison. None of the others ever cared like that, not even Alesha. I like you too much to tell anyone."

"I never drink at work," I said quietly, paranoid that another patient might overhear.

"Oh, I know. It's okay. I'll never tell anyone." She winked at me, before getting on with her drawing. After a short pause, she said. "I think magpies might be my favourite birds. They're so clever. Pepsi brings me things for me to make my own nest. Sometimes I wish I could. It'd be a lot cosier than this room. Maybe I could make a little nest in the woods somewhere and live on my own. That way no one would bother me and I wouldn't bother them."

"Would you like that?" I asked.

"Maybe. As long as Owen could visit. He came today, actually. He's disappointed in me for hurting myself."

The mention of Owen worried me. What if he'd told Isabel that I'd visited her home? Would Isabel feel that I'd crossed a line? What if she went to Chi and told him what I'd done? I searched her face for any evidence that she knew, but Isabel's expression was blank. I leaned back in my chair and tried to relax. Why would Isabel tell Chi anything? Then again, it was odd for her to bring up the drinking, too. She seemed off today. It wasn't often she talked about anything as negative as this; usually she focused on the positives. Perhaps it was the wave of depression that had gripped her all week.

"It gets claustrophobic in this place sometimes," she said. "There are too many people here. I can't walk down the corridor unless there's someone with me. The only time I'm alone is at night and in the bathroom. It's suffocating."

"I know it might feel like that," I replied. "But it's in your best interest for the time being."

"*My* best interest? Or is it in the best interest for the rest of the world?" She rolled her eyes. "I am a *murderer,* after all. At least, that's what the legal system decided when I was fourteen years old." She tapped her pencil on the top of her desk and lowered her eyes.

"Have you been thinking about your conviction, Isabel?"

"More than usual, yes," she said. "Maybe it's because of those bitches out there stamping on my feet when I walk past. Pushing me into walls. Leaving notes in my room that tell me I'm the devil. Maybe it's all piling up on top of me. I can't breathe." She tapped the pencil so hard I was worried it might break or hurt her wrist.

"I'm sorry that's happening to you," I said, and meant it.

"It's not your fault." She threw the pencil onto the desk and turned so that her body faced me, crossing one leg over the other. "I remember more about that day now."

"You do?" Though I tried to play it cool, my heart responded to my excitement. She remembered?

"Not everything—a few little bits here and there. Can I tell you what I remember?"

I rubbed sweaty palms against my thighs. "Yes."

"It was warm and sunny. I was wearing a white sundress that I didn't like very much, but Mum wanted me to wear it because the Earnshaws were coming and they were important. I wanted to wear jeans and a t-shirt but that didn't 'convey the right image.' Owen was forced into a smart shirt with buttons that he kept undoing. Mum wanted them done up right to the collar, but Owen felt like it was strangling him. When the Earnshaws arrived we were supposed to line up like tin soldiers and say hello. We were supposed to pretend we were a happy little family."

I tried to imagine what the Fieldings had looked like that day. Had they stood with forced smiles on their lips, cheeks straining with the effort? In my mind, the white house was so dazzling it created an eerie backdrop to their plastic perfection.

"Why did you have to pretend? Didn't you live in a happy home?" I asked.

"It was okay," she said with a shrug. "But Dad was always working, and Mum seemed spaced out a lot of the time. Neither of them was that bothered about spending time with us. That's why we used to play on our own a lot. Owen liked to play hide-and-seek in the woods near the duck pond. Sometimes he used to pretend he was a wolf and I was Little Red Riding Hood. I even had a coat with a hood that I used to wear."

A shudder worked its way through my body. I think I physically trembled, because Isabel gave me an odd look, as though she had noticed my revulsion.

"It was perfectly innocent," she said defensively. "We liked the Grimm fairy tales. Sometimes we'd pretend we were Hansel and Gretel, leaving breadcrumbs through the trees. Owen believed in fairies for a while. He even built them little houses out of twigs and leaves."

Was I reading too much into their innocent games? If I didn't know a little girl had been brutally murdered on the Fielding property, would I think playing fairy tales was creepy?

"Did you play those games on the day Maisie died?" I asked.

"We didn't go down to the duck pond right away," she said. "I remember Mum had bought some finger food and laid it out on the kitchen table. The French doors were open, and Owen and I ran onto the patio with Maisie. She was eating a sausage roll and chasing us around with greasy pastry fingers. What was she wearing that day? Was it a yellow sundress? I seem to remember daisies, but I'm not sure. Maybe it was red. Or maybe I remember the red from… other things." She was lost in her memories now, staring beyond me at the wall above my head. "When Mum opened a bottle of champagne, the adults moved onto the patio, and we got bored of the small space, so we chased each other around the lawn for a bit. They'd finished the bottle by the time we decided to show Maisie the duck pond. They were drinking those adult drinks with lots of spirits in them, and we were pretty bored by then. Plus, Mum was mad at me because I'd tumbled down the hill and had grass stains on my dress. When she took me into the bathroom to clean me up, she told me I was too old to be running around with my brother and that I should start acting like a lady. I had an image to uphold, and that image didn't include grass stains."

I thought about Isabel's mother sitting at the dining table while her husband controlled everything. Maybe the woman felt she'd at least had one thing she could try and control: Isabel. But when Isabel was taken away from her, she cracked.

"Anyway, we took Maisie to see the duck pond. The previous owners had it built, apparently, and Dad let us buy some ducks to house there. It was a pretty big pond that stretched out where the lawn dipped. We'd never been allowed to go to the pond on our own. Not until I was twelve, anyway. From then on, I was deemed old enough to make sure my little brother didn't drown. I always loved that pond. Dad used to take me when I was little. He'd hold my hand and carry a few slices of bread to feed the ducks." She paused. "We didn't go very often. Later, I'd go with our housekeeper, who was always reluctant to sit on the grass and feed the ducks. She was afraid of birds."

"Do you remember what happened when you were at the pond? How did you end up in the woods?"

"It was Owen's idea." She turned her head to the left and stared at her bedroom wall.

I followed her gaze to see what she was staring at. It was an image of a magpie.

"He wanted to play a game," she said in a quiet voice. It was as though she was in a trance. Had she forgotten I was there?

"What sort of game, Isabel?" My heart was pounding now. I was so close to finding out the truth of what happened the day Maisie died. Isabel was the key to it all, I knew she was. If she would just tell me…

"I…" she started. "I think I remember." In one swift motion, she dropped her head into her hands and began to groan.

"Isabel?" I stood up, alarmed at her reaction.

Isabel rose from her seat so that we were both standing face to face. Her cheeks were wet with tears, which she brushed away quickly.

"Do you remember?" I asked.

She nodded. Her shoulders were slumped and her mouth was slightly open, as if in shock. "I… I want to tell you." Her bottom lip trembled as she spoke.

I stepped closer. "You can trust me."

"I know I can." She moved towards me. "Please, hear my story."

"I will," I said.

And before I knew it, I was moving into her room.

PART 2

Sometime in the middle of the night, the alarm sounded out through Hutton village. The high-pitched blare woke many from their peaceful slumber.

Not once in fifty-two years had the alarm rung out. Some didn't even know what it was about, but many others did, and they knew it meant only one, terrible thing.

A patient had escaped from Crowmont Hospital.

CHAPTER
20

L et me check that again.

One. Two. Three. *Rattle. Rattle. Rattle.*

The door is definitely locked, but as I turn away from it, my skin itches so badly that I want to check one more time. I allow my fingers to run over the heavy-duty locks that have been installed on the thick wooden door. No one is getting in through that door.

But what about the windows? I have this issue before I go to bed every night. The ground floor windows are the perfect way to break in. One large brick, and the single pane of glass would smash with ease. I pull the woollen blanket around my shoulders and try to ignore the seeping, cold dread in my veins. It's time to go to bed.

These days I take a mug of Ovaltine to bed with me. The boxes of wine are gone. They don't mix well with my medication. I'm on medication now. That's part of my life.

Six months ago, Crowmont Hospital security found me half-unconscious and delirious on the floor of Isabel Fielding's room. The door was locked and Isabel was gone. Sometime in the night I'd swallowed eighteen 100-mg clozapine tablets; after the medical professionals pumped my stomach at York Hospital, I spent two hours hallucinating that a flock of birds was attacking me. The doctors were forced to restrain me, which only allowed the birds to peck out my eyes while I remained immobilised on the bed.

Sometimes, when I drift into sleep at night, I still feel the sensation of their beaks pecking against my eyelids.

The six months that have carried me kicking and screaming to this moment—checking the locks, closing the curtains, barricading myself into my bedroom—have been a period of revelation and realisation. Perhaps I should begin with what I remember, because there's a lot that I don't.

After recovering from my overdose, I was told by the police that Isabel Fielding had escaped Crowmont Hospital wearing my clothes and using my pass. At first, I didn't understand what they were saying to me. I wasn't even sure it was real. How did Isabel leave the hospital impersonating me? How did she get past the gates? But the police told me it was late—after midnight—and Isabel kept her head down through the corridors, flashed my pass to the receptionist, collected my car keys from my locker, and drove my car out of the front gate.

The guard saw my unique yellow and green Fiat Punto and automatically opened the gate. Why would he suspect that the woman inside, with the same colour hair and same build, would in actual fact be someone else? She had on my clothes and wore my pass around her neck.

How did she have my clothes?

How did she have my pass?

How did she know which car was mine?

How did she know which locker was mine?

The police asked me these questions over and over again, but I couldn't answer any of them. The last thing I remembered was sitting outside Isabel's room. She'd told me that she remembered more about Maisie's death. I was about to go into her room.

And then nothing.

Then birds pecking at my face, their clawed feet landing on my chest. Beaks tearing at my skin. Claws scratching. Feathers flying. It was furious and painful, and I never want to go through anything like that again. Why would I take the clozapine? Why would I have done that to myself? I know the potential side effects, and I understand exactly how dangerous such a large dose would be. I don't understand anything. All I know is that a patient had escaped on my watch, and now I don't know what to believe.

The revelations kept coming. A few days after Isabel's escape, after I'd recovered from the overdose, I was interviewed by a detective, DCI Murphy, who clearly believed I'd allowed Isabel to leave before taking an overdose out of remorse for my actions. The stubborn part of me scorned this theory, because I would never take an overdose, not after witnessing first-hand what it could do to a person.

But then I was admitted to Oakton Hospital, a psychiatric facility in Harrogate.

The rooms were locked at night, and I was forced to wear clothing without any buttons, zips, or draw strings, exactly like the patients at Crowmont. I padded around in slippers and was only allowed in the communal area if I behaved appropriately.

After being the nurse for so long, I discovered what it was like to be the patient.

It was in this new hospital that I was introduced to a therapist, Dr Ibbotson, who remains my doctor to this day. Now, however, the sessions are weekly and I don't live on the ward anymore. During our sessions, he sits with his long pianist's fingers idling on his knees as he listens attentively. Even as I think about him now I become nauseated, not because he is an unpleasant man, but because of the shameful things he has forced me to realise during our therapy sessions.

On my way up the stairs I close my eyes tightly to try and block out the memories of his patient, vacant expression as I gradually realised the lies I'd been telling myself ever since moving away from Hackney. It was Dr Ibbotson who had finally forced me to confront the truth, and I think I'll always hate him for that, despite how it has helped me in the long run.

It's cold tonight. September brings with it the promise of winter; the cold bite of the wind seeps in through the single-paned windows. I'm alone in the cottage. Tom was taken to a foster family while I was under psychiatric care. Even at the time, I knew it was for the best, because I want Tom to be safe, and being around me isn't safe anymore. But the lack of his presence in the house is vast, and if I dwell on how much I miss him, I begin to feel myself spiral down into the kind of despair that only a box of wine can fix. At least now I understand that the wine doesn't fix anything. It's a masking-tape patch that only works until the corners begin to peel again.

Every night at nine pm I call Tom's mobile to check he's safe, and then I inspect the windows and doors to be sure they are all locked, take my Ovaltine upstairs, turn off all the lights, and get into bed. It's not much of a life, but the routine helps me feel somewhat protected from whatever is out there lurking in wait.

I'm not sure what I'm waiting for. I'm not even sure if I'm in danger. I'm not sure if I know what's real and what isn't. All I know is that I need to feel safe. I need to know she—or he—isn't coming for me. I don't know which Fielding is the most dangerous—perhaps they're all as dangerous as each other—but I know they're all out there and at least one of them is a murderer.

Back when I was in the psychiatric ward, Dr Ibbotson worked

hard to confront the white lies and delusions I'd been telling myself. In a clean, white room with a desk more like a school table than the kind of desks you see in movies about therapists, he coaxed out of me the truth that I'd locked away for a long time.

"What do you remember about the funeral?" he'd asked as he sat cross-legged with a small notebook balanced on his knee. His long face was relaxed and neutral. His eyes blinked every now and then, which was the only movement of his inert form.

"I held Tom's hand next to the grave. My father's aftershave travelled downwind and smelled so strong that my stomach flipped over and I felt sick. I was crying a lot. I remember the wind on my wet cheeks. Everyone was in black."

"You smelled your father's aftershave," Ibbotson said. "But you told me it was a funeral for both of your parents."

"That's right," I said. "But I sensed that my father was there. I don't understand why. I've never believed in ghosts. I… I'm not crazy, I swear." I recognised the irony of my words, given where I was, but I was convinced that it'd been the drugs in my system after being found in Isabel's room that had made me crazy. Everything before was… It was hard and stressful and I'd made mistakes, but I hadn't been crazy. Had I?

"I need to go through what you've told me about the crime your father committed," Dr Ibbotson said, followed by a slow blink. "Your father stabbed your mother before killing himself. Both your parents died in the murder-suicide crime. Later, you attended the funeral of both your parents, where you sensed your father's presence."

"That's right. I don't understand why we're talking about this again." I ran my fingers through my hair, pulling at the ends in frustration. Therapy isn't supposed to be easy, but rehashing my parents' violent deaths didn't seem to be helping me. It was simply dredging up my old feelings of grief and guilt, despair and darkness.

"Leah, I need to show you something, and it's going to be difficult for you to see."

My fingers tightened around my hair. "Show me what?"

Dr Ibbotson flipped to the back of his notebook and retrieved a piece of paper with a black and white image on the front. Some sort of photocopy. He glanced at it briefly before placing it on the table and sliding it towards me. "This is a copy of the article that was printed in your local newspaper. Could you read that for me?"

I was already reading. With my head bent low, and my white fingertips clutching the sheet, I read the words and then I read them again. "This is wrong. This has been doctored. It's wrong." When I heard the tremble in my voice, I put the paper back down on the table and pushed it away. "It's wrong."

"Are you sure?" Dr Ibbotson clicked the button on his pen and lowered it to his notebook. I hated the thought of him writing his secret observations about me in his little pad.

"This article says that my father was arrested after Mum died. It says that he was alive. But that's not true. My father killed himself."

After Dr Ibbotson had finished writing his notes, he skipped again to the back of his notebook and retrieved another slip of paper. Again, he gave it a little glance before placing it on the table and sliding it across to me.

With trembling fingers I reached across and lifted the small, glossy, rectangular paper. A photograph, printed on cheap card, of my father. He was fatter, balding, and was wearing an ill-fitting jumper, a shade too bright for his pale skin. It was him all right, but it also wasn't him. I knew every expression on my father's face, from the amiable man who helped his neighbours to the drunken lunatic who terrorised his family, but I didn't recognise the slack expression on this man's face.

"This photograph was taken of your father last week in the high-security hospital where he's incarcerated. Your father was found guilty of the murder of your mother, but he was not found to be mentally fit to serve his sentence in prison. He was taken to Broadmoor Hospital where he is kept in a secure wing. Your father attended your mother's funeral under police custody."

"No." I shook my head. "No."

But deep down I knew it was true. As Dr Ibbotson was talking, I remembered that day with my father's aftershave drifting to me on the wind. I remembered Tom's cold hand in mine, and the fact that I didn't want to look to my right, where my father stood in handcuffs, stooped over so that his tears fell onto the grass. His sobs had been so loud that we'd barely heard the celebrant. I remembered thinking that I wished it was him in the ground.

When Dr Ibbotson gently took the photograph from my hand, I realised that I'd been clutching it so tightly there was a tear in the corner.

"What's happening to me?" My small voice was an echo in the white room. I felt like a shadow of the woman I used to be.

"I think you have been experiencing a nervous breakdown. I think you have had a psychotic break, which resulted in various delusions and hallucinations."

"So I'm crazy."

"No," he said, leaning closer. "Your mind is a little chemically imbalanced right now, but with the right medication, we can get you back on track."

I leaned forwards, resting my head in my hands. "I can't trust myself. I don't know what's real and what isn't. What if I let Isabel out deliberately? What if I'm as bad as all the others? Like the ones Alfie told me about? What if I'm like them?"

"Alfie?"

"A porter who worked on Morton Ward at Crowmont Hospital. We took cigarette breaks together, and he used to tell me about all the serial killers and murderers who stayed in Crowmont."

"It's interesting that you would want to hear these stories. Do you believe *you're* a murderer?" Dr Ibbotson asked.

"Yes," I said without hesitation. "I never stopped him, did I? I let him kill her. Mum would be alive if…"

"Your father killed your mother, Leah. You didn't do anything wrong and it was never your fault." He scribbled more into his book. "We need to talk about this Alfie."

"What about him?"

"He has the same name as your father."

No, no, no, no.

Dr Ibbotson flinched for the first time as I snatched the photograph back. I don't know why I needed the photograph to remind me; I know what my father's face looks like, but at the same time I needed to be reminded again so I truly understood. The man in the photograph was an older, fatter image of the man I'd shared every cigarette break with. Oh, I'd managed to change a few things—the slightly more narrowed eyes, thinner lips, thicker hair. But it was him, all right. All this time, I'd been haunted by the man I hated most on the world, and I hadn't merely conjured him with my broken mind. I befriended him, too.

"I feel sick," I said. "All those conversations with… with Alfie. They were all in my mind."

"Do you want a glass of water?"

"I'll be all right."

"Tell me if you need to stop." Dr Ibbotson had pushed a box of tissues along the desk towards me. "But I think it's time to talk about your father now."

I'd nodded, agreeing with him. "The first thing you need to know is: Tom isn't just my brother. He's also my son."

TRUE CRIME JUNKIE

Isabel is free

by James Gorden

Wow, I don't know what to say. I've spent so much time going through the Maisie Earnshaw case, talking on here about my suspicions about David and Owen Fielding, speculating whether Isabel Fielding might be innocent, but I never imagined this would happen. Did you?

Isabel Fielding is free, but not in the way I ever thought this would happen.

So, what do we know?

We know that a nurse (who will remain nameless for her own sake) entered Isabel's room and the door was closed. Now, the police haven't told anyone how long the nurse was in the room with Isabel, but we do know Isabel escaped the hospital at 1:30am. She left the hospital wearing the nurse's clothes, using the nurse's pass to get through the ultra-secure (pah!) wing of the hospital. She then retrieved the nurse's belongings from her locker, got into her car, and drove away into the night.

Meanwhile, the nurse was found after taking an overdose of anti-psychotic medication.

What the hell happened in that room?

Did the nurse believe Isabel was innocent? Did she set her free and then take a bunch of drugs as an after-party? Was the nurse using before Isabel was set free/escaped? Or did Isabel mastermind this entire venture?

Whatever happened, Isabel Fielding is now out there in the world somewhere. We'd better hope she really was innocent, or the world could be in trouble.

What do you think?

COMMENTS:

TrueCrimeLover: The nurse let her out. How could a trained nurse be so stupid as allow a prisoner to escape? It doesn't make sense.

JamesGorden: We all have off days…

Bundy's Bitch: Isabel did it. She's the mastermind behind it all. She's been waiting for some low-hanging fruit to pluck and this nurse came along at the right time.

RedRose: It was her brother. He blackmailed the nurse and got Isabel out. Bet they go on a crime spree now. Like Bonnie and Clyde, but Lannister style.

JamesGorden: Um, eww…

CHAPTER
21

"I was thirteen when I gave birth to him. The whole thing was a blur. All I remember is the screaming, not just from me, but from Tom too. His red little face all screwed up in anger. That's all it was: screams, blood, and my mother holding my hand. There's no father filled out on the birth certificate, and I never told my mother who the father was. I never told her, so I can't blame her for not knowing. I can blame her for not leaving when he continued to hit her, but I can't blame her for what he did to me. Perhaps if I'd told her she would have left him, at last, and she'd still be alive today."

"I'm not sure you can blame yourself for anything. You were a child," Dr Ibbotson had said kindly.

"No, I suppose not. But I had a chance to speak up. I was thirteen years old. I had to talk to the police, but I refused to tell them who the father was. In the end, they gave up with me and moved on to another case. I had my chance to tell them and I didn't."

"Why didn't you?"

"I was embarrassed!" I'd let out a hollow laugh that echoed off the walls and came back to me. "And I think some part of me still loved him, my father. I didn't want him to go away. This was all before he became very violent. Before the drinking got worse. He was still… he could still be, sometimes, a loving father." I inhaled loudly, sickened by my own words. Sickened by the fact that I missed him, no matter what had happened, no matter what he'd done. "It only happened one time, and sometimes I wonder if he even remembers what he did. Sometimes I feel like I made it all up in my mind. If it wasn't for Tom's existence, I think I might have blocked the whole thing out."

"You blame yourself for what happened." It wasn't a question because it was so obvious. I knew it myself, and I had for a long time.

"I begged Mum to raise Tom herself. No one knew I was pregnant, they just thought I was fat. Then, when I stopped going to school, a rumour spread that I'd been admitted to hospital after a suicide attempt. They said I was fat and depressed and wanted to die. They weren't wrong. I did want to die." I took a deep breath, composing myself as the memories came flooding back. It wasn't a time I liked to remember. When it came to Tom, I mostly tried to convince myself that the pregnancy and the labour had never happened. "I didn't hold him as a baby. I never breastfed him. He wasn't mine, I told myself. He was my little brother and I had no reason to feed him. That was Mum's job."

"And you've never told Tom any of this?" Dr Ibbotson asked.

"No. Are you joking? How could I tell him?"

"It would be very hard," he admitted. "But this isn't a unique case, sadly. You're not the first person to survive this kind of abuse, and Tom isn't the only child born from rape. If you want to tell him, you can."

My eyes had burned as I'd met the doctor's gaze. My skin burned along with them. Every part of me needed to shed tears, but I couldn't. "I always believed that Tom was born with the birthmark as a punishment for what happened to me. It was my fault."

"Birthmarks are a result of pigment cells and blood vessels. It could be genetic, but it's certainly nothing to do with anything you've done. You're not to blame, Leah. Think about that. You're not to blame."

But I didn't believe him. I couldn't.

The birds are quiet in the mornings now. They're either building their nests for the coming winter, or migrating away to a sunnier clime. The birds are quiet, but the spiders are restless. I hear them scuttling around my room at night. Except that I don't, not really.

Dr Ibbotson told me that one of the most common hallucinations in schizoid disorders is seeing insects. That makes sense when I think of the ants I'd witnessed invading the kitchen. Tom told me he'd never seen them, which always seemed bizarre at the time. Then there were the bats swooping through the sky at night and the insects I saw stealing around the hospital.

They weren't real. It was all in my head.

We're working on getting my anti-psychotic medication exactly right. It's a process. The latest had been doing well, until I started hearing the spiders. It's September, which is when they always come into the house to escape the rain, so I saw a couple of real ones. I even made myself hold one in my hand to prove it was real. But the fear of holding it triggered something in my mind, letting the hallucinations back in.

I get up, shower, dress, and eat breakfast. One of the other patients at Oakton Hospital told me all about overnight oats, so I'm trying them. She was right; they're delicious. No more hangovers for me. I start the day with water, oats, and a morning check that everything is in order. I need to know that no one broke into the house while I was asleep.

As soon as I wake, I have to check that the windows and kitchen door are still locked. Most importantly, everything must be as I left it before I went to bed. I need to know that I didn't sleepwalk and touch anything.

The sleepwalking seems to have stopped, but I no longer trust myself or my judgment, which is why the rituals have become so important to me. Perhaps the sleepwalking component of my psychosis was more wine-induced than it was the mental illness.

As I'm about to open the kitchen door, the phone rings. I know who it is even before I answer, and as usual, I steel myself for whatever they might have to say.

"Hello."

"Leah, it's James Gorden."

"Hi, James."

"There's no news."

"Thanks for calling."

"No worries. I'll keep my ear to the ground."

I hang up. I hate how James talks as though we're living in the movies. I still think he believes this is all a game. But on the other hand, he does tend to have good contacts, and he tells me more than the police do.

After Isabel escaped Crowmont a huge manhunt ensued, but I was mostly unconscious or delirious as helicopter lights swept Hutton village and the surrounding area. Tracking dogs searched the moors and the woods. Police visited every train station, bus station, and petrol station in the area. The public were encouraged to come forward with any information. Isabel's most recent photograph was plastered all over the news.

There have been sightings. London. Manchester. York. Edinburgh.

People everywhere think they've seen her face, but they're mostly either mistaken or crazy. DCI Murphy, who is running the operation, told me about one real sighting, or at least a possible one; that was in East London, three months ago. Since then, there has been nothing new. She's vanished. Some days I wake up feeling positive enough to believe she's innocent of the murder, and now she's living somewhere abroad, grateful for her newfound freedom. Other days, I wake up believing a psychotic murderer is out there somewhere, and that one day she will catch up with me in a sick game of cat and mouse. Sometimes I tell myself that Isabel doesn't care about me in the slightest, that all I was to her was a means to an end. But I never quite believe it. We'd developed a connection while at Crowmont Hospital, and I can't shrug away the feeling that our fates are intertwined with one another.

But when you can't even trust your own memories, it's difficult to know what to believe.

Is Isabel innocent?

Am I innocent?

Is David Fielding a murderer?

Are *all* the Fieldings murderers?

The police scoured the Fielding property, and found no trace of Isabel, and no reason to suspect any of them of a crime.

And yet, I still find myself checking David Fielding's social media accounts on a regular basis. Where is he? What is he doing? The man travels on business a lot, tweeting from London, posting a picture of his lunch on Instagram from a bistro in Paris. Wherever he visits, I search for news articles of missing people, just in case. Even after all this time and everything that's happened, I still can't quite let it go.

At least now I understand why I became so obsessed with the Fieldings. It was a distraction from what was going on in my head. But now that Isabel is out there in the real world and I know what has been happening to me, I don't feel safe anymore. I don't remember what happened in Isabel's room before I was found that morning. I've imagined every possible scenario. I've imagined Isabel telling me a terrible story, so disturbing that I gave her everything—my clothes, keys—and abandoned the career I'd proudly built over the years to ensure she got her freedom. I've imagined Isabel overpowering me and forcing me to hand over what she needed. But in none of the scenarios can I figure out how I ended up with 1800mg of clozapine in my system. Was Isabel trying to kill me? Was I trying to kill myself? If it was the latter, where did I get them from? I'd have had to steal the tablets, which would mean it was all premeditated.

But what I do know is that I can't rule out the suggestion that Isabel tried to kill me, which means she could do it again at any time without any warning at all. And along with my fear of what Isabel may or may not be capable of, I still have the creeping, chilling feeling that violent David Fielding is out there, still angry with the way I interfered in his family's life. Now he believes I let his dangerous daughter go, and maybe he wants revenge for that act.

Whenever I search for David Fielding's name, I find myself clicking on the same link over and over again, because I can't help myself.

The YouTube video begins with an advert—usually for pregnancy tests or the latest diet food—which I eagerly skip after watching it for the allotted time. Then David's face pops up on the screen. It's Newsnight, and Kirsty Wark sits behind a desk in a dark studio with David to her right, lounging on a black sofa. Blue lights illuminate his face in an eerie glow, while the studio audience watches with interest. Kirsty introduces David, explains Isabel's past, and talks to him about the failings of the NHS. I've seen this video so many times I could almost quote it.

"I don't blame the NHS, but the truth is they failed her, and they failed my family. The NHS budget has been cut so many times that security measures in these facilities are appalling." He throws his arms up and the audience claps along.

I find myself balling my hands into tight little fists. What does he know about working in a psychiatric hospital? What does he know about any of it? He never even visited Isabel.

"We don't feel safe in our own home anymore," he continues. "My wife cries herself to sleep at night because she thinks Isabel is going to come home. She wants her home, she really does—we never stopped loving Isabel. But we know what she is, and we know how dangerous she is, especially when she isn't taking her medication. Some nights, I lie awake staring at the ceiling, truly believing that Isabel is going to come home and kill us all."

His expression seems off. As always, I pause the video and stare into the man's eyes, observing the concern on his face. It could be my paranoid imagination, but David Fielding strikes me as a man who has observed and imitated what a concerned expression should look like. There he sits, with his eyebrows knitted, his jaw clenched, and the barest hint of moisture in his eyes. I can't stop staring at him as he tricks the entire audience. I'm convinced he's a sociopath. *Convinced.*

With a sigh, I click the play button and allow the video to progress to the part I love to hate: the part about me.

"And what about the nurse who was in charge at the time?" Kirsty asks. "Do you blame her? It says here that Isabel was on twenty-four-hour surveillance at the time. How could this have happened? Isabel left wearing the nurse's clothes, carrying the nurse's pass. It's almost unbelievable what happened."

"No," David replies, shaking his head and looking down at the ground. For dramatic emphasis he lifts his head and stares directly into the camera. "It's not unbelievable, not if you look at the facts. Since Isabel's escape, the nurse has been admitted to a psychiatric facility. She's deeply disturbed. Do I blame her? No. She's ill. She should never have been allowed to work. How could her mental illness go unnoticed? Why didn't anyone see that this woman was unfit to be a nurse?"

"But what do you believe happened in that room?" Kirsty prompts. "Did Isabel overpower the nurse?"

David shakes his head again. "No. I don't believe that. This nurse was just disturbed enough to let my daughter out. The nurse was deluded enough to believe that Isabel is innocent, and in her sick state she let a dangerous criminal into society."

"You think she acted out of some sense of justice? She freed your daughter intentionally?"

"Yes," David says. "That's exactly what I believe."

CHAPTER
22

I f there's one good part of this chaotic mess I'm in, it's that I've managed to keep Tom away from it all. After I was found delirious and drooling on the floor of Isabel's room, and later committed to Oakton Hospital, Tom was taken into foster care. At seventeen years old, Tom could legally live on his own or ask to come home to me, but I've suggested that he stay with the foster family until everything is settled. I've met them a few times since leaving the hospital, and they're good people with a lot of patience. Tom is happy with them for now.

They live ten minutes outside Hutton in a pleasant, five-bedroom house situated away from major roads, with a long-stretching back garden and a brown fence. Mary and Gavin have three children, two of whom have left home for university, and have been fostering children for the last five years. When I was told that Tom would be taken to a foster home, I imagined a care home filled with lurking evil in the older bullies and the abusive staff, but this couldn't be further from my fears. Mary's cocker spaniel, Rusty, greets me as always with a friendly bark and tail-wag as I open the gate to the garden, and their youngest daughter Cora waves from the swing at the end of the lawn.

"Hi, Leah." Mary is drying her hands on a tea towel. Her hair is messy, more grey than black, and she has deep lines around her eyes, but she also has the easy, relaxed smile of a woman who has lived well. "Tom's upstairs. He's excited about seeing you. Go on up."

"Thanks." I rub my hands on my jeans, always feeling awkward whenever I see Mary or Gavin. I'm never sure what they know about my past. Do they know about Tom? Do they know what my father did to me all those years ago? Do they know that Tom is my son and my brother?

I keep thinking about Dr Ibbotson's words during my therapy sessions. He has this idea that telling Tom who his real father is would help me heal from the guilt I carry. He thinks that I no longer feel guilty about the actual abuse, and that my current guilt stems from the lies I told to protect Tom from the truth. But how can I do that to him?

"Hey, stranger," I say, poking my head around his open bedroom door. As always, I find myself choking up when I see him, especially in this spacious, pleasantly decorated attic room, nothing like the poky rooms in the cottage with scatterings of mould in the corners of the ceiling.

Tom is sitting at his desk with his back to the door. When he hears my voice, I see his body jolt with surprise and his hand moves swiftly to the mouse to click off the web page he was looking at. I don't get a good look at the page, but I see enough to know it isn't porn, which is a relief.

"Everything all right?" I ask.

My son has his father's eyes, which are currently red and blotchy.

He tries very hard to wipe away a tear before I step into the room, but it's too late, I've spotted it.

"Hey, what's going on?" I hurry over to the desk and stretch my arm across his shoulders, squeezing him to my waist. "What's happened?"

A few moments pass before Tom composes himself enough to be able to talk. "They're all fuckers and I hate them."

"Hate who?" I move away and sit on the edge of his bed, all my focus on Tom. A hot blast of protective emotion spreads over my skin, prickling the hairs on my arms. I don't know if it's motherly or sisterly, and perhaps I'll never know. All I know is that I want to hurt whoever has hurt him.

"Them. The people who made this." He clicks the mouse and the website pops up again.

This time I get a good look at the entire page, which is cruelly called 'Tommy's Jugs' and contains photographs of Tom from school in unflattering poses, zoomed in so that his unfortunately large and flabby pecs are showing through his t-shirt. Some are zoomed in to show his birthmark and double chin.

"It gets worse," Tom tells me.

He clicks onto a separate page where there are Photoshopped pictures of Tom's face put onto the bodies of sumo wrestlers, hippopotamuses, pandas, and anything else round-shaped. He scrolls down the page slowly so I get a good view of the imaginative cruelty inflicted by teenagers.

"People can upload whatever they want. They're all from different people at school. Dozens of them."

"Do Mary and Gavin know?" I ask.

He shakes his head.

"I'm going to fucking kill them," I say, and for a fleeting moment I actually want to murder the little bastards who think it's amusing to demoralise and target a vulnerable young man like Tom. "Wait, hold on, go back one."

Tom scrolls back up the page, past a Photoshopped image of him on a mobility scooter in a mall in America, and another image of him next to an enormous cheeseburger, to the one I want to take a second look at.

"Stop."

"What is it?" he asks.

"Nothing, just… that one's a bit weird. Different to the others, don't you think?"

"I guess so," he says.

The picture is of a large, fat bird with a red chest. A robin. The bird's head has been replaced with a picture of Tom, which I notice is the same picture of Tom used in a few of the other images. But more care has been applied to this Photoshop. The composition is more pleasing to the eye and the background is pretty. The bird is on a branch next to the window of a house that looks a little like the cottage.

The position of the bird looking in the window of the house is unnerving and artistic. It's too familiar.

"Shut it down," I say.

Mary and Gavin are kind enough to go with me to the school to speak to the head teacher, Mr Kallas. We want to show a united front against the bullying Tom is facing at Hutton Comprehensive.

"I never expected this from a rural school," I admit, as we sit in the office that overlooks the rugby pitch. "The level of maliciousness is frankly worrying. And from A-level students! They should know better."

"I completely agree." Mr Kallas lifts his hands. "The creators of the website will be excluded. It's without a doubt the most shocking incident I've ever seen here at Hutton School. I'm so sorry Tom has had to go through this."

The meeting consists of the head teacher, as well as a school psychologist, one of the governors, and a police officer, PC Abbott. The police are involved to try and work out who set up the website. None of them seem to believe me about Isabel Fielding, but I'm told they're also looking into the origin of the bird image. I don't hold out much hope.

When I let out a heavy breath, Mary reaches across and places a hand on my arm. I can't bear to think of Tom going through all this. Knowing he's safe has been the one good part of this mess, and the one thing I think about when I'm on my own in that cottage that makes me happy. I miss him, of course I do, but knowing he's safe is everything. Everything.

Someone is trying to take that away from me, and I think it's Isabel. And if I'm right, it means she was guilty all along.

"He wants to leave," I tell the head teacher. "But there's nowhere else he can attend to sit his A-levels. He doesn't have a car yet—we can't afford one—and all the colleges are over an hour on the bus. Please, sort this problem out so my…" I hesitate. "…brother can continue his education. He's done nothing wrong. I'm the one who's made the mistakes and that's probably why they're targeting him again."

Mr Kallas's sharp blue eyes hit mine, and I know he's thinking about the escaped psychotic criminal from Crowmont Hospital, and my stay in the psychiatric ward. I'm sure he's one of the people who whisper about me in Hutton village. I see them all, casting guilty glances my way before they disappear behind their hands to talk about me. They all wonder if I did it. Well, so do I.

"I know his home life has been disrupted recently," Mr Kallas says tactfully. "But his grades are still decent and I can see he's trying hard. We like Tom very much here. He has a flair for creativity and his essays are very thoughtful. You're doing a good job raising him, Leah."

The words thump me in the chest, and my chin wobbles as I stem the desire to burst into tears. I might be Tom's mother, but I've never felt like it. Yet, at the same time, I *have* raised him, because my parents weren't fit to do the job themselves. I *have* raised him, and I don't want to let him down. Not now.

Mary passes me a tissue.

TRUE CRIME JUNKIE

Road trip
by James Gorden

The last sighting of Isabel Fielding was in the northeast of London two weeks ago. Your intrepid blogger decided to travel down to the area in the hope of catching a fleeting glimpse of the woman herself. What did I expect to see? An innocent woman enjoying her freedom? An innocent woman with nowhere to go and no one to see, living homeless on the streets of London like so many others? A guilty woman searching for her next victim? Evading the police with clever disguises?

Or, most probably, I wouldn't see her at all. But I had to try.

So I took a copy of the photo the police supplied when Isabel escaped, and I walked the streets of London asking people if they'd seen her. During that time I was mugged once and assaulted twice by the helpful people of London town, but no one recognised her.

It has been a week since I set up in a cheap B&B (no expense account for me! Get on Patreon, you lovely lot), but I'm still hopeful. Isabel Fielding is out there, and I want to be the one who finds her.

Meanwhile, guess who else is in London? According to

his Twitter account, David Fielding is in London on business. While he has a meeting in the Gherkin, his daughter is lurking somewhere, out there. Does he know? Has he come to meet her? Is it a coincidence?

Who knows?

Maybe I'll be the one to find out!

COMMENTS:

Bundy's Bitch: James, get over yourself, you're not going to be the one to find Isabel. She's clearly being funded by her dad. I bet she's getting plastic surgery right about now.

TrueCrimeLover: James, BE CAREFUL. These people are dangerous!

CHAPTER
23

There is a point, above the cottage, above the abandoned farmhouse, above the village of Hutton and all the countryside that spreads out below, where I can find peace. It's a quiet place, away from the main path, where the cold wind stings my skin, and my lungs get that good ache that reminds me I'm alive.

That's where I am right now, letting all my fears drop away one by one. Isabel rolls down the hill away from me. Tom gets lost in the grass. Money seeps into the soil. I'm free.

Seb shifts near me, pushing his hands deep into his pockets. Since Isabel escaped from Crowmont, he has accompanied me on the occasional walk, showing his support with silence as always. His silence is as familiar and warm as a well-fitting glove. When I sit down on a rock jutting out of the hill, he sits next to me and our legs casually brush together. The intimacy is there, but we haven't acted on it yet. I'm not ready, and I think he senses that.

We're not looking at each other, but I see movement out of the corner of my eye and know he's turned his head to face me. I do the same until we're looking into each other's eyes. What do I say to the man who has quietly saved my life? Without Seb I would be homeless and afraid with no one in this world to count as a friend.

My phone rings, rudely breaking the silence. I dig into my pocket and answer the call.

"This is DCI Rob Murphy. You asked me to look into one of the posts on the bullying website in connection to Isabel Fielding."

"I did," I reply. "And?" My leg moves away from Seb's as I feel myself close in and withdraw from him, preparing myself for the worst.

"The post was made from a public library in East London," says the detective. "Whereas the website and the other posts were all created in and around Hutton. You might be right about Isabel's involvement in the website. I don't know how she might have heard about this website, unless she's been keeping tabs on social media. Does your brother have a Facebook profile?"

"Yes, of course he does, he's seventeen. He has so many social media accounts that I can't keep up. I haven't heard of half of them."

"Tell him to disable them all," Murphy says.

My throat is raw. Here is my worst fear coming to life in the place I find peace. I can't bear it. "You need to keep him safe."

"And you, Leah. If Isabel is stalking you both, you will need to be careful. Is there someone you can stay with?"

"No."

"Then I'll see what manpower we can spare. And you call me on this number every night to tell me you're safe. Is that clear?"

"It is."

"I'm not happy with you still being in that house," Murphy says with a sigh. He's mentioned this before in previous conversations, but I've always been pretty insistent on staying at the cottage. I want to be close to Tom, and I don't want to give up the job Seb has given me. "Isn't there a hotel you can stay in?"

"I can't afford it," I admit.

Seb looks at me sharply with eyes that scrutinise me. I'm sure he's wondering how much money he can offer me before I get offended and clam up. A small shake of my head hopefully puts those thoughts out of his mind.

"I feel safe here," I say. "I have the Braithwaites' farm a few minutes away. She doesn't know where I live. I don't use social media and I never told her." It's true, but there were things I revealed in the hospital that she might be able to put together. My other worry is that David Fielding could use his power and connections to find out exactly where I am.

"You have my number," he says, before hanging up.

I'm convinced that the pity he feels for me runs deep. As far as DCI Murphy is concerned, I let Isabel go, thinking I was acting as some white knight there to save her from her conviction. For all I know, he could be bang on the money. I truly believed Isabel was innocent and that the murder of Maisie Earnshaw should at least be re-opened. The email I sent to the police didn't help my case. There it was, in black and white, with underlying tones of obsession between every line. Everyone knew my interest in Isabel bordered on creepy, and my conduct at the hospital hadn't been great either. I'd received a warning for arriving late to work, and my colleagues had noted my often slightly dishevelled appearance.

DCI Murphy is proceeding on the basis of Occam's Razor, whereby the most logical and probable solution is most likely the truth, just as James Gorden had explained in Costa on that warm spring Saturday. I am beginning to come to the same conclusion.

Back at the cottage, Seb leaves me with fresh milk and eggs so I can at least eat, but I'm not hungry. I ring Tom instead and cringe when I hear the note of worry in his voice.

"Leave the school," I urge. "I know I told you not to, but it's different now. If you're in any kind of danger whatsoever, keeping you safe is more important than any exams or sticking it to a bully. While you're in school Isabel knows where you are. There's one school in Hutton village and she'll figure it out. At least, if you're home with Mary, Gavin, and a police escort, I don't have to worry about you."

"Come stay with us."

The phone is slippery in my sweating palms. I want to, but wouldn't doing that put him in even more danger?

"Mary and Gavin are nice people, but I think that might be pushing it a bit far, matey."

"They'll be fine," he says, his voice high-pitched and frightened. "They'll understand."

"Hey, who's the big sister here? I'm supposed to be the one telling you what to do."

"Not that I ever did what you told me to do," he points out.

I let out a laugh. "You weren't so bad, little bro. I have the Braithwaites up here. They've got my back, as well as tractors and diggers, and about a hundred pigs out for blood. I'm going to be fine."

A short exhale is all I get for the attempt at humour.

"Leah, can I ask you a question?"

"Of course you can. What is it?" Despite common sense telling me otherwise, I'm gripped with fear at the thought that Tom has somehow figured out the truth.

"Did you let her out? I won't blame you if you did. You were ill, and you thought you were doing the right thing for someone who was innocent. It's okay, you can tell me."

"I wish I could tell you, but I don't remember anything that happened in the room before she left the hospital. It's all gone from my mind."

"What does that feel like?" he asks.

"Horrible," I admit. "Like someone stole the memories intentionally. I guess it's like coming home from holiday and realising someone has burgled your house. But it's all right. I'll get over it. I'm doing better now, and I'm figuring out what's real and what isn't. Things got kinda blurry for a while there."

Tom sighs. "Sometimes I wish I believed Dad had died too."

My heart thumps. "So do I. And then I feel horrible, like I'm as bad as him."

"Me too."

"Tom," I say, and my voice breaks. "I swear I'm not drinking anymore, okay? I'm sorry you had to see me like that before it all happened and I lost my job."

"It's okay."

"Thanks."

"You're not like him, you know. You don't have whatever it is that he has."

My hand gropes down to grip the kitchen table and my eyes fill with tears as I stare out the window. "That means a lot."

"It's just the truth."

"Still it means a lot." I wipe away the tears with the backs of my hands and try not to sniff so that Tom knows I'm crying. It results in a dribble of snot working its way down my lips. "Hey, I have to go work in the farm shop. I'll call you tomorrow, okay?"

"Yeah, speak to you tomorrow."

The afternoon runs on without incident as I spend it weighing meat, counting eggs, and gift-wrapping jam jars. It's a relief to have this time so I can try and shut off my mind from everything else. Later on, after eating toast and butter over the kitchen sink, watching Pye stalk confidently along the dry stone walls around the cottage, I suddenly realise that I haven't heard from James Gorden today.

SARAH A. DENZIL

Leaving the toast on the kitchen counter, I retrieve my phone and pull up his number. It's strange that he hasn't called. We've fallen into a routine that hasn't been broken since I was released from hospital.

His phone rings, but there's no answer. I take a bite of my toast and try again. Still no answer.

Before trying the third time, I hurry around the house, checking the locks on the doors and the windows. Everything is shut, locked, and nothing has been disturbed. I get James's answering message yet again, but this time I leave a message asking him to call me.

Without hearing from him I don't feel safe, so I check the locks and the windows again, pulling all the curtains shut. There's half a slice of toast left, but suddenly I don't have much of an appetite. I grab my laptop and quickly send off an email to his website. Maybe his phone is out of battery or he hasn't got signal. That's when I read the latest blog post. James is in London, in the same area where Isabel was last sighted.

CHAPTER
24

In a room that stinks of bleach, I look down and see the leather restraints around my wrists and ankles, holding me down onto a bed. A thin white robe covers me from neck to knees, but the material is so flimsy that the cold breeze easily penetrates down to my bones, chilling me to the core.

I remember the last time I felt this vulnerable, and it isn't a memory I wish to revisit. In that memory I was restrained too. Not with leather, but with hands. Willing it away, I close my eyes and concentrate.

There's a reason I'm here like this, but I'm not sure what it is. Is it to find the missing piece? I know there is one but I don't know how to find it. Maybe someone will let me go and I can explain to them that I'll be fine when I find the missing piece. That's all I need, I'm sure of it. But the room is empty, apart from me restrained to the bed in a hospital gown.

I can't look behind me because I can barely move my head, but I hear a strange sound, as if the air is moving. Perhaps a fan has been turned on, or some papers dropped to the ground. It could be a flap of wings, but I don't see how a bird could get into the closed room. For some reason the sound fills me with dread, and a cold sensation spreads up from my toes, like someone is slowly pouring cold water over my skin.

When the flapping sound starts again, I try my best to bend my neck back so I can see behind me, stretching as far as I can, with my eyebrows lifted so I can get a better view. But it's no good. I barely get past the pillows. Air ruffles my hair as the flapping intensifies until I can actually feel the direction of the movement coming from behind me. It's obvious now—there's a bird in the room with me, and I don't like it one little bit.

The restraints remain firm no matter how much I tug them. The leather is thick, and I can't seem to break free. A flutter of the wings puts my teeth on edge as the sound reverberates ominously around the empty room, building in volume as though the room is filling up with winged creatures. And then the squawking begins—a frenzied cawing that rings from one corner to another. Why can't I see these things? Where are they coming from? How are they getting into the room? Sweat dribbles its way down my face, burning my eyes, as I yank at my restraints, sending my body into a spasm.

The air moves again, and this time I feel the brush of a feather against my ear, causing me to recoil and twist my neck as I try to move away from its touch. I yell, hoping the sudden noise might scare it, or them, away. But whatever is in the room with me isn't your average disease-riddled city-dwelling pigeon—it's much worse, much more evil, and makes me think of all those supernatural omens I once scoffed at.

One for sorrow.

The rhyme is one we all know, isn't it? I learned it from my father who learned it from his mother. One for sorrow. Two for joy. Three for a girl. Four for a boy.

Good morning, Mr. Magpie.

I say the words out loud as if I'm in school assembly addressing the teacher. Perhaps if I say it the creature will spare me, but somehow I doubt it.

A feather brushes my cheek and I close my eyes, shivering in my restraints. They aren't coming off no matter what I do, so my body goes still, giving up. A weight lands on my chest, its claws digging deeply through my nightgown and into my skin. I'm cold all over, struggling to breathe. *This is what it's like to die*, I think suddenly, in a surreal, hallucinogenic epiphany.

When I open my eyes, I see what I'd feared before I closed them. The magpie is the largest I've ever seen, with tiny black eyes above its fearsome beak. It cocks its head to the left and regards me with malice. When it ruffles its feathers and puffs up its chest, ripples of blue spread along its wings like a slick of oil.

It takes a step, and the weight of its foot feels like a heartbeat. My breath catches in my throat as it angles its head down and attacks my flesh with its beak.

My screams are drowned out by the chorus of birds as they descend from the ceiling to cover me from head to toe.

I am a feast.

Are nightmares the mirror image of a broken mind? If so, my mind is in pieces.

Almost every night I dream of the terrible hallucinations I experienced in hospital following Isabel's escape. The flapping of wings can reduce my legs to jelly and my insides to water. Whenever I go to work through the farm, I walk as far away from the chicken coops as I can, dreading the sound of their clucks and crows.

I open the farm shop and go indoors, turning on the lights and starting up the till. Before Isabel escaped I was never someone who enjoyed cleaning or tidying, but now I need to keep my hands busy at all times, so I set to work, dusting down the counter and rearranging the displays. Seb says the shop has never been so clean.

It's another quiet day, which means I jolt every time the bell breaks a long silence. My eyes immediately seek out the face of the person entering, which doesn't really put our shoppers at ease, but I still can't help myself. They are all strangers today. The shop attracts a few regulars, and it supplies some of the pubs in the area, but today most of the shoppers seem to be tourists picking up treats for their holiday cottages: free-range eggs, expensive preserves, cheeses arranged in hampers. They come in couples and leave their border collies tied up outside while they peruse the aisles, deciding between Stilton and broccoli pies or cheddar cheese pastries.

By the time the day ends, I'm tired, and Seb hasn't called in at lunchtime like he often does. I didn't eat much today. My sandwich is half eaten, wasting a nice slice of ham from the deli counter. Rather than throw it away, I decide to wrap it up and take it home. Throwing away food is not something I can stomach. Those who haven't always known if they can afford their next meal cannot bear to waste even a morsel that many others take for granted. As I'm closing up for the night, I realise how odd it is for me to work amongst wealth while poverty knocks at my door.

As soon as I'm home, I try calling James Gorden again but there's still no answer. There are no new emails in my inbox, and I have one text from Tom telling me about his day with Mary and Gavin. I'm relieved that he decided to stay at home rather than go into school. The three of them binge-watched sci-fi shows on Netflix. Reading his message makes my chest feel tight. I miss him. I even miss the loud music at night and the teenage scowl greeting me in the mornings.

Today has been a lonely one, but I'm lucky to have people who care enough to make sure I'm safe and healthy. Seb has given me a home, a job, and most of the time he feeds me, too. Tom never goes a day without checking in with me. As I examine every lock and window in the house, I remind myself of that.

The sun begins to set as I lock the kitchen door and rattle the handle, turning the house gradually dark as I move systematically through the cottage, turning on the lights and closing the curtains. Each of the doors, even the internal ones, are closed, trapping me in the tiny space of the living room. I need them closed because if someone is in the house, they'll have to open the door to move through the house and then I'll hear them. I pull each curtain straight, and let my fingers trail over every surface, checking everything. Are the pictures as straight as I left them? Is the TV remote in the same spot? Has someone moved the coffee table an inch to the left? Is my bedding tucked in the way I do it?

Usually, after I've been through the entire house, I can relax knowing that no one has broken in and I'm completely alone, but this time that sense of relaxation never comes. My checks always end in Tom's room, which is always the hardest to make sure no one has entered because I never quite remember where he left everything. I don't tend to touch anything in his room, so I have no memory of how his belongings ended up where they did.

After finishing Tom's room, I go back to the kitchen and begin again, taking it slowly, letting my eyes roam over the mugs on the kitchen counter, into the living room where magazines are stacked up by the sofa, into the narrow hallway with the coats on the wall, up the stairs to the bathroom where shampoo bottles stand precariously on the edge of the bath, to my room with my clothes in a heap, to Tom's room where his posters stare down at me. It's no good. I don't feel relaxed.

Something is out of place. Something is different.

But what is it?

CHAPTER
25

Dr Ibbotson stretches his long fingers like he's at a concert preparing himself for a performance, before lifting his right leg over his left and settling into his seat. Now that I'm no longer an inpatient at the hospital, I come to meet him once a week in his office, which is decorated much more pleasingly than the hospital room with the table. I get to sit in a luxurious leather armchair, and Dr Ibbotson sits behind a large mahogany desk. There are artistic watercolour paintings of poppies framed on the wall behind his head, and he has a full wall of bookshelves filled with textbooks and psychology journals.

"Are you still having the nightmares?" he asks.

I nod my head. "Not every night, but frequently."

"Have you heard any voices or seen anything that you suspect is a hallucination?"

"No voices. No hallucinations that I know of. Sometimes I hear spiders moving around the house."

"But you feel confident that you can distinguish between what's real and what is your mind playing tricks on you?" He taps his pen on his notebook and leans back.

"I am," I say, a little tentatively. There are times when I see a magpie in the sky, or ants in the grass, and wonder if it's all in my mind. "It's small creatures I'm never too sure of."

"Look for them acting in unusual ways. You understand the laws of the universe. The basic laws of physics. If an object begins to break those laws, it's a hallucination."

I nod. "I know that, but I don't think my hallucinations ever broke any laws of physics. They were… dull, I suppose. Sometimes I wish I saw crazy things, but I didn't. I had conversations with a man and I saw ants in my kitchen. They were normal."

"That's true," Dr Ibbotson admits. "Perhaps you need to understand your own triggers. Such as thinking of your father or Isabel. Alfie was always the personification of your father. He spoke to you about murderers residing in the place you work, which could be because your father represents the way you see your darker side. What do you think?"

"That makes sense," I say, squirming in my seat. Thinking about my dark side isn't something I care to do, but I'm all too aware of how everything is linked to my father. My main vice is drinking, which I have in common with him, as well as similar psychological issues. Sometimes I wonder whether I have the same violent nature buried deep down inside, and I wonder what it would take to wake that violent nature from its slumber. Why shouldn't a monstrous side lie sleeping within me? I have everything else from my father.

"I know it was me who looked up all those criminals. I used to get drunk, go on the laptop, research all the infamous residents of Crowmont Hospital, and then pass out on the kitchen table." When

I say it out loud the shame makes my cheeks burn. I brush my fringe away from my forehead to stop it sticking to my damp skin. "But I don't understand why I made up that *man* to tell me all the stories of the murders."

"Perhaps because your subconscious mind never wanted you to realise how much you enjoyed learning about those crimes," Dr Ibbotson suggests. "Why do you think that is?"

"Well," I say, thinking. "Because of Mum. She was a victim of a senseless, horrifying crime committed by her own husband. After she died, there were reporters and busybodies all talking about it, and I hated it. I hated them for gossiping about my mum's death like that, but at the same time..." I trail off, still not wanting to admit it.

"You're just as fascinated by murder as everyone else," Dr Ibbotson finishes for me.

This time, I turn away as I nod.

"Leah, it's normal to feel like that."

"It's sick."

"It feels like that to you because you're so close to a victim of murder. It's personal and painful. But human nature is to be curious about things we don't understand, and most people in the world don't understand why one person would choose to take another person's life. You're right, it *is* unpleasant to see how people can gossip about the victims and perpetrators of such crimes, but in a way it's helping them to deal with the horrors of everyday life. Do you understand?"

Honestly, hearing him say it is a relief. "I do."

"You are allowed to be interested in murder. You are allowed to wonder why these people committed these crimes. We're all fascinated by it. You're not a bad person for wanting to learn more."

"No," I say, "but I am crazy enough to hallucinate an entire person, so I can talk about it."

He lowers his head and raises an eyebrow. "You know the C-word isn't allowed in this office."

I roll my eyes, but I'm smiling at the same time.

"Tell me more about what you've learned about your triggers," Dr Ibbotson asks.

"Well, I know that my parents are the main triggers. The stress of Mum's death is what started this whole thing off. I convinced myself my father was dead and had some sort of psychotic break. My sleeping patterns became erratic. I drank too much, which didn't help, and I began to hallucinate bugs and people who don't exist. Then…" I pause.

"Go on." Dr Ibbotson senses that I have new information to tell him, and he leans closer in anticipation.

"There are a couple of things I heard that, now that I look back, I don't think were real. I was talking to Isabel once and she started saying very dark, worrisome things about her room and feeling trapped. It was out of character for her at the time and I don't think she said it at all. And then there was another occasion when I was walking away from Chi, the charge nurse, and he said something that was out of place."

"What did he say?"

"He said that Isabel was innocent. It wasn't like Chi. He never gave his personal opinion about the patients. But at the time it felt so real."

"This is good progress," Dr Ibbotson says.

"When Chi said that about Isabel, I… I felt so strongly about her innocence. I was obsessed with it. She never seemed like a criminal to me at all. She was a young girl who needed… who needed my protection."

"Do you think you have a strong urge to protect others?"

I rub my palms on my thighs. "I think I do. But I couldn't protect her—I failed."

"Isabel?"

"No. Mum."

Dr Ibbotson nods. "I see. But you do realise that you were the child. If anyone needed protection, it was you."

"I forced her to raise Tom. If I hadn't done that, maybe she would have had the strength to leave him."

"The past is the past, Leah. You are not responsible for any of the bad things that happened to your mother, including her death. It was an unfortunate sequence of events, that's all."

I know he's right, but for some reason I can't shift the guilt. Maybe I'm not ready to yet.

"Tell me about your day-to-day life. Are you happy?"

The temptation to tell him everything is fine is overwhelming, but my desire to get better means I have to force myself to talk, even if it's painful. "I'm afraid. I still don't remember what happened in the room with Isabel. I don't know if I let her out voluntarily, or if I was somehow coerced. I don't know where Isabel is, and I don't know if she's guilty of killing that little girl or if she's innocent. I'm frightened. What if she's obsessed with me and she comes to find me? What if the rest of her family are obsessed with me and want to kill me? They might think I know too much and it's best I'm dead. Or they might want to hurt someone close to me like Tom. I just don't know."

"That must be very stressful. Have you thought about moving away?"

"Yes," I reply. "Of course I have. But I don't have the money. Seb lets me live in the cottage basically rent-free and employs me in his farm shop. It's a nice job that I enjoy, and it keeps my mind off everything else that's happening, like Tom's bullying website." I think about the image that I'm sure Isabel posted and shiver. "The nights are hard. I check the locks and I check the windows, but sometimes I still feel like someone has been inside the house."

"That's a common feeling. When we're afraid, we often feel as though we're being watched." He leans back in his chair, frowning for the first time.

"But not everyone has worked closely with a prisoner from a high-security hospital who has now escaped and is out there in the world somewhere," I reply. "She could be anywhere. And she could be watching me."

CHAPTER
26

r. Ibbotson's words are on my mind as I work in the farm shop the next day. It's another quiet shift, but I've brought my laptop to make the most of the free wifi. The fact that James hasn't emailed me back is still concerning. He's not a man who tends to be away from the internet for long stretches of time, and he isn't picking up his phone either. The blog hasn't been updated for a while, which is strange because it picked up traffic after Isabel's escape. The whole thing makes me uncomfortable.

I decide to call DCI Murphy and mention James's disappearance. Other than the Fieldings, I don't talk to James about much else. We don't chat about our lives or gossip about celebrities. There isn't a lot I *do* know about James, beside his obsession with Maisie Earnshaw's death. Before I call DCI Murphy I decide to do a bit of poking around on his private Facebook page to see if I can work out what might be going on. Perhaps he's gone home, or he's moved in with his parents, or he's gone on holiday. Somehow those options seem unlikely given how obsessed James was with Isabel's escape, but it's still possible, and I don't want to waste police time.

James Gorden's personal page turns out to be mostly private, but he has posted the odd public update about the blog. We aren't friends on Facebook, but I can view his friends, of which he has many from all over the world. One post jumps out at me on the page, from a woman in a cowboy hat. It says: "Hey James, when's the next blog post out? Have you seen any child killers wandering around? Lol!"

The casual nature of the post makes my blood run cold, as does the implication. His audience are waiting for another blog post, which means it must be taking him longer than usual to update his page. And the reference to the child killer fits in with his last blog post, which said he was hoping to find Isabel in London.

What if he did find her?

What if he found *any* of the Fieldings?

What if he's been hurt?

I call DCI Murphy immediately and tell him everything I know. Part of me expects to be treated like a crazy woman, but he takes all the information and sounds serious when he says he'll look into it. When I hang up the phone I feel both better and worse. Better because I've unloaded some of the responsibility I feel I owe to James, and worse because now my suspicions are being treated seriously.

Neither James nor I should have got ourselves messed up in this dangerous, chaotic situation, and perhaps now we're paying the price for allowing ourselves to be involved. Leaning back in the chair behind the counter, I wish I could turn the clock back and never move to Hutton. But then I would never have met Seb, and perhaps I'd still be thinking that my father was dead and hallucinating ants crawling up the walls.

A sudden influx of tourists makes the afternoon speed along a little faster, and at the end of the day, I decide to buy a pair of reduced price Wellington boots from the country clothes section of the shop. With winter around the corner, the boots will come in handy, and the fact that they're a distasteful neon pink colour that no one wants to buy, and therefore a fraction of their usual price, means I can just about afford them. I put the money in the till, pack them up, and then start locking up the shop. Before long, the money is in the safe and the doors are locked.

Seb had warned me he'd be busy for a few days, settling in new pullets in the chicken coop and pigs in the pig pen. The Braithwaites are beginning to prepare themselves for Christmas. Turkey, chicken, and bacon are all popular around the festive time, pulling in quite a bit of profit. Though Seb still calls round at the cottage and goes on the occasional walk with me, he doesn't stop by the shop as often, which means I usually have to walk through the fields alone. Winter weather pulls the nights in, so I make that journey through the twilight hours as the darkness descends.

This is the part of the day I hate. It's a good ten-minute walk from the farm to the cottage, through sodden grass and dirty tracks. I hurry along at a brisk pace, my nerves on edge, jumping at every slight sound coming from the fields. If a pig squeals in the distance I let out a gasp. If the birds overhead flap their wings my stomach flips over in terror. It's during these long ten minutes that I imagine my own death over and over again.

By the time I reach the door my hands are trembling and the keys rattle loudly when I fish for them out of my bag. A low growl sounds behind me, causing me to flinch so violently that I drop the keys on the doorstep and spin around on my heel, the box of boots hitting the overgrown weeds next to the doorframe.

"Oh, for God's sake, Pye."

The fat ginger cat hisses at me before lifting his nose in annoyance.

Now I know why the scruffy tom is so mad—I've forgotten to throw him a few scraps from the shop on my way home. Every day I put out a little bowl of free samples, usually homemade pork scratchings or small portions of cooked meat. At the end of the day, I give what's left to the cat, but I'd forgotten to pick up the leftovers today.

"You'll just have to wait," I say, retrieving my keys from the step.

Feeling frazzled and a little sweaty as I finally get the door open, I fight my way into the small space and dump the boot box on the table as I look around for something to feed to the cat. Snatching open cupboard doors, I try to remember whether there was a tin of tuna left, but there wasn't.

"Sorry, Pye, the cupboards are bare because Mummy's poor. You'll have to make do with a saucer of milk."

The cat grumbles loudly as I take the milk out and place it down on the garden path, even batting at my hand as I move away.

"You ungrateful little sod."

But I can't help but watch the cat melt into a kitty as he laps up the milk. For a fraction of a second I think about trying to stroke the little bugger, but I like my fingers intact, and I've lingered outside on my own in the dark for too long as it is.

I hurry back into the kitchen, shut the door, lock it, check it twice, remove my shoes, and gasp. *What have I done?* Without thinking about it, I snatch the shoe box from the table and throw it onto the floor.

"Fuck it, Leah!" I yell at myself in frustration.

I hit myself on the forehead with the heel of my hand. I can't believe I'm such an idiot. All this time and my father's superstitions are still ingrained in me. Even now I berate myself for an act as trivial as putting a pair of new shoes on the table. Perhaps I should put the box back on the table and tell my father to go to hell.

The last time I put a pair of new shoes on the table I was fifteen years old and proud of the fancy platforms I'd bought from New

Look for twenty quid in the sale. They were gorgeous—purple with stripes along the heel. Mum was in the kitchen and I wanted to show her, so I put the box on the table and lifted out the shoes as she gasped at how pretty they were.

"WHAT ARE YOU DOING?"

Dad had been red-faced and drunk, staggering through the doorway at a speed that alarmed us both. He swept the shoe box from the table with his arm before staring me down with wide, bloodshot eyes. Spittle had collected in the corner of his mouth, and his breath was as stale as sour cider.

"Sorry," I mumbled, not sure what I was supposed to be sorry about.

"You *never* put new shoes on the table!" He grabbed me by the ponytail and yanked me back until my neck felt like it was going to break.

"Alf!" Mum screamed in terror.

"She needs to learn. She should know! She's old enough to know what you don't do. That's bad luck you've brought on the family now. Do you understand that? It's bad luck."

"Yes, Daddy. Yes, I understand. I promise I won't do it again."

And now I am here, and Mum is dead, and he is locked away. He was right. It had brought bad luck on the family, but not in the way he'd thought.

Well, what did he know? Why should I live that way? I glance at the shoebox, but for some reason I can't bring myself to do it. Instead, I grab the kettle and fill it with water from the kitchen sink.

In the cottage kitchen, the sink is beneath the window that looks out over the garden. One of the more pleasant aspects of living in the middle of nowhere is standing in this very spot doing the breakfast washing-up, looking out over the fields beyond the house. A golden glow of morning sun brightens the dewy fields in the morning, picking out highlights in the rolling hills. My own private art gallery. But in the dark, the hairs on the back of my neck begin to stand on end. Perhaps the memory of my father has spooked me, or perhaps the cat scared me with his growl, or perhaps my subconscious senses someone out there watching me.

No, it isn't only the memory of my parents; there's another reason why goosebumps are spreading over my arms. The superstition may have started it, but now I realise that there's something different about the darkened view outside the window, and it's on the windowsill.

It's difficult to make out in the dark, so I have to lean over the sink to get a closer look. My abdomen presses painfully against the kitchen counter as I push myself towards the glass, lifting up on tiptoes.

Three dead birds are lined up on the outside windowsill, their lifeless bodies on their sides as though they've been placed there with care.

I trip over my feet, staggering away from the glass, almost knocking the kettle of boiling water onto the kitchen floor. With my arms flailing madly, I do manage to grasp hold of the hot kettle for a moment, burning my hand in the process. Luckily, it doesn't tip over onto the floor, or I would be covered in burns from head to toe. But as I flail back, I hit my head on the kitchen table and land on my backside, twisting my ankle underneath my body. Pain blooms from three separate areas, the worst of which is my head. When I reach behind to check on myself, my fingers come back bloody.

Dr Ibbotson's advice is to take deep breaths and count to fifty when I'm feeling overwhelmed and anxious. I do this now, but I'm too afraid to close my eyes at the same time, so I struggle to concentrate on the counting without blocking everything else out.

After three more long breaths, I check on the cut at the back of my head. It's painful, but it isn't too deep, I don't think. I won't need stitches. After wiggling my toes and gently moving my foot I conclude that my ankle isn't broken, and the burn on my hand is sore but won't kill me. I use the kitchen counter to help me back on my feet before drawing the curtains and retrieving my phone.

Seb answers after one ring, and is at the cottage in under fifteen minutes. During that time I limp back and forth along the kitchen, worrying he'll think I'm as crazy as I feel.

"What's happened? Are you hurt?" he asks. As always, his voice is low and barely above a whisper, but there's an urgency to his tone that I'm unaccustomed to.

"I fell and hit my head, but I'm fine."

"You're bleeding," he says, moving closer to examine the wound. "I'll get the first aid box."

"No, don't. There's something I want you to do first," I say. "Can you open the curtains and look out on the windowsill? There are three dead birds there. Will you look at them, and tell me they're there?"

Seb doesn't answer, merely walks slowly over to the kitchen window. He opens the curtains with both arms, drawing them back dramatically. I hold my breath as he peers through the glass with his chin angled down towards the windowsill.

"There's nothing there."

I hurry to his side. "Are you sure? I don't understand. They were there a moment ago. I… I don't understand."

"Maybe you should sit down for a moment. I'll pour you some tea."

"This can't be happening again. I don't understand why this is happening." I can't stop saying it. "I don't understand."

Seb puts the kettle back on the stove and takes two mugs from the cupboard. "It's all right, Leah."

I run my fingers through my hair. "I'm hallucinating again. I can't trust my own eyes."

CHAPTER
27

"You must think I'm a lunatic," I say, staring down at the clay-coloured tea in my Snoopy mug.

"I don't think you're a lunatic," Seb says. "But let's think about all the options. Let's go through them all and then make a decision. Okay?"

I nod.

"You saw three dead birds," he prompts.

"Yes. On the windowsill. They were all lined up and laying on their sides. It frightened me because of Isabel and the birds she used to draw for me. When I got scared, I staggered back and hit my head on the table. The fall caused me to twist my ankle, and when I reached out to try and break my fall, I burned my hand. Then I called you, shut the curtains, and the birds disappeared."

"They were gone by the time I got here," Seb says.

"Or they never existed."

"That's possible too."

"I'm a lunatic."

He shakes his head. "You're not. Let's say the birds *did* exist. I went out and checked to see if they'd fallen off the ledge, and there was nothing there. I checked all around the garden and found nothing. That just means they didn't fall off."

"Or that they never existed."

"One possibility is that they died on the ledge, but in the time between you shutting the curtains and me arriving, a different animal took them away, like that stray tom out in the garden," he suggests.

"What are the odds of three birds dying in the same spot?" I ask. "Seems quite unlikely."

"That's true," Seb replies. "Another possibility is that someone put them there and then removed them while the curtains were closed."

I don't like that possibility; I think I prefer it to all be a hallucination. My fingers wrap around the mug for warmth.

"The other possibility is that the stress you're under caused you to hallucinate them. Or that the medication you're taking isn't working anymore."

"I'm not sure I like any of those options," I say. "Either I'm crazy, or I'm being stalked, or that cat is terrorising me."

Silence lingers in the kitchen as Seb hangs his head. It's impossible to know what he's thinking with that neutral expression on his face.

"I wish I knew what was real and what wasn't."

"It's real to you," he says. "And that's what matters, isn't it?"

Seb stays on the sofa for the night. I offer him Tom's room, but am secretly relieved when he insists on taking the sofa so we don't mess up any of Tom's things. It's hard enough as it is to check that no one has been in Tom's room since he left, but if someone else had stayed there too, it would be impossible. Perhaps Seb is aware of that, or senses that I'd prefer Tom's room to stay exactly the way it is. Or maybe he just doesn't want to sleep in a teenage boy's bed. Teenagers aren't generally known for their cleanliness.

Seb is out as the sun rises—farmers don't get a lie-in—leaving me alone in the cottage. With one eye on my watch, waiting for nine o'clock, I drink tea until the regular working day begins. I don't particularly want to, but I force myself to call DCI Murphy. There's no update on James, except that the detective has asked for help from the police in East London to look into James's disappearance. It seems none of my business to report James as missing, seeing as I'm neither a family member or a friend, but I can't ignore what he set out to do and the fact that he has gone silent.

"Anything else?" Murphy asks.

"There is one thing," I say cautiously.

"Go on."

"It's silly, really."

"Anything that can help the case is important. Finding Isabel is important. Tell me."

"All right." I take a deep breath. "There were three dead birds on my kitchen windowsill last night. Three regular garden birds. Small ones. I didn't have time to note what kind they were, but they were the size and shape of birds like a chaffinch or a robin."

"Isabel had an obsession with birds, didn't she?"

"Yes. She used to draw me a bird every day. She told me they had different omens, mostly good ones. Isabel always focused on the positive." I hesitate. "But…"

"What is it?"

"The birds disappeared. I fell down after I saw them because I immediately thought of her and it frightened me. When I got back up they were gone. I called Seb Braithwaite and he came to check I was all right. He looked around for the birds in the garden, but there wasn't a trace of them. I… I could have hallucinated them. I'm still taking antipsychotic medicine."

"Okay. It's still good that you told me," he said in a kind but slightly disappointed voice. "I'll have a team come out to dust for fingerprints and check for footprints. If it was Isabel, this could be very useful."

"And you'll continue look into James's disappearance?" I ask. "Will you let me know if you find him? I'd like to know that he's safe."

"Of course I will. It's good that you called, Leah."

I can't help but note the slight note of condescension in his voice, but I don't think it's malicious, or that he notices he's doing it. It's nothing I haven't heard before. Every doctor and every nurse talks to me like I'm a child. Maybe I *am* a child now that my mind is broken. Are our bodies the real indicator of adulthood? Isn't it our brains that distinguish the child from the adult? I was a nurse long enough to know that a child can exist in an adult's body, and the difficulties that come along with that. When I put down the phone I start to cry.

But crying isn't going to get me anywhere, so I dry my eyes quickly, wash my face, clear away the breakfast dishes, and open my laptop. For the first time in a while I have the urge to watch the video of smug David Fielding condemning me for the release of his daughter, and calling for NHS reform because she escaped, but I don't watch it. Instead, I check his Twitter account to see where he is today. According to the account, he was drinking coffee in a Costa in Harrogate, which means he is out of London and further north. What does that mean? If Isabel is moving in the same direction as her father it might mean they were both coming north. Then again, if the birds were real, she was already here.

I close the laptop. None of this is working. I can't track David or

Isabel from his Twitter account because there is no way of verifying the information he posts. I need James. He's the one who can travel to the suspected area and report back to me.

The sound of a van pulls me from my thoughts. The postie walks with a whistle towards the front gate and then pauses, staring at the bushes where Pye waits for him.

"Get t'fuck, kitty," he shouts, opening the gate quickly and shuffling up the path, leaping once into the air as Pye rushes out of the bushes with his hackles up. Tom and I used to watch this scene every Saturday, giggling into our mugs as the poor man protected his legs from the oncoming claw attack.

The letterbox rattles, and the postie hurries back down the path, stomping his feet to scare the cat away. I haven't had post for a while, so I decide to get up and investigate. The only post we receive here are bills and pamphlets about local events in Hutton village: line dancing in the village hall, cider tasting at the Queen's Head. I skip through the scant pile of envelopes until I find one embossed with the North Yorkshire NHS Trust, and my heart drops to my knees. I don't need to open it to find out what's inside. They've set a date for my misconduct tribunal, which will be the date I officially lose my job as a nurse. Right now I'm suspended, but once the tribunal goes ahead, I'll be surprised if I manage to keep my job. A dangerous criminal escaped on *my* watch. That doesn't go unpunished.

But what I can't stand is the idea of Chi going through the same thing. He didn't do anything wrong, but his judgment has already been called into question. The police don't name names, but they've already dragged Chi over hot coals for his decision to hire a nurse whose father resides in Broadmoor, and his decision to put Isabel on a ward with slightly fewer restrictions than the intensive care ward. But what do they expect a hospital to do with a patient who has shown no signs of violence for years? Are they supposed to keep her isolated forevermore? What if there's another patient who needs to be in the intensive care ward more than Isabel? Are they expected to turn that patient away because they're short of beds? None of them understand what it's like or the pressures facing the staff, but they love to throw their opinions around all the same. Everyone becomes an expert on how to care for a patient once there's a crisis like this.

I put the letter to one side and try not to think about it.

I spend the morning in the farm shop before leaving early to meet the police team to check on the garden and the windowsill where I saw the birds. After they've taken a statement, I decide to leave them in the garden as I go for a walk to clear my head, but the wind unnerves me, tricking me into thinking there's someone behind me when the breeze whistles through blades of grass.

When I return to the cottage I'm on edge, climbing the walls and feeling the oppressive weight of them. Despite the cold, the air feels stale, but I daren't open a window. For the first time in a long while, I crave alcohol. A soothing glass of wine would take the edge off and put me at ease. But the house has been stripped of all alcohol, so instead, I settle for a mug of hot chocolate and a blanket wrapped around me on the sofa. Seb calls to check on me in the evening. He's stuck at the farmhouse with a birthing horse. Part of me considers going to watch the event, but the other Braithwaites frighten me. The other brothers, with their weathered-faced farmwives, regard me with suspicious eyes whenever I work in the shop. I'm convinced they see me as an insane scrounger who has seduced the youngest son into my bed.

Time ticks slowly by until I feel the pull of sleep. I was worried it wouldn't come for me tonight, but the boredom of the day has taken its toll. Before I make my way upstairs, the doors and windows need to be checked. I go through it quickly, rattling the handles and yanking the curtains shut. After getting into bed, I get up and check my bedroom window again to be sure, and then I settle into the bedcovers.

My dreams are filled with birds, as usual. A gulp of magpies cluster around my body, perching on me from neck to toe. I try to wiggle myself to scare them away, but I can't move. When I try to count them, I get lost and have to start all over again, beginning with the first line of the rhyme—*one for sorrow*—but forgetting the rest. They peck at me and claw my skin, flapping their wings until a cloud of loose feathers forms around me. There must be dozens of them with their beady little eyes.

When I come to, I can't move and my breath comes out in a ragged pant. It's perhaps a second or two until my muscles release, but the moment is stretched out with panic. I'm drenched in sweat and breathless by the time I can sit up in bed. I bend over, pressing my forehead against my knees as I slowly recover from the dream.

That's when I notice it.

My head snaps up. *Something is different.*

I throw the covers back and place my feet on the bedroom floor. It's cold. The heating is off and winter is creeping into the house, cooling the old floorboards. But I don't bother looking for a dressing gown. I shiver as I walk through the bedroom and into the hallway, flicking on the light switch.

Something is different.

But what is it? I inhale slowly, trying to gauge whether there's a slight difference in the scent of the house. The air is always somewhat musty, but is there more of an earthy smell than usual? Or is it rot? I'm not sure. I move slowly through the hallway and down the stairs, my feet a bare whisper on the floorboards.

When I reach the bottom of the stairs I notice the tickle of fresh air on my ankles and neck. Is there a window open? That can't be possible—I checked every window and every door in the house, and I shut all the curtains. If there is a window open, it means someone has either forced it open or broken the glass. My heart begins to pound.

I'm on high alert as I quietly open the door into the kitchen. By now I'm certain that the fresh air is definitely coming from the kitchen. It's dark in the room. There are no streetlights outside my house, not like when I lived in Hackney; it's only moonlight that ever comes in through the windows, but the curtains are shut as I thought they were. I listen carefully for the sound of an intruder, but the house is silent. Until a soft bang, like the sound of a door gently closing. Has someone slipped out of the house as I've been coming down the stairs? I grope for the knife block, knowing it's on the kitchen side somewhere near here. My fingers wrap around the handle of one of the knives.

The house is silent apart from my breathing and the blood rushing through my ears. I approach the wall where I know the light switch is, terrified of switching it on, but equally terrified of remaining in the dark. Without the light I can't defend myself, but I don't want to know what's going on. I want to be in my bed relaxed in slumber, not here, frightened for my life.

My fingers reach the switch, and I flick it on with a little gasp.

The room is empty, but the kitchen door is slightly ajar. That's why there was a breeze coming through the house. When I move closer, I see that the door has been forced open. There's a gouge in the wood where a crowbar or some other implement has broken the lock and opened the door. I need to be careful not to destroy any evidence, but I need to check that there's no one out there. Taking a deep breath, I hurry forwards and open the door with my fingertip.

What I see on the doorstep leaves me bloodless and limp. When a high-pitched scream breaks the silence, it takes me a moment to realise that it's coming from me.

CHAPTER
28

James Gorden stares at me with his eyes and mouth wide open. He's as shocked to be there as I am to see him. I drop to my knees and the knife hits the ground, clattering slightly on the tiles.

"This isn't real," I whisper. For the briefest of moments I reach towards James with a trembling hand to touch him. Then I retract it and move away from the door. "No. You're not real. This is in my mind."

James simply stares at me as I talk to myself, his face as bloodless as mine feels. He's the same milky pallor of a full moon, with his features in the shade of the dark. Only the orange glow from the kitchen light casts any colour, except for the feathers.

The feathers are the same iridescent blue of the feathers in my dreams, except they aren't moving anymore. They are still and lifeless. As dead as the birds I saw on the windowsill.

I close my eyes and open them again, trying to process what I'm seeing. There, on my doorstep, is the severed head of blogger James

Gorden, and in his mouth is a dead magpie.

That's exactly what I see, and this is why I'm crazy.

"It's not real."

The smell seems real. It smells like a hospital room with a dying patient, except that the bleach of the hospital has been replaced with the earthy scent of decay. James must have been dead for a while because he doesn't look anything like the corpses I've seen as a nurse.

"Stop it. Stop it." I clamp my hands around my ears and try to stop myself from justifying this, from analysing it like it's real.

Moving back from the door, I press myself into the corner of the kitchen and draw my knees up to my chest. None of this is real; it's a hallucination. It has to be. What's the alternative? That Isabel has delivered James Gorden's severed head to my house in the middle of the night? Isn't that insane? Of course it's insane because *I* am insane.

When I close my eyes and open them, James is making a sound, like a groaning sound. The bird is wiggling, as if trying to break free from between his teeth. The sound of wings flapping against my window turns my skin to ice. It's all too much. I close my eyes and I don't open them again.

This is what she's done to me. She's worn me down until my mind is broken. Perhaps I'll never know what she did to me in that room, or whether I'm as much to blame as she is, but the outcome will always be the same: I'll always be the woman cowering in the corner of the kitchen, curled up into a ball, staring into the dead eyes of my ally. I'll be the one with the crippling hallucinations stripping me away step by step until I'm so far removed from reality I'm not even here anymore.

There are footsteps coming up the path. I lift my head in an instinctive reaction to the sound, even though my mind is elsewhere.

Am I talking? I'm not sure. Someone says, *It's not real*, but I couldn't say whether it's coming from my lips, or whether I hear it in my mind.

How long have I been here? The darkness of night has turned into the pastel blue of morning. My eyes are glazed from lack of sleep.

"Leah!"

Smash.

Footsteps again. Quicker. Quicker, *quicker*.

"Leah!"

Then comes a gurgling sound followed by a splash. I can see the back of someone doubled over. Those thick canvas trousers that belong to Seb. He always wears them because they're durable. He straightens up and turns to me, still outside the house, still only visible through the open door. He's staring down at James on the doorstep, and for a moment I actually believe that James is real, but then I remind myself that this is all in my head, and I let out a snort.

"It's not real."

"Leah," Seb says again. This time he looks up at me with sad eyes, and I can't bear the pity. "It is real. I'm going to phone the police."

"You're not real either."

The Seb standing by the door ignores me and collects a mobile phone from his pocket. He takes a step back and puts the phone to his ear. It's so convincing that I have to remind myself how elaborate my hallucinations can be. None of this is real—not James's head presented to me like a suckling pig, and certainly not this version of Seb who looks at me with sad eyes and says my name in a desperate, longing kind of way. It's like Alfie all over again, nothing more than my broken mind playing tricks on me.

"I'm going to stand out here," Seb says, after hanging up the phone. "I don't want to disturb any evidence, so I can't come inside, but everything is going to be all right. The police are on their way." He stops talking and waits, but I'm not sure what he's waiting for. Maybe he expected me to acknowledge him, but I'm not going to. "It's going to be all right." Another pause. "I… I'm not one for words at the best of times, and I've never known what to say in bad situations like this. I'm a doer, you know that. When the animals are in trouble, I know what to do or who to call to help. I don't like standing by and watching others sort out a problem, I like to get stuck in." There's comfort in his voice. The low depths of it soothe me deep inside, but I can't allow myself to be taken in by my fraudulent imagination; by these falsities that are nothing more than a conjurer's trick performed by the synapses in my brain. "You've no idea how much I want to come into the house right now and… and… well, do *anything* rather than be stuck out here. But I won't. If there's a chance to catch her, I won't risk it."

"It's not real!"

"Leah. Leah, it is real. It's very real, I'm sorry to say."

"No."

"Yes." I hear scuffling as he paces back and forth. "I can't bear this."

"You're not real," I whisper to myself.

Dr Ibbotson told me to learn my triggers. Isabel, Father, Mother. Those are my triggers, but I don't see how that helps right now. What triggered this? I don't understand.

When the police car pulls up, the siren seems out of place in the quiet countryside. Sirens were commonplace back in Hackney—I heard them every day, and sometimes at night. But this is a peaceful place, not to be sullied with the violence of the city. I'm shocked to hear them, not just because of the sound, but because two police officers climb out of the car. If this is still all a hallucination, it has become infinitely more complicated. Why? Why would I make up police officers, too?

"We're going to need SOCOs down here," I hear one of them say with a note of panic in her voice. "I'll call it in."

"Is … is that a head?" says another.

"I was sick. I hope it doesn't mess up the crime scene." Seb this time. "And I dropped a bottle of milk."

"If you could take a few steps back, sir. There might be evidence in the vicinity of the … remains."

"Okay, no problem. There's a … a woman inside. Leah. She found the head, but I don't know when. She's frightened and upset. Please, help her as soon as you can."

"Is there another entrance into the property?"

"No. The back room is used as a living space. The sofa blocks the door."

"All right, well, I'll go and see if I can talk to her. Leah? Is it Leah? My name is PC Abbott, and I'm here with PC Fisher. How are you doing in there?"

"I keep telling you all it's not *real,* but no one will believe me."

"It's real, Leah. Don't you remember me? I spoke to you at Hutton Comprehensive School about the bullies targeting your brother. Sit tight for now, okay? We'll be in to take a statement. Stay warm and keep yourself comfortable."

The police officer turns away as she speaks into the walkie-talkie attached to her jacket. I can't say how long it is before the next car arrives but soon there are several, with people walking around, measuring, whispering, barking orders, and taking photos. I sit there watching it all unfold, shivering so hard my teeth chatter together.

When the head is taken away, Seb is the first one through the door. He throws his jacket over my shoulders and kneels down next to me.

"It's real, Leah. I'm real." He touches my face, my hair, and pulls me into his shoulder, proving that he is in fact a real person, warm, with a heart beating hard and fast beneath his ribcage.

"James," I say, my teeth still chattering. "She killed him."

"Hello, Leah." DCI Murphy stands over me with his hands in his trouser pockets. "Were you the one to find James Gorden?"

"Yes."

"Okay. And about what time was that?"

"Hold on a minute, mate. She's freezing cold and in shock." Seb gets to his feet and stands between me and the detective.

"The paramedics will be in shortly, and PC Abbott is making a cup of tea. Unfortunately, I need to ask these questions as quickly as possible. This is a very serious crime and we need to move quickly."

"It's okay," I say. It's hard to focus on anything, but now that I know it's real, I feel more able to speak. "I don't know what time it was. I woke up in the middle of the night and came straight downstairs. I would have checked the time, but I was frightened. I could tell something was wrong, but I wasn't sure what it was. When I came downstairs, I realised that the door was open. Someone broke in. Then I saw James and… Well, I lost it. I've had a psychotic break recently and have suffered some hallucinations, as you know."

"Did you touch the remains?"

"No."

"Okay," he says. "And did you see anything else? Did you see a person outside the house? Or inside the house? Think carefully. It could be nothing more than a fleeting shadow."

PC Abbott presses a hot mug into my hands. "There was no one here. I went down the stairs slowly, so if it *was* Isabel, she had time to leave before I reached the kitchen."

"Can you explain why there's a knife on the kitchen floor?"

"I took it out of the knife block to defend myself when the light was off. When I turned the light on and saw… James… I dropped it."

"Thanks, Leah. We'll let the paramedics see you now."

"Catch her," I plead.

"We're searching the area. We're bringing in dogs. If she's here, we'll find her."

CHAPTER
29

I lean against the cold window of the car as rain splashes down on the windshield. It's three days since James Gorden's severed head was found on my doorstep, and I'm returning home for the first time. After the shock of finding him, I decided it was best to voluntarily check myself into Oakton Hospital, but they felt that I was fit to come home already. After two long sessions with Dr Ibbotson, he told me that my reaction had been normal, and I was doing well given the trauma I'd been through.

Mary and Gavin offered me a spare bedroom after the event, but I can't bring this to them, not when Tom is with them. If anything happened to him I could never forgive myself. Since I don't know where Isabel is and what she might do next, I told Mary and Gavin to take Tom away for a few days. And rather than move into the Braithwaites' farmhouse, Seb has agreed to stay in Tom's room until they catch Isabel, whenever that might be. I'm beginning to think she'll outwit us all.

There have been no sightings of her in Hutton or any of the surrounding areas. The lack of CCTV cameras out in the middle of nowhere hasn't helped much, but the police did find tyre tracks on the road before the turning to the farm. A car was parked there, and it's believed that Isabel walked the head up to the cottage to place on my doorstep. She *walked* the ten minutes it takes to get here, carrying a human head. I can't even begin to imagine the darkness it takes to do that.

Why didn't I see that darkness? I spent hours with her every working day, and I saw nothing but a remorseful young woman who was not capable of murder.

Patients can't hide their true selves for such a long period of time. It's impossible. At least I thought it was until I met Isabel Fielding. She played me from the very beginning, using her talent as an artist to trick me into believing she possessed empathy. Then she studied me, got to know me, slimmed herself down to resemble me, all so she could walk out of Crowmont Hospital without a single person stopping her. She hurt herself on purpose so I would volunteer myself for suicide watch. She waited for the perfect moment to put her plan into motion. She knew Chi had been busy with new patients, and she knew the night security guards didn't know me as well as the day security guards.

If only I could remember what happened in that room. Did I help her voluntarily? Was I stupid enough to still believe that she was innocent?

James Gorden is dead because of me. The lone question remains whether I was forced to let Isabel go, or whether I did it voluntarily. As far as I'm concerned, one of those options makes me a murderer, and I'm not sure I can live with myself if it turns out to be true.

The rest of James's body hasn't been found, despite the police bringing in cadaver dogs to search the area. What if she sends me another part of his body next? A foot. A hand. Worse. There are times I'm so sure I can smell his decomposing flesh that I believe the head is with me again.

Even Pye the cat seems somewhat subdued as Seb carries my bags up the garden path. He sticks to the bushes, growling softly, rather than running and pouncing on our feet as we make our way to the kitchen door. I could do with the distraction of a feral cat, because I don't particularly want to look at the spot where I found James staring at me. Then again, the image is burned into my mind, so what does it matter? Every time I close my eyes I see the head, with every pore, every drop of blood, every magpie feather in perfect detail. I wish I could remember my mother's face in such detail.

"Are you okay?" Seb is standing on the spot where James's head had been placed a few nights ago. He has one hand on the door handle and the other around the handle of my bag.

"I'm okay," I reply, hugging my body for warmth.

"I'll light a fire for you."

Following him into the kitchen is easier than I thought it would be. Placing my foot on that step was a moment I'd been dreading, but in reality it lasts a mere second and then it's over.

Seb turns on the central heating, lights the tiny log fire in the living room, and then sets to work changing the locks on the kitchen door. Meanwhile, I walk through the house touching nothing, simply observing. Home has never been a familiar concept to me. My childhood house never truly felt like home because it was the place where my abuser lived. The string of dingy bedsits I lived in after leaving my parents' house never felt like home either. When you're sharing a room with two drug addicts and an illegal immigrant, it's hard to think of the place as a home. I felt more at home with the other nurses on my course, and then later in a shared house with friends. But they moved on, switched jobs, and left me stranded.

Tom is home to me. This is our home, that we made, together. Our home has been violated by Isabel because I let her in. Not into the house, but into my life, into me. I'd wanted to help her, and she twisted that gesture into ugliness. The last few months have been confusing and disorientating, clouded by my grief and insecurity, but for the first time in a while I feel like I'm strong enough to get through this. Now that I understand where my home is, I'm prepared to fight to keep it.

I take blankets and spare duvets out of an old wardrobe and strip Tom's bed, preparing it for Seb. Then I go downstairs and prepare a chicken Seb brought up from the farm shop. The kitchen is filled with the sound of Seb's drill. My father had always been handy with DIY work, which means the sounds of drills and hammers leave me feeling a strange sense of uneasy comfort, reminding me of the good and the downright awful memories of my father. But now isn't the time to dwell on those. I flick on the radio and hum along to a song I like while the potatoes bubble away on the stove.

Seb cleans up after he's done. He's silent most of the time, moving clumsily through the house, a little unsure of himself. His head is almost always looking at the floor, occasionally lifting to meet my eyes.

"Dinner will be ready in fifteen," I call through to the living room as he's taking his tool box away.

There's a brief pause in his step before I hear him moving again. I've come to love his reticence because the silence soothes me.

Exactly fifteen minutes later, Seb is back with clean hands and combed hair. He smiles when I place a plate of roast chicken down on the table, and then waits patiently as I finish sorting my own.

"I would offer wine, but I don't actually have any in the house," I admit sheepishly.

"Water's fine."

"The bird you brought is tasty. Is it one from the shop?"

"Yes."

"Good." I'm hungry. The mashed potato is a bit lumpy but I hardly notice as I take large forkfuls at a time. Seb does the same, leaning over his food like a protective puppy.

"What does your family think of you staying here?" I ask. It's a subject we haven't dared to broach before. Though I see the others around the farm, I have no idea what they make of Seb giving me so much attention.

"It's none of their business," he says.

"They own a stake in the farm, though," I point out. "And here I am riding on your hospitality. You practically let me live here for free. I wish there was more I could do but—"

He calmly places his hand on top of mine. "That's for me to worry about."

It's been a long time since a man laid his hand on top of mine, and my face flushes with heat. Good heat. A good touch. I want more, but I know it's too soon for that.

"In case I haven't said it before: Thank you. And I'm sorry for the trouble I've brought here with Isabel and the… James's… Well, you know." It feels absurd to think the words "severed head" but somehow that has become my reality now.

"You're welcome." He stares back down at his food.

"There's… there's something I want to tell you." Somehow, the tasty roast chicken has lost its appeal, and instead of taking large forkfuls of food, I end up moving it gingerly around my plate.

Seb, sensing a change in the atmosphere, lifts his gaze from his meal.

"I feel like I need to tell someone, because I've never told anyone before," I admit. Now I put the fork down because there's no point in me eating anymore. "But I feel like if I say it, I'll feel better."

"What is it?" There's a note of urgency in Seb's voice. He's worried for me.

"It's not about Isabel or anything like that. I still can't remember what happened the night she escaped, and you know everything else. You've been *there* for everything else, through it all with me. It's about my past. When I had… my breakdown, I convinced myself that my father had died. As you know, he committed a terrible crime before we moved here. He killed my mum with a knife. Something snapped, and I couldn't process it." I take a sip of water. "He was arrested and convicted of murder with diminished responsibility because… well, because he's crazy. He's in Broadmoor now."

Seb places his fork down on the table. "I… I'm sorry." For the first time he seems completely surprised. His usual plaintive expression is replaced by a furrowed brow.

"The reason why I couldn't cope with it all is because of my childhood. It wasn't a happy one. It was violent and horrible." I can't look at him anymore. I can only grip the kitchen table instead. "What I'm trying to tell you is that Tom is my son."

"Okay."

I look up. Seb's eyes are trained on me, a question across his face. Has he realised?

"He's my son and my brother. I was thirteen."

It's miniscule, but it's there—a ripple of anger spreads across his face, working its way from his clenched jaw to his throbbing temple. He takes a moment, a still, extended moment, and then he lets out a long sigh.

"I'm sorry," he says.

"It's okay. I just wanted to say it out loud."

"And now you have."

"Now I have."

This time, I reach across for his hand.

CHAPTER
30

I t's easy to fall into a routine when you have someone to fall into it with. We eat breakfast together before the sun rises. I fall into step with his early mornings and nights. I drink tea in the kitchen as the sun rises, and then go to the farm shop where I serve tourists and locals. At the end of the day, I call Tom to check he's safe, watch logs burn in the fire, and discover more about Seb.

He likes to read more than he likes to watch movies or TV. His favourites are pulpy science fiction novels from the sixties and seventies, because they're short and he doesn't like to sit still for long periods of time. He smells like cow dung at the end of the working day, but his shower gel has a pleasant earthy scent. He always dresses nicely for dinner, and he washes up the dirty plates at the end of the day. He likes his tea milky and his coffee strong. His favourite biscuits are stem ginger and lemon from the farm shop. He knows how to make chicken stock by boiling the bones.

And he knows that I gave birth to my father's child when I was thirteen.

I dropped that bomb on him and nothing changed between us. It's a small step, but it makes me begin to believe that one day I can tell Tom without breaking our relationship.

I'm getting stronger every day, even though I know Isabel is out there waiting. It won't be long until we meet again, I know that, but at least I'm becoming strong enough to face her.

It's six pm, and I'm warming soup on the stove for our dinner together. Seb is in the shower washing away the muck of the day. When the landline rings, I hurry into the living room to pick it up from the handset, my mind rushing through different possibilities. Tom would call my mobile phone; Mary or Gavin might call the landline, which would mean Tom is in danger; or it could be DCI Murphy.

"Hello?"

"Leah, this is DCI Rob Murphy. I'm calling to tell you that we've made an arrest in connection to James Gorden's murder."

The relief is so quick and so sudden that I melt down onto the sofa, still clutching a wooden spoon. "You found her."

"No," he says. "We didn't. Leah, Isabel didn't kill James Gorden. Owen Fielding did."

"What?"

"We found his fingerprints all over the door handle on your kitchen door and three of his hairs on James Gorden's head. We found his footprints in your garden."

"What?"

The wooden spoon falls onto the carpet, splashing me with tiny droplets of vegetable soup.

"That's as much as I can tell you right now," the detective says. "The media will be all over this." He sounds tired. "Keep in touch, Leah, okay? If you hear anything else at night or see anything suspicious, contact me right away."

"Okay, I will."

Seb walks into the room as I'm placing the phone back onto the handset. He must see the pallor of my face and the spoon on the floor, because he hurries to my side and places a hand on my knee, crouching down so he's at my level.

"What's happened?"

"They've arrested Owen Fielding for the murder of James Gorden," I say. "He's the one who did it. His fingerprints were on the kitchen door. He walked here with the head, and he put it on the doorstep." Numbness spreads through me. I disconnect from the words coming out of my mouth, still in a state of disbelief. "It's so… strange. The way the head was arranged with the bird… I just assumed it was Isabel."

"Owen is Isabel's brother?"

I nod my head. "He visited her at the hospital quite frequently, and I think they used to speak on the phone. They always seemed quite close. He knows all about Isabel's love of birds because she used to draw him pictures whenever he came. The first time I saw him visit, she drew him a magpie and he chastised her because magpies are manipulators. Maybe she was trying to tell me something."

"Or maybe she just liked the way magpies looked. It'll do no good obsessing over this."

But I already am. I'm thinking back to that bizarre night at the Fieldings' home, with Owen hungover around the house, talking to his housekeeper like she was a piece of dirt. He'd always seemed like an entitled shit, but was he also a murderer? Perhaps Owen was sick of being overshadowed by his sister. Maybe he wanted some of the spotlight.

I turn on the television and flick across to the news channel.

"They're reporting on it already," I say, turning up the volume.

"... hearing reports that Owen Fielding has been arrested for the murder of James Gorden, a blogger known for writing opinion pieces on the Maisie Earnshaw murder. James's severed head was placed on the doorstep of the nurse who freed Isabel Fielding three months ago. Unfortunately, the rest of his body has not been discovered. It's thought that Owen Fielding has not only confessed to killing James Gorden, but also to killing Maisie Earnshaw seven years ago, exonerating his older sister, Isabel Fielding. We will be hearing more about this case when the updates come in."

"What?" The enormity of the situation comes crashing down on me. "It wasn't Isabel?"

"It wasn't Isabel," Seb says softly.

"It wasn't my fault," I whisper. This changes everything. I take a deep breath, trying to process what is happening. "I spent so long wondering how I could have got everything so wrong. If Isabel was guilty, why did I have such a connection with her? Why did I like her? How could I have come to care about a person who could murder another human being for fun? I know this doesn't make everything right, but it means I wasn't completely crazy. Doesn't it?"

"I don't know what it means," Seb replies. "But if you're safer than you were yesterday, that's a good result in my mind." He pulls me into his arms, and we sit together watching the news reports come in. By the time either of us move, the soup is burned dry and the fire has died. Seb goes over to check his phone.

"I'm sorry to do this to you, but I have to go to the farm." He stares down at the phone with a frown on his face.

"Is everything all right?"

"It's fine, but George found some injured cows out on the top field. Looks like they got tangled in wire. We were missing a few after milking today, and I left him as he was going to investigate. The emergency vet arrived a few minutes ago." His head turns up to meet my gaze. "But I can stay here if you need me."

I can tell by the worried expression on his face that he's torn between doing his job and being my knight in shining armour. But I feel stronger than I have in months. I don't need the knight.

"You go. Stay there tonight and keep things calm. Sounds like they need you there."

He nods. "Only if you're sure."

"I'm sure."

When he reaches out and brushes a few fingers down my cheek, I begin to wonder if this is the true start of something real between us. It's as though a barrier has been knocked away, and we're free to finally meet each other for the first time.

But it can wait.

CHAPTER
31

It's my first dreamless sleep in months.

It had been raining when I went to bed, with the raindrops pattering against the glass. When I wake, the raining has stopped, but there is a rhythmic sound in my room. Breathing.

The sharp edge of a knife rests against my throat.

"Hi, Leah."

It isn't possible. I checked every lock and every window before bed. After the news, I was so sure that I was safe, to the point that I sent Seb away, but now my worst fear has come to pass. It leaves me with a strange sense of calm spreading all the way over my body. This was inevitable, and I've always known it.

"Hi, Isabel."

She shifts her weight from one foot to the other. I can't see her in the dark, but I can hear her soft breathing. I know the knife she holds to my throat is far sharper than any of the knives in my kitchen, because I feel a slight trickle of blood run down my neck.

"What did you do to the cows?" I ask.

"They're quite stupid animals," she replies. "Easily led. A little bit like you. Time to get out of bed, sleepyhead. Go slowly now, because I'm not moving this knife even a little bit, and I definitely don't want to slice your head clean off. At least not yet." Her voice is almost exactly like I remember it, filled with positivity and innocence, but the slight change creates a new edge to it, one of malice.

"How did you get in the house?" I ask.

"After the police were done, there was a gap of a few hours where the door was still broken and no one was around. They'd already searched everything, dusted the whole place for fingerprints and photographed all your not-so-pretty belongings. The forensic team had dismantled their white tents and cleared away their tools. There wasn't a church mouse in the entire cottage. I slipped in, went upstairs, and I waited."

"You lived in the attic?" I should be trembling with fear, but I'm strangely calm as I sit up in bed, moving slowly enough for her to be able to track the knife with my movements. Then I flick on the lamp by the bed so I can see what I'm doing.

Isabel stands close to me, with her right arm outstretched, keeping the knife trained on my skin. She's dressed in plain jeans and a blue jumper, both clean but crumpled. Her hair is different again, now short and bleached blonde. The innocence of her usual facial expression has moulded into cold determination. There's more life in her flushed cheeks and bright eyes than there ever was before.

Now I see it.

The extra weight around her middle, the dull grey sportswear, the pastiness of her skin, the mousy hair colour—it all made her seem so insignificant and harmless. It's strange how your first impressions of a person can so dramatically alter your view of their past behaviours.

I knew all about the crime she'd supposedly committed, but the past became diluted by the way I saw her day in, day out, that innocent creature with a gentle heart and wasted talent, locked in a cell like a bird in a cage.

"You took your time coming back from the hospital. You've no idea how ravenous I am for a decent meal. But first we have a job to do. I want you to stand."

I know that every part of Isabel is enjoying telling me what to do. Being in control suits her.

"Put this on."

She tosses me the dressing gown that was slung across the bottom of the bed. I pull it on over my nightie.

"We're going to take a walk." The lamplight catches her eyes as she smiles down at me.

For the first time, I feel afraid.

"Where are you taking me?"

As I walk slowly, she slips behind me and rests her elbow on my shoulder, guiding me forwards with her free hand on my waist. Her body feels harder than I thought it would. Has she been exercising? Preparing herself for this moment?

"You'll see."

We negotiate the stairs and the hallway into the kitchen. The house is dark and quiet, sadly missing Seb's presence. At least Tom isn't here.

"Put on your Wellington boots. It's going to rain and I don't want you getting cold."

"You're so thoughtful," I say, letting the sarcasm drip heavily into my words.

"I know. I am, aren't I?"

Isabel leans down with me as I pull on the bright pink boots. God, they look ridiculous in this situation, but if I have any chance of escaping, thick boots might not be the worst choice of footwear. After putting on the boots, we walk together towards the door. My eyes scan the surface of the table for anything sharp I can slip into the pocket of my dressing gown. There's a small dinner knife, but I need to distract Isabel to get it.

"It was clever, slipping into the house like that. But it was risky. What would you have done if you hadn't hidden in the attic?"

"Oh, the same. It just wouldn't have been quite so clean and tidy."

A shudder ripples through my body as I wonder what that might have entailed. I have visions of Isabel leaving my house drenched in blood, smashed windows behind her. Or Isabel with orange dancing in her eyes as she watches the house burn.

I bump into the table leg and Isabel's knife cuts slightly deeper into the skin on my neck.

"Watch what you're doing," she snaps. "You're not supposed to die yet. If this knife slips, it could sever your artery, you idiot."

But as she's busy chastising me, I slip the knife into my pocket. It's not much, but it's something.

"Unlock the door for me," Isabel says calmly, gesturing to the keys resting in the bowl next to the door.

We move together as I retrieve the key and push it into the lock, almost as though we're slow dancing together. Her body brushes against mine, and I'm ashamed of the pulse that shudders up my spine. The biting chill of October cuts through my scant clothing as we exit the house, and rain begins to sputter down from the knitted clouds above. There's no moon or stars, merely foggy darkness. I don't know what time it is, and that leaves me feeling disorientated. She has the upper hand in every way, and all the control.

"You're not doing too badly for yourself, Leah," Isabel says as we walk out of the garden and up towards the moors. "A hunky farmer has been staying with you, that brat of a brother is out of the picture, and you've got yourself a job. It's a demeaning job in a shop for people richer than you, but it's still a job. Well done, you!" She talks to me in the saccharine voice of a patronising adult talking to a child, setting my teeth on edge.

"You're also doing well for yourself. You're free, you're obsessed with me, and you're jeopardising your freedom by taking the time to come and kill me. Even I wouldn't be that stupid."

"Even you," she agrees. "I have my reasons."

"Care to share?"

She whispers in my ear. "Maybe later."

I wince as her hot breath tickles the hairs on the back of my neck.

"Why did your brother confess?" I ask. "Did you kill James?"

"Keep walking, Leah. We've got quite a way yet."

"Why did Owen bring the head to my door? Why didn't you do it yourself?" I'm not sure whether I'm asking to keep her talking, or whether the curiosity is burning me so badly that I need to know.

"Concentrate." Her word is a hiss in my ear, caressing against my skin like the flick of a snake's tongue.

We're out of the farmlands and into the moors now. Isabel must have memorised this route, because it's tricky in the dark. She's even moved the knife an inch away from my throat in case I slip. The footpath continues up an incline, and although it isn't a difficult path, there are still a few slippery rocks to negotiate. It's a route I've walked many times.

"You're taking me to the abandoned farmhouse," I say.

"Do you remember when you told me about this place?" she replies. "You walked up here in your sleep and woke up amidst dust and cobwebs."

"I wasn't well," I admit. "Neither are you."

"I'm fine. You're completely bonkers, but I'm just fine. I've chosen the path I want to take, and it's this one right here with you. I wouldn't have it any other way."

"It's not the path I want to take, Isabel. I want a happy life with people who love me. Maybe you could have had that once."

She lets out a snort. "I believe you've met my family, so you already know how absurd that statement is."

"We make our own families."

It's the first thing I've said that gives her pause; I can tell, because her step falters. Is it possible that there's still a shred of humanity left inside her?

"I feel sorry for you because you never got the chance," I continue. As I talk, my foggy breath steams the space in front of us. My words are punctuated by my breathing as we continue up the hill, my legs tired from the long climb. "If Owen *did* kill Maisie then your family is foul. All of you are damaged, and I think I know why. It's your father, isn't it? He's the one who has turned you both into the people you are now." I want to say 'monsters,' but decide against it. "Your childhood was taken away from you. Were you told to lie about what happened to Maisie? Were you told to say you forgot to protect your brother? Why was he the one who got to be free?"

"You know nothing about it," she says.

"Then tell me. Maybe I can understand. Maybe telling me will lift a weight that you've carried all these years. I don't know who you are, Isabel, but I would like to find out."

"Spoken exactly like someone who would say anything to save her own life."

The house is barely visible through the dark, its outline a crumbling square up ahead. We're completely isolated now, surrounded by the moors on every side. Even if I shout and scream at the top of my lungs I'll never be heard from here.

"What about all the time we spent together at Crowmont Hospital? What about then?" I ask, hoping to keep her talking as much as I can.

"It was all an act."

"All of it?"

She hesitates. "Yes."

Isabel pushes me into the house, roughly shoving me with her hands. The knife is behind me now, its point jammed into my side, just far enough to hurt but not quite hard enough to break my skin. She ignites an electric camping light, and the room is flooded with a soft glow. In the centre of the room is a chair with rope already arranged around the arms.

Opposite the empty chair is another chair, but there is a person sitting on this one. Isabel pushes me so that I face that person, and for the first time, I scream.

CHAPTER
32

APRIL 2017

"**D**o you remember?" I asked.

She nodded. Her shoulders were slumped and her mouth was slightly open, as if in shock. "I… I want to tell you." Her bottom lip trembled as she spoke.

I took a step closer. "You can trust me."

"I know I can." She moved towards me. "Please, hear my story."

"I will," I said.

And before I knew it, I was moving into her room.

But then I hesitated. "I can't go into your room; it's against the rules. I need to stay out here so I can do my job professionally and effectively," I replied, moving back to my chair. The words came tumbling out as though they were rehearsed, and they made me sound like I was in control, but inside I felt unsure of myself. The truth was that I was exhausted, and I wasn't sure I was thinking straight. This great mystery had fallen into my lap when I'd taken this job, and any piece of the puzzle was like a lifeline for me. I needed to know.

"Don't you trust me?" Isabel sounded hurt. Her small voice carried all the notes of a wounded animal. She even sniffed away a few tears. "After all this time? You know I'm not dangerous. You know who I truly am. I'd expect some of the others to treat me like a freak, but not you."

"I do trust you," I said. "But I want to keep you safe, that's all."

"Please come into the room. I don't want anyone to overhear. What I want to say is all for you, Leah, because I trust you more than anyone else in this world. Do you understand?"

I nodded, and I can't deny that the words felt good to hear. Trust wasn't a feeling that came my way very often. I lived with a teenage boy who hated to tell me about his day, and I'd spent years with two parents who never trusted anything to me, not even their love, which felt good to admit. Even about Mum.

"All right. One minute. That's all."

Knowing that the CCTV cameras in the hallway would be monitoring this very moment, I went against all my better judgement and stood up from my chair. It scraped back more loudly than I would've liked, but it was the middle of the night, and I hadn't heard anyone moving around the hospital for hours.

My heart was beating too fast as I stepped into the room, and I could feel the alcoholic sweat seeping from my pores, all the wine coming out of me. When I glanced down at my hands, I saw that they were trembling beneath the fluorescent light inside Isabel's room.

"I was eight years old the first time I found one of Daddy's pictures." Isabel sat on her bed with her hands folded on her lap. She was bent over, making her body appear smaller than ever, especially with her recent weight loss. "I didn't understand what I was looking at or why he would have drawn an image so terrible. I didn't understand why anyone would want to hurt another person like that. I was so innocent, you see."

"You were a child," I said, taking another step closer. "You were innocent. What was the picture of?"

"I'll show you." Isabel stood up from the bed and walked around me to get to her desk. She rummaged through a few illustrations piled up on the surface and lifted one to examine. She stood there for a moment, contemplating the image between her fingers, then she sidestepped to the left and walked straight towards me with the paper still in her hand.

When she got close to me, I took another step back closer to her bed. "What is it?"

She moved again, and I moved one more pace back so that my legs were touching the side of her bed. Then she raised her arm and passed me the picture.

I took it slowly from her and, at the same time, she pushed me back onto the bed. Before I had time to react, she moved catlike to the ground, lifted a long, thin object—some sort of rope—and wrapped it around my wrist.

"Isabel, what—?"

Before I could say another word, a sharp implement was jammed beneath my chin, pressing my head up.

"In case you're wondering, I spent a lot of time making this shiv, and it is sharp enough to make you bleed. Here." She pressed the implement into my collar bone beneath my blouse, and a small red flower of blood bloomed there. I winced at the sharp pain, though it was little more than a pinprick. It was a display of strength, not intended to truly hurt me.

"Don't do this, Isabel," I warned. "You've been doing so well. I… I sent an email to the police telling them I thought you were innocent. If your father is behind all this he'll be arrested and you'll be freed. If you let me go now, I won't say anything about this. You won't be punished."

But she simply smiled. "You'd like it to be Daddy, wouldn't you? Daddies are naughty, they deserve to be punished. At least yours did." Quick as lightning, she moved down and tied my arm with another long rope, which I now realised was made up of strips of bedsheets. The long, narrow pieces of linen had been previously attached to the legs of the bed before being tied around my wrists, which wrenched my arms apart and pulled my chest down towards the bedroom floor. I had to lift my chin to meet her eye as she stood over me and pushed her shiv harder against my throat. I couldn't quite make it out, but I suspected it was made from a sharpened toothbrush handle.

"You've been planning this for a long time, haven't you?" I said as I struggled to keep my backside from slipping off the duvet cover. My arms already ached from being pulled across the length of the bed. I wasn't sure I could remain in this uncomfortable position for much longer.

Isabel smiled as she retrieved the paper I'd dropped while she was tying me up. Triumphantly, she held it up to my face so I could see it.

On the paper was a perfectly executed drawing of me sitting in this exact position with my hands bound to the bed. In my mouth was a bird. A magpie.

"Magpies are deceptive and intelligent, but you know that, don't you?" She put the illustration back on her desk before stroking my face. When she leaned towards me, I saw the cold determination in her eyes. "Poor Leah. You have no idea what you've been going through. I saw it straight away. Your pinched little face, so scared, so full of pain. I smelled the alcohol on your breath, saw the dark circles beneath your eyes. I sat on this bed and I watched you hallucinate wood lice crawling along the floor. You've been having a nervous breakdown, dear Leah." She took a step back and pouted. "Daddy killed Mummy, wah wah wah!"

"Isabel, let me go or I'll scream."

She lurched towards me, her face feral and terrifying, and lifted the shiv to my eye. "Do that and I'll cut you, starting here. How quickly do you think security will get here? How much time do you suppose you have? I could gouge your eye out by then. Do you want to live with one eye?"

It was the first time I feared for my life. Everything I had once believed about Isabel's character was stripped away and I saw her for what she really was—a killer.

And then she laughed. "Oh, silly me." She hit herself in the forehead with the palm of her hand. "I almost forgot." She bent down and collected another strip of bedding. Then she leaned towards me and forced it into my mouth, gagging me. The sight of her psychotic laughter sent shivers up and down my spine. "And I'd better take care of this." She walked over and closed the door to her room. "We'd better work fast before they notice you aren't there. How long is it until someone comes to give you a comfort break? Oh, I forgot, you can't answer. Let's get this moving, then."

I watched in horror as the girl I'd once felt so protective of came back to me and snatched my nurse's pass from the clip on my shirt pocket.

"Even looks a bit like me, doesn't it?" she said, showing me the photograph. "When I first laid my eyes on you I knew you were perfect. We're around the same height, similar hair colour. I had to lose some weight and cut my hair like yours, but we're a pretty good match. Of course, I had to take bets on you not coming into work with platinum blonde hair one day, but you don't strike me as the adventurous type. Besides, you have, what, three work outfits in rotation? You couldn't afford a fancy hairdo even if you wanted one." She stroked my cheek again. "Poor, poor Leah. Skint, living in a rundown cottage on a farm outside Hutton village with her little brother. Yes, that's right, I know a lot about you. It's a Fiat you drive, isn't it? Let's have the car keys, then. I wonder if I can remember how to drive. Luckily, Daddy always let us have a go in his car when we were kids. I'm sure I can remember where the pedals are. Oh, wait. You haven't got the keys. What's the number of your locker?"

I shook my head.

Isabel pressed the shiv against my neck. "What's the number?"

"Fifty-two," I mumbled through the gag.

"Very good. Now, I'm afraid there's one small matter to deal with and it's going to be tricky." She knelt down in front of me and began pulling off my shoes, then the socks. "I wonder what you look like naked, dear Leah. You don't seem to have a bad body. The tits aren't bad. You're a little bloated from all that wine you've been glugging away." She laughed. "Would I fuck you? I don't know, maybe. Maybe I will. Now." The laugh that came from her was high-pitched and disturbing, the kind of laugh a child would make, but twisted with malice. "It's a shame we don't have enough time."

Her hands groped up my legs until she reached the waistband of my trousers. I was trembling all over, making a whimpering sound behind the gag. Her fingers nimbly worked the zip and clasp, before she yanked them down my legs. Then she changed out of her own bottoms and into mine. She pulled her top off, and dropped it to the floor.

"Do you promise to be a good girl?"

The shiv pressed into the fleshy part of my face beneath my right eye, and she leaned closer so I could see her small breasts swinging beneath her bent shoulders. The bra she wore was flesh-coloured without underwire, more like a training bra than a grown woman's lingerie. I almost felt sorry for this girl who had grown up in institutions, who was broken, lacking humanity, lacking love.

"I promise," I mumbled.

By now I knew what she intended to do, but I was too afraid to stop her. Looking back, I can see that I had a choice I decided not to take. Isabel would never have escaped if I'd screamed or shouted; even

244

with the gag, there were enough people nearby to hear the sounds and alert security. But I knew I'd be horribly maimed and possibly killed if I made that choice. It was the safer choice for everyone else, because I knew that by being silent I was letting a dangerous criminal out into society, but I was too afraid to stop her. It was ingrained in me to freeze up. It happened on instinct. Every time my father had hit me when I was a child I was so scared that I never fought back. It was a constant source of shame to me that I'd never fought back whenever I found myself cornered by a bully. Not everyone has it in them to deal out violence in response to violence. Not everyone has that kind of strength. And over the years, as the shame worked its way down into my very core, it made me believe that I was never good enough and that I deserved it.

I deserved it.

When I looked up at Isabel's face, I saw his face leering down at me.

She untied one of my hands, quickly slipped my shirt sleeve over my arm, tied me back up and then repeated the process on the other side. Then she slipped it over her body and began fastening the buttons.

"Oh, isn't this lovely," she said. "You started wearing brighter colours because I told you to. Such a sweet, sweet Leah. For a minute you actually believed you were worth something, didn't you? There you were, my crusader, my saviour, turning up at my family's house with accusations to make and a finger to point." She took the picture of me tied up and folded it, then put it in her pocket. "You liked me and you couldn't cope with the idea that I'm a killer, so you obsessed and obsessed, anything to avoid dealing with your own problems." She slipped her feet into my shoes. "Leah, the nurse, the protector of people." She stepped closer and lifted my head so that we looked deeply into each other's eyes. "You can't fix me."

Then she bent down to the floor, lifted a loose piece of tiling beneath the bed, and retrieved a small bag.

"I have a parting gift." She smiled at the bag as she rose to her feet. "I've been collecting them for a long time. I hope you like them." The bag rattled and I understood what were inside.

I shook my head.

"I think you need them, if I'm honest. You're a little… you know." She rotated her finger next to her temple to indicate my insanity. Then, she unfastened the bag and poured the pills into the palm of her hand. "Open up for Mummy."

Isabel ripped the gag from my face, forced my teeth to part and rammed the pills down my throat before pressing her hands over my nose and mouth. I spluttered and choked, but could do little more than swallow the sour tablets.

"You bit me a little," she said, pouting like a little girl. "That was ouchy. Naughty Leah. I hope these kill you now. Maybe they will, I'm not sure. It would certainly make things easier for me. But on the other hand, if you live—which, personally, I'm rooting for—we get to meet again. And that, Leah, is something I'm looking forward to very much."

With her hands cutting off my oxygen, I began to feel woozy. My arms were tired, aching all the way down to my fingers. My body was heavy and tensed all over. I'm not sure how long she held me like that, but I was barely aware of her removing the bindings from my wrists and tucking them beneath her—or rather, *my*—shirt. Then, as the room began to melt away, she kissed me on the lips and left.

CHAPTER
33

James Gorden's decomposing, headless body is sitting opposite me, propped up on a chair with his hands placed neatly in his lap, as though posing for a school photograph. The corpse is bloated and sagging, like the balloon remnants from a child's party. I only recognise him from the t-shirt, a large baggy thing with a Harry Potter lightning bolt across the chest, and, of course, the fact that there's no head.

My mind flits back to the day I saw my first dead body on the job. For a short period of time I worked as a geriatric nurse in a nursing home, and the sweet old man I'd been caring for slipped away as I was changing his bedsore dressings. There was an awful rattle in his chest, followed by a peaceful sigh, and then every part of what made him who he was left his body in an instant. It was simple and quick. Relatively painless. It was the way most people would wish to leave this world.

I look at James's corpse and wouldn't wish his fate on even the worst of us. It's violent and disgusting. Degrading. Isabel wants to show me her power, and she's succeeded.

Now she stands between me and James, with a small table to the right of her hip. She turns to the table and flips open a cloth. Underneath, I see a set of sharp knives, which she caresses lovingly.

I need to keep her talking. Distract her from the torture implements I see on the table.

"Did Owen help you? How else could you get James here? Was there some sort of pact? You've suffered the last seven years in incarceration. Maybe it's his turn to take the blame. But if you did arrange that, why are you jeopardising your chance at freedom by taking me? You know I'm in touch with the police, and you know that Seb Braithwaite is looking out for me."

"Shush, Leah. Don't tire yourself out. It's going to be a long night." Her eyes never move from the set of knives on the table. She brushes a lock of hair away from her face and sighs as though staring at a lover.

I decide to try a different approach. "You found this place because I gave you directions to it, didn't you? I was stupid enough to tell you all about my life, and where I lived, what was close by. I told you about the morning I woke up here, and you brought me back because I told you that story."

"It's nice and secluded," she says. "And it reminds you of a low point in your life. It felt poetic."

"It was clever. Everything you've done has been clever. You lost weight, changed your hair, and you pretended to be me. You waited for the perfect moment and took your chance." If there's one thing I've learned from working with sociopaths, it's that they love to be reminded how cunning they are. Now is the right time to begin feeding her ego.

"I did. Perfect opportunities never fall into one's lap. We don't wait for fate, we force fate's hand. That meant waiting and waiting until the right moment came where I could steal my own fate. It meant waiting for you, Leah. You're the one who made all of this possible. My perfect nurse." She takes a step closer and I cringe away from her. She shushes me again as she strokes the length of my face with her warm hand. "Just the right amount of damage. Just the right amount of neediness."

"I wanted to believe you were innocent," I admit. "More than anything."

"I know, sweet girl." Isabel's touch is almost comforting as she wipes away the tears on my cheek.

"I was your nurse. I only ever wanted to help you. That's my job."

"That's what nurses do, isn't it? They help people. They help the sick and make them better. No matter what they might have done." She crouches down so that we're face to face. "Did you think you could make me better?"

"I don't know."

"I think you did." She smiles.

When she moves away, I almost miss her hand on my cheek, and then realise how fucked up that is. After the months of fearing for my life—checking the locks with obsessive compulsion, dreaming of the birds pecking my flesh, jumping at every slight noise, seeing her face whenever I'm in a crowd—it's almost a relief to finally be her prisoner. I've been caught up the Fieldings' dark web for so long that I always knew this was inevitable. This has been my fate for since I set foot in Crowmont Hospital, and now it's all going to end. The guilt, the pain, the grief, and the worry that has plagued me, made me itchy inside, is finally going to be cut out of me until there's nothing left.

But if she does succeed in cutting me into tiny pieces, who will be left for Tom? He'll live his life never knowing the truth. Or worse, one day he'll need his birth certificate, and he'll see my name and realise I lied to him all those years. But the blank spot where the father's name should be will confuse him for the rest of his life. He'll never understand. He'll never know.

Don't I owe it to him to fight?

"Do you want to know why I went to London, Leah? I'm surprised you haven't asked." She picks up the smallest knife and plays with it between her fingers.

"To hide from the police? I think if I was on the run I'd choose the most populated city in the country, too."

She points the knife at me. "Yes, that was certainly a perk, but that wasn't the only reason. I looked you up. You're quite the celebrity in your home area, did you know that? I found newspaper articles about you on the internet. Public libraries are a great way to waste time when you're on the run from the police with no money. I learnt a lot there. I learnt that your father didn't die. Remember that touching story you told me about sensing his presence at his funeral? That's because your broken mind didn't recognise that he was real, you silly bint!" She starts to laugh.

"I already know this," I reply, anger beginning to replace my fear.

"I visited your mother's grave."

Warmth spreads through my arms as the anger continues to flow through my veins. But confusion comes along with it. "What? Why?"

"To put flowers on her grave, of course. What, did you think I would dig her up?"

"Shut up!"

Isabel's eyes narrow. "You have a bit of a weakness for Mummy, don't you? Is that what all this is about? You couldn't save Mummy from bad Daddy, so you want to save everyone else instead? My poor little Leah wanted to save me too because I was so innocent."

"You lived a lie," I retort. "You're the one who's messed up. You don't even know who you are. You can insult me all you like, but I'm not the one without an identity. Yes, I want to help people, and yes, I had a psychotic break, and no, I couldn't save my own mother, but you're desperate to prove yourself. Who are you trying to impress, Isabel? Daddy?"

She slashes the knife towards me, brushing the fabric of the dressing gown with the sharp edge. "You don't know me!"

"You have a bit of a weakness for Daddy, don't you?" The satisfaction of hitting her squarely with her own attack brings strength back into my limbs. I'm not dead yet. There's still a chance.

Isabel stares at me with eyes wide and wild, her nostrils flaring in anger. She's gripping the knife so tightly that her knuckles shine bright white.

"Is that why you're so obsessed with me?" I ask. "Is it because we're so similar? Did your father hurt you when you were a little girl? I remember what you said to get me into your room at Crowmont. You told me you found pictures belonging to your father when you were a little girl. Was that part true? Did your father enjoy hurting little girls, Isabel?"

Isabel shakes her head. "Not little girls, no."

"But he likes to hurt people."

Isabel's head turns to the left, where the abandoned old house remains shrouded in darkness. When I came for my walk up to this place all those months ago, I walked through the downstairs of the house. I know that if you walk through that darkness you reach another room, some sort of sitting room or lounge. Why is Isabel looking in that direction?

I struggle against the ropes, sensing a change, but they're tight and my mind is racing so quickly that I can't seem to think straight. Every part of me goes cold, chasing away that brief feeling of strength. I'm listening intently, waiting for what will happen next, because I know things are about to change.

The low chuckle ripples through the room, too low to be Isabel. It belongs to a man. It's followed by footsteps moving slowly, dragging along the dusty concrete of the old house. The ropes chafe my skin as I struggle against them, panicking. James Gorden's headless body sits in front of me as a reminder of what I may become.

"Isabel," I whisper. "It's not too late to let me go. It's not too late to stop this."

Isabel's eyes flick across to mine, but there is no pity in them. She exhales through her nose once. A sad, bitter laugh.

"I told you to stay away from my family. I did warn you." The sound of his voice alone causes my stomach to flip over in fear. He was always the most dangerous.

My premature feeling of hope dissipates. How can I possibly expect to escape with Isabel *and* her father as my captors? Ever since David Fielding pinned me up against his kitchen counter and met my gaze with his own I've been terrified of him. The cold edge of his voice has haunted me in the long, lonely nights at the cottage. I'd recognise his voice out of a thousand others.

The slow, dragging footsteps continue to echo around the small space. Isabel licks her lips and strokes the knife handle with her thumb, already anticipating the family fun that's about to begin.

I brace myself as David Fielding steps out from the shadow. There's a scrape of footwear across concrete which alerts me to the fact that David isn't alone. He's pushing a smaller, dumpier figure ahead of him.

"Tom!"

I'm frantic, jerking my body in the chair, pulling at the ropes, chafing my skin and drawing blood. How did they find him? I told Tom to go away with Mary and Gavin, even insisting that they not tell me where they were going. But now my worst fear has been realised.

My poor, sweet son is held hostage in front of David, a gag over his mouth and tears running down his cheeks. His jeans are damp at the crotch and his hands are pulled behind his back. David holds a knife to his neck.

"I'd calm down if I were you, Leah." David's voice is dark and dangerous. "Otherwise, I'll gut your little brother."

CHAPTER
34

David kicks Tom's feet out from under him and ties his ankles together. I'm silently screaming as my son sits there squirming and shivering. I'm trying desperately to keep my mind clear. There's no point in panicking anymore. The stakes are too high. I have my son to think about, and I cannot stand the sight of David bending over him with a rabid grin on his face, while all the time Tom's eyes are on me, pleading and terrified.

I turn to Isabel. "This is between you and me. Let him go." The power in my voice surprises me.

But Isabel lifts her arms above her head, twirling the knife in her fingers like it's a baton. She's dancing to the sound of Tom's tears. "I don't want to."

"Why are you doing this?" I plead. "Why? You could be free. You could go anywhere you like, and your father could carry on living his own life, business as usual. Rich. White. Entitled to anything he wants. But you're jeopardising all of this for me. What's so special about me?"

Isabel's head moves sharply towards me. "Because you cared, Leah. Now I care about you, too."

"This isn't caring." My voice is a screech so high-pitched it disturbs me. "This is sick."

Isabel and David exchange smiles. I feel deflated. There's no reasoning with them. I'm in the presence of murderers who enjoy this, who are enjoying my fear and my desperation. I'm *feeding* them.

David moves away from Tom and places his arm around his daughter. "Stop fighting it, Leah. Fighting never works. I've been fighting who I am for years, but not anymore."

It sounds appealing, giving up, but my son is frightened and alone in the corner of the room, sitting in urine-soaked jeans. I need to think carefully about what I know, and what I can do to get us out of this situation. First, what I know: Owen Fielding confessed to killing Maisie and James. I can't trust that to be true. The Fieldings strike me as cunning criminals with souls as dark as molasses. They've made some sort of pact. Owen's confession was a distraction to allow Isabel time to capture me. She wanted me to drop my guard. This is a last hurrah. They don't intend to get out of this unscathed; instead they've given up and they're taking me down with them.

I need more time.

I need to get Isabel to talk.

"All right," I say. "I'll stop fighting. I know that you're going to win this no matter what I do. I'm just sorry that I got involved with any of you in the first place. You drew me into this mystery and made me question everything, and now I want you to give me answers. Isabel, what happened to Maisie Earnshaw? What happened that day? Don't let me die without knowing, because I spent months agonising over what might have happened, and now you can finally tell me."

"Shall I tell her?" Isabel asks her father.

David moves over to the table with the knives and perches on the edge. "If that's what you want to do."

Isabel walks over to me, still fingering the knife, and draws it along the lapel of the dressing gown, cutting into the fabric, barely grazing my skin. Despite my attempt at bravado, I let out a small gasp, wincing as the blade draws a small amount of blood. "You were right, you know. When I told you I'd found my father's pictures as a child it was the truth. But he never hurt me. He used to draw pictures of the women he tortured and killed. They were hidden in a locked drawer in his home office. I was an inquisitive child who noticed that Daddy always carried a key that didn't unlock any of the doors in the house or his cars, or his work office. I also noticed that sometimes he lied to Mum. He'd tell her he was working late, but he'd come home wearing different clothes or shoes. I was seven, but I was already smarter than my mother.

"One day I created a diversion. I waited until Dad placed his keys on his office desk, and then I pushed my brother down a set of steps. When I screamed, Dad forgot to pick up his keys from the desk in order to run to my brother." Isabel directs her lazy eyes to her father. "Got to make sure the male heir isn't dead." She turns back to me. "While Mum and Dad were busy checking Owen was okay—which he was, because I only pushed him down a few steps—I ran into his office, tried the suspicious key in his locked drawer, and found the pictures. I kept one of them underneath my mattress and used to look at it at night."

A little girl, and a drawer filled with tortured women. Most people could never comprehend the darkness, nor the way Isabel was drawn to it. But I've been touched by darkness myself, and the thought of her sleeping on top of that picture makes me feel sick. I almost pity her. Then, I see Tom trembling in the corner and that pity fades away.

"Why weren't you frightened?" I ask. "Most little girls would be."

"I'm not most little girls," Isabel says proudly.

"And you." I direct my gaze to David. "James told me he'd always suspected you of kidnapping and killing homeless women over the years. Was he right?"

David ignores my question. "Did you enjoy the meal you had with us, Leah? Did you like it when I wrapped my fingers around your neck? I've been so looking forward to doing it again."

His words are so cold that they reach into my chest and wrap around my heart. I ignore the sense of dread spreading over my skin. There's no time for fear anymore. I have to ignore it and keep Isabel talking while I figure out how to get the knife out of my dressing gown pocket.

"What are you, Isabel? If you're not like most little girls."

She lifts her face to the ceiling of the crumbling house and runs her fingers through her hair. "You know what I am, Leah. I'm a god. I turn people into beautiful things."

This surprises me. I've never heard anyone claim to be a god before, not in the years I worked at Whitmore, nor even from my father's drunken mouth. But it makes sense, in a warped, sadistic way.

"Beautiful birds," I whisper. "That's what you did to Maisie. You turned her into a bird."

Isabel sits down on the floor so quickly that for half a second I think she's collapsed. She takes a lock of her hair and strokes it between her fingers. "I'd been telling Owen for months that Daddy was special and liked to turn people into art, but he didn't believe me. Owen always said that people couldn't be made into anything beautiful because all people are ugly. We'd been experimenting with animals in the woods, seeing if we could make them more beautiful or uglier. Sometimes Owen would tie me up like the girls in Dad's pictures, but it never worked out right. I could always get out. I wanted to prove to Owen that we could make a truly beautiful *thing*. Magnificent." She stops stroking her hair before giving it a little tug. "Then, Maisie came along."

"You dragged Maisie into the woods like one of your animals," I say. "Then you hit her on the head with a rock, removed her clothes, and carved wings into her back. You did it *with* Owen."

"And now she's a beautiful bird, not a dirty little girl," Isabel says triumphantly.

"And you," I say to David. "You knew what your children were, and you did nothing about it."

"My daughter is an artist," he replies. "A glorious artist."

Tom is watching us in the corner, calmer now, his chest moving up and down less rapidly. Good. My talking to Isabel is giving him time to calm down. My fingers inch around the arm of the chair towards my pocket where the knife is hidden. I ignore the pinch of the ropes and continue.

"But killing Maisie was reckless. You put the family in jeopardy, Isabel," I point out. "Your father didn't need the attention. In fact, I bet you had to give up your hobby for a little while. Didn't you, David?"

"It was put on hold," David admits. "But Isabel was brave enough to take responsibility for what happened, and she was clever enough to get out of it."

"Then why have you given up? Why take me? You know you're not going to get away with this. It's too high profile. The police have been checking up on me every day. What are you doing?"

"My little girl has suffered all these years." David hops off the table and walks towards me, his chin angled down and his eyes gravely determined. My fingers grope the fabric of my dressing gown, reaching for the knife. "She deserves to take whatever she wants in recompense for that suffering."

"Now it's Owen's turn to protect the family."

"Well, he's hardly innocent now, is he?" David pokes James's body in the stomach and laughs.

"Is your wife in on it? Is she a killer too? What is this, Family von Trapp the Halloween edition? You think you're gods, but you're sick." My heart hammers against my chest as David closes the gap between us and grasps my throat in one hand. I'm forced to sit there, helpless, as he squeezes hard, his face growing red with the effort.

"Let me ask you a question, Leah." His eyes are glossy and wide, with the whites of his eyeballs shining through the darkness. He's excited, I realise, exhilarated by the death that surrounds him. What kind of person finds joy in pain? What kind of person comes alive at the thought of taking life from another? "Do you remember the victims? Do you remember the names of the people serials killers take? No? The world will know my name. The world will know exactly who I am. You're nothing. You're the bug we'll grind into the dirt."

"Daddy!" Isabel grabs hold of David's shoulder and wrenches him away. "Don't be so silly. She *is* something. She's a beautiful bird. She's mine."

My throat rasps as I drag in the dusty air, burning me all the way down to my lungs. The lack of oxygen has made me woozy and the room spins. A sad moaning lament escapes from Tom on the other side of the room. He's calling my name through his gag.

I need to stay strong for him, but my eyelids are drooping. A soft hand caresses my face, then wanders down my chest, brushing the outline of my breasts, before reaching my hands. For an awful moment I think she might find the knife, but instead, Isabel is beginning to untie my wrists. Before hope floods back in, David moves behind me and puts a knife to my throat.

"Don't try anything, Leah," he warns.

"What… what are you doing?" I mumble. My throat burns so badly that my words are a hoarse whisper.

Isabel pulls me to my feet, shushing me gently. She tucks a lock of hair behind my ear as she pushes me forwards. With horror, I realise I'm walking straight towards James Gorden, the smell of him hitting the back of my injured throat. His sagging body moves and squirms in the chair, infested with maggots. I start to heave, almost vomiting onto my chest, until Isabel strokes my hair and calms me down. She moves me past James's body to the centre of the room. Here I get a better view of Tom. He's quiet and watchful with his eyes trained on mine. There's a glint of anger in them. Good, I think. I'll be angry too.

Isabel stops me and moves away, but I can't do anything because David is behind me, his sharp knife pressing into my skin. I'm not sure what's going on, but I wish I'd kept Isabel talking for a little while longer so I could've managed to get the knife from my pocket.

It's too late now. Isabel is pulling ropes down from the ceiling. I didn't notice it because the room was so dark, but Isabel and David have set up some sort of rig with climbing equipment. Isabel tests it once, and then moves back to me, sliding the dressing gown down to my feet. I begin to whimper.

"Hush now, Leah. You're about to be part of something beautiful, there's no need to be afraid."

My nightgown is split open at the front with her knife and pushed over my arms and onto the ground. I turn away from Tom, ashamed of my naked body in front of my son.

Isabel taps my breast. "Better than I thought." Then she takes hold of one wrist, wraps the rope around it, and clips the rope into the pulley system above my head.

When my second wrist is held in place with the rope, I find myself yanked open, like da Vinci's Vitruvian Man. They both move behind my back and someone pulls on the rope so that it's taut.

"Now," Isabel says in a cheerful voice. "Shall we begin?"

CHAPTER
35

Before she starts, there's a moment so quiet that I can hear the rain on the dilapidated roof a storey above me. Tom's breathing is raspy through the gag, but both David and Isabel are silent movers, giving nothing away. I can't see them, I can't hear them. A solitary drip of water comes down from the ceiling.

I crane my neck, examining the pulley system. Hooks have been driven into the plaster above, and through the hooks is the climbing rope. The rope slips through the system, pulling my arms and legs apart, fixed at some point behind me so that I can't move the rope no matter how hard I try. I'm sure the ropes are excellent quality, which means cutting through them won't work. Besides, I'm naked now. I don't even have the knife I took from the table in the cottage.

But what about the hooks? Could that be a weakness? This building isn't exactly safe even without the added pressure of the pulley system. The light is dim, but I think I can make out a few cracks in the ceiling; some are bad enough to let water drip onto the floor. Perhaps if I try to pull the hooks out, I'd bring the ceiling down with me. It could hurt Tom, but could also give me an advantage over the Fieldings, and I can't think of any better ideas.

"Tom will watch you get your wings," Isabel says brightly. "And then you will watch while we kill your little brother."

We're going to die unless I try to escape from these ropes. I have to pull these hooks from the ceiling, even if I pull half the building down in the process.

Isabel slowly draws the knife over my flesh, gently touching me with the blade so that it tickles my skin. She's practising a pattern along my shoulder blades, like a tattoo artist testing out her canvas.

Don't scream, I tell myself. *Whatever you do, don't scream.*

"Everything's going to be all right," I say, with my eyes directed at Tom. He's trembling again, and I need him calm if we're going to get out of here.

She wants me to scream, I can feel it coming off her in waves, the eagerness. Can I be strong enough not to? *Focus on getting out.* Carefully, I assess the strength of the ropes binding my wrists, gently pulling on them to test the strain. The water drips down from the ceiling less than a foot away from where the hooks have been screwed in. That gives me hope that there's weakness in the old plasterboards or the rafters above me. Even if I could loosen one of the hooks far enough to get an arm free it would be useful. Maybe I could knock one of them out and grab Isabel's knife. But what if they get to Tom first?

"Remember how you told me that your father was superstitious?" Isabel's breath tickles my neck.

"Yes."

"He always said hello to magpies. But to me, it's simply good manners to talk to birds. They're wonderful creatures, why not address them? Birds are a hundred and fifty million years old. The original dinosaurs. They deserve our respect, don't you think?"

"Yes." My biceps strain as I pull on the ropes above my head, but I can't allow any of that strain to show in my voice. I'm not a strong woman; I don't attend fitness classes or go to the gym, but I am toned from restraining patients when I have to and being on my feet most of the day. Since I've been working at the farm shop I've spent the daylight hours carrying goods, moving tins, lifting sacks. *I'm stronger than I think I am. I'm stronger than I think I am.*

When the knife slices into my flesh for the first time the sharp pain takes my breath away. *I won't scream for her, I won't.* What Isabel doesn't realise is that the deft slicing of her knife distracts me from the strain in my biceps, allowing me to pull even harder. But at the same time I'm aware that flexing my shoulders and back would be noticeable to Isabel. Luckily, she mistakes it for a reaction to pain.

"Relax, dear Leah," she soothes as the knife swoops down to my waist. "I need to draw feathers. You need to keep still."

"Want me to hold her?" David offers.

"No," she replies. "You keep an eye on the boy."

Pull, Leah, pull as hard as you can, I think, screwing my eyes tight and gritting my teeth. With my eyes shut, I see Alfie leaning against the wall with a cigarette hanging out of the corner of his mouth. His hands are pushed into his trouser pockets, and he scrapes the concrete with the toe of his shoe. I'm watching him with sweat pouring down my face, blood streaming down my back, and the muscles in my arms feeling as though they're going to pop, but he doesn't seem to register any of that. He lifts his chin and looks me straight in the eye.

"The Hackney Hacker," he says.

Shut up. The words don't escape my lips.

"Alf Smith was a family man, a decent man. On the street where he lived with his wife and two children, he was considered a friend to everyone. Always up for a laugh, Alf would be in the pub at the

SARAH A. DENZIL

end of the street most nights, singing West Ham chants until the pub was filled with a lively, boisterous spirit. But then he'd go home and everything would change."

A groan of pain rises up from my belly and out of my mouth. I feel spittle in the corners of my mouth, but I keep my eyes screwed shut because I don't want to see Tom's face.

"Alf once dreamed of being important. But the accident in the factory changed all that, didn't it, Leah? He became a different person. He turned meaner and meaner until one day he snapped completely, and hacked his wife to death, almost chopping her head off with the knife. Who found her, Leah?"

"Tom," I whisper.

"That's right." Alfie lifts himself from the wall and takes a step towards me. "You've always been a victim, haven't you, Leah? But what about him?" He nods over to Tom, crouched and afraid. The scenery in my mind is half the abandoned house and half the carpark outside Crowmont Hospital.

"I don't want him to be," I admit. Leah and Tom Smith have been ground down into the dirt for as long as I can remember, but it's because we've let them grind us down. No one with an unbroken spirit can truly be a victim. They can hurt you physically and emotionally, but you're no one's victim if you remain in possession of your whole self. Of your willpower.

Why has it taken me so long to realise that?

When I open my eyes, I allow myself to scream, but the scream isn't one from pain, it's from determination, because I can feel one of the hooks slipping.

"One for sorrow," Isabel recites to herself as she continues to carve into my skin. "I carved this same pattern into Maisie's skin, you know. The police never released that detail, did they? It's a good job, or you'd never have believed I was innocent little Isabel."

264

Shut up, I think. *Shut up about your stupid obsession with birds.* A little ceiling dust hits my forehead. Tom's eyes are on mine and they are intense. He knows what I'm doing. He sits up with his back straight and his bound wrists resting on his knees. He hunches his shoulders and moves himself into a position where he can move easily or reach up to protect his head. He must see the ceiling straining.

"Two for joy."

I scream again, hiding the sound of the plaster cracking above me. One of the hooks is half out and there are fine lines moving across the surface of the ceiling.

Isabel raises her voice. "Three for a girl."

And the ceiling opens. I drop to the ground to cover my head. The pulley system collapses around me. Plasterboard, dust, and debris rains on top of my naked body, bruising me in the back, shoulders, and side. But as I fall, I knock Isabel back, which gives me an opportunity to take more control. Both Isabel and David are protecting themselves from the falling rubble. I can't rest for even a moment. I need to get my head up and find a weapon. Wishing I could at least check on Tom, I force myself to turn towards Isabel. She's on her back with an arm thrown up to protect her face. The knife is no longer in her hand. I scramble across the floor, searching through dust and debris for the knife.

There's a scuttling close to me. David. He's on his feet. I roll to the left and narrowly miss his foot as he attempts to kick me. My hands quickly grope along the floor. The knife must have fallen close to Isabel, unless she opened her arms and threw it in the heat of the moment.

"What did you do, Leah?" David says in a low growl. "If you've hurt my daughter—"

My skin is slick with mingled sweat and blood, and the dirt that has made its way into the wounds on my back will make me vulnerable to infection, but I can't worry about that now.

David lurches closer and grabs hold of one of the ropes still attached to my wrist, yanking me towards him, causing a jolting pain to run all the way down my arm to the elbow. I'm pulled onto my feet, with David pressing his face against mine. The spit from his heavy breathing collects on my upper lip.

I have no chance of finding the knife with him holding me so tight. Even though I wriggle and squirm under his grip, I'm still attached to the rope and he has it tight in his fist. He's taller, wider, stronger, and fitter. There's no way I can beat him.

Just as I'm about to open my mouth to tell Tom to run away as fast as he can, David lets out a strange high-pitched exhale, like air coming out of a balloon. His grip on me loosens as he gropes around his back, searching for something. Not giving him even a single second to right himself, I pull the ropes from out of his hands, kick him as hard as I can between the legs, and then push him down.

Tom stands behind him, his bound hands reaching towards me, trembling from head to toe.

"I … I stabbed him," he says. "I stabbed him."

"It's all right." I pull him into a hug, ignoring my nakedness and the ropes attached to my wrists and ankles. "Isabel."

She's still on the floor, her head lolling to one side. I crouch down and feel for a pulse. It's still there, but she seems to be unconscious. Moving quickly, I grab a knife from Isabel's torture table, crouch back down next to Isabel and search for a phone. There's nothing. Next I try David. He lies in a pool of his own blood, his glassy eyes staring up at me. He's dead, which I try to ignore as I search his jacket pockets. No phone. I try his jeans. No phone.

"We need to get out of here. But first I need to get out of these."

Isabel's knives are sharp, so cutting through the ropes takes moments. Then I pull David's jacket off his dead body and wrap it around my shoulders. I'm freezing cold, covered in blood, and sore all over my body, but my mind is clearer than it has ever been before.

"Come on." I take Tom's hand and hurry out of the house. I don't know what other structural damage was done to the house when the ceiling caved in, but it's certainly not safe to stay there.

"What about her?" Tom says, nodding at Isabel's unconscious form lying amidst broken pieces of plasterboard and crumbled bricks. "If you… If you kill her, this is all over."

I turn over the knife in my hand and consider it for a moment. "If I kill her, it's murder."

"But after what she did to you, she deserves it."

"I can't, Tom. I just can't do it."

CHAPTER
36

Sharp, slanting rain hits my sore skin with nature's needles. Tiny pinpricks of agony spread across my face and my bare legs. With my left hand I grip Tom, and with my right hand I grip the knife. I'm not so much running as tumbling; rushing downhill away from the dilapidated farmhouse. My eyes sting from the plaster dust, my back is sore from my cuts, and David's jacket chafes every injury when I move, but I will not stop. I'm all too aware of Isabel left behind in the house; unconscious, but for how long?

As a trained nurse, I couldn't bring myself to kill her. Not after spending a good portion of my life protecting the vulnerable. I couldn't take a life, and I feel weaker for it because I'm running away from the house, and I'm looking over my shoulder in fear.

"How far is it to the Braithwaites'?" Tom asks. His palm is sweaty inside mine, despite the chill of the wind bringing the rain down. He must be as high on adrenaline as I am at this point.

"I know I can walk there in forty minutes. If we run, maybe twenty. It's mostly downhill."

"I think I hurt my ankle when we were getting out of the house."

I've been concentrating so hard on getting away from the Fieldings I haven't even noticed that Tom is limping. "Do you need to stop?"

"No," he says, biting his bottom lip. "Let's get away from… away from what's in that house."

I turn back once more while the house is still visible through the dark, before the shadows engulf it. The ramshackle door is slightly open. Did I leave the door open?

"We need to keep moving." It's becoming a mantra.

The wind whips David's jacket open as we hurry down the hill, exposing my abdomen to the rain. Whenever my back is turned towards the direction of the house, a slow tingling feeling works its way up my spine, and every moment I expect a hand to grasp my shoulder. I anticipate her whisper in my ear—*one for sorrow*. Tom is struggling, I can see that. He winces every time his foot is caught on a slight bump on the path. My bare feet will be torn up by stones by the time we reach the Braithwaites', but I'm beginning to feel numb from the cold, which helps.

There's no light on the moors. Even the Braithwaites' farm is dark tonight. There are no lights on in Rose Cottage either, not that I'm sure I can even see it from where we are. I imagine we're still high up in the hills, but it's hard to know if we've drifted sideways, seeing as my only way of figuring out which direction we're heading is if we're going down or up. It hits me for the first time: We could get lost. Twenty minutes away from the farm is fine if you know which direction you're heading, but there's no way of knowing in the dark. I can't see any of the landmarks I use in the daytime.

"Leah," Tom whispers. "Can you hear something?"

We stop suddenly, and my feet sink into the soft, muddy ground. We're definitely away from the path now because I haven't felt stones on my soles for quite a while. Both Tom and I are panting from the effort of hurrying away, but I need to concentrate, so I slow my breathing down and strain to listen.

It's quiet, but not quite silent. Wind whistles through foliage, and rain patters against David's jacket. Tom is trying hard not to breathe loudly, but he's still out of breath from hurrying down the hill.

I *listen*.

My body is in tune with nature, ready to identify any sound that doesn't belong. I know these moors, I've walked them before, and I've spent time with Seb, sitting, thinking, listening. I know how to listen.

The footfall is soft, barely perceptible above the wind and rain, obviously made by someone who doesn't want to be heard. When I whip my head around, the grass stirs, and feet move hastily, but there's no one there.

My heart kick-starts another rush of blood to my extremities, warming me. Adrenaline surges through my body and heightens my senses. We need to get out of here as fast as we can. I don't know where Isabel is, but I know she's following us. Pulling on Tom's hand, I urge us on, putting a finger to my lips for us to make our way quietly. If Isabel can merge into the shadows, we can too, and staying quiet will help with that.

There's nothing but shapes on the moors, from the looming rocks to the sudden slopes and the sporadic trees. It occurs to me that Isabel might not be the most dangerous thing on the moors—we could fall into a ravine, or trip and break an ankle. I'm not sure what to do, whether to run wildly downhill until we come to civilisation, or find a place to hide and wait out the night, praying that Isabel doesn't find us. Or, if she does, finish what we started and plunge this knife into her heart.

"Leah."

My name is an echo through the noise of the wind rustling the moor grass, but as it works its way into my mind, every muscle in my body stiffens. Tom lets out a whimper. I squeeze his hand to reassure him that I'm here before spinning around in search of her.

Nothing but darkness.

"Stop hiding, Isabel." If I can at least know where she is, maybe I can stop whatever it is she's planning to do. My mind is filled with images of her moving towards me at preternatural speed, slashing my face with her fingernails, feasting on my flesh with her teeth. In my head she scuttles on all fours like a sick, deranged monster from a horror film.

The reality is just as bad.

As I search desperately for her, a hint of blonde hair emerges from the long grass on the moors, followed swiftly by her torso. She dives towards me with her own knife outstretched and her teeth bared. In the split second that it happens, I push Tom away and steel myself for her attack, her shadowy figure launching at me like a feral cat. I'm more vulnerable than her, half-naked, half-frozen, and wounded, but I won't give up without a fight because if she kills me, I won't be around to protect Tom.

"Get out of here!" I shout to him. "Run down to the farm and phone the police."

As Isabel slashes the knife towards my face, I fall onto my backside and dive away from her. I'm scrabbling back up the hill when she comes at me again, falling to her knees by my feet. I kick her in the shoulder, knocking her on her back and roll headfirst, managing to sink the knife into her thigh. Isabel screams in pain and a swell of blood escapes the wound. I'm vaguely aware of Tom running away in the distance. Good—now all I have to think about is Isabel.

I lift the knife, ready to strike her again, but Isabel is swifter than I anticipate, slipping away from me and staggering to her feet.

"You don't give up, Leah," she says. "I always thought you would, but you keep on going. You never gave up on me, did you? Always looking for a way to make my life better. Most nurses wouldn't give a crap about trying to prove my innocence, but you could never let it go. I almost admire you for that."

I climb to my feet and steady my arm with the knife. No matter what I do, my hand keeps shaking. Isabel, however, remains cool and confident despite her wounded thigh.

"You're not a killer. We both know it, but you don't appear to be able to face up to it." She closes the distance between us with a step. "It's time to give up now. Tom won't make it to the farm, will he? He'll get lost on the moors and I'll slaughter him after I've killed you."

"No, you won't." My voice is surprisingly strong.

"I will." Her blonde head bobs up and down as she nods. "This has always been inevitable since the first moment we met. I love you, Leah, but we can't both live, so it's going to have to be me."

"You're wrong."

"Why?" She tilts her head to the right as if genuinely confused by the notion that she might lose.

"Because Tom is my son, and I'm never going to give up until he's safe."

Her brief moment of shock is all I need to get the advantage, but Isabel is not someone taken off guard easily. As I'm about to plunge the knife between her ribs, she kicks my feet from under me and we tumble together down the steep slope of slippery grass. Her hand is in my hair as we gain momentum, but neither of us can get our knives in the right position to do any damage. Finally, a rock stops our fall, and we split apart. I tumble farther than Isabel, landing on a hard surface. Rock. It's slimy as I struggle to my feet, shuffling and slithering while attempting to stay balanced. As I force myself upright, I advance a few steps, gliding across the smooth stone, unstable and out of control. My toes kiss the edge of the rock after coming to an abrupt halt. When I realise where I am, my heart skips a beat, and I panic, scurrying two steps away from the edge. Through the dark, cloudy night, I can barely make out the cliff. Tom and I wandered farther away from the path than I'd thought, coming to the edge of the gorge that works its way through the valley on the moors. If I'd slipped any further, I'd be dead.

Isabel rights herself, lifts herself up and dusts herself down. The knife is gone from her hand, lost in the fall. But her determined look tells me that she hasn't given up. She's coming for me.

I'm going to die.

It's not the first time I've had that thought tonight, but it is the moment that feels the most immediate. It happens so quickly that I can count the number of breaths I take.

Breathe. Isabel's hands are forceful against my shoulders, forcing me towards the edge. *Breathe.* She shoves me back. My shoulders lean so far over the edge that I'm completely off balance and about to fall. *Breathe.* My heel is inches away from the drop. *Breathe.* I drop my left shoulder, throwing my weight to the side. With the last remaining strength in my body, I use the momentum of my dive to throw Isabel away from me and over the cliff to the depths below.

Breathe.

Her scream pierces through the rain as she flies over the edge, hands scrambling to grasp hold of me, the rock, anything. They find nothing but air. The look on her face etches itself into my memory, an image I'll never forget for the rest of my life. Half-drowned in shadow, she finally transforms into the wild animal she always wanted to be.

For a few precious moments, Isabel is a bird in flight.

CHAPTER
37

By the time I make it to the farm, I'm limping on torn feet, doubled over from pain, my teeth chattering against the freezing cold. The only warmth comes from my own blood running down the backs of my legs, mingled with rainwater and mud. Seb rushes out of the house, hastily dressed in pyjama bottoms, a jacket, and a pair of boots.

"Tom?"

"He's here." Seb wraps his arms around me and lifts me as I begin to collapse.

I wake to the sound of sirens pulling into the farm courtyard. Paramedics are here for me. They bundle me up and put me on a stretcher with Tom joining me in the back of the ambulance. Headlights and torches light up the courtyard like a festival at night, the beams bouncing off the guns of the armed officers.

It takes me a moment to remember what's happening and where

I am. Then I see her face in the darkness and the echo of her screams as she plummeted down into the ravine.

"Isabel," I whisper.

Tom leans over me and squeezes my hand. With the lines of concern between his brow, he appears older than ever before. When did he become a man?

"What happened to her?" he asks.

"She's dead."

The dark depths of unconsciousness pull me away from the harsh light of the ambulance. As I drift into slumber I feel Isabel's bony fingers dragging me away.

When I was Isabel's nurse, she lent me a book about birds to read while she was in her art therapy sessions. In that book it said that magpies are capable of grief. They are clever and cunning birds, too, but the thought of them grieving their lost ones certainly provides an alternative view to their perceived maliciousness. Isabel has always been the magpie, but I wonder whether the grief I feel for her counts in this instance. Even as Isabel was torturing me, I saw a glimmer of humanity hidden behind a soiled past, and I think I'll spend my lifetime wondering whether she was a product of her childhood and incarceration, or whether she'd been born a magpie imitating a human voice.

I'm in a private room the size of a small hotel room, with a large glass window overlooking York. The hospital smell permeates every ion, and it's never quiet because there are always nurses bustling through the ward. Outside, the minster stands proud in the centre of the city, a reminder of what stood before us and will stand long after we're gone. Isabel still looms as large as a cathedral, with my life firmly covered by her shadow. I need to know what happened to her that night on the moors. I need to know if she really is dead.

What I do know is that in the abandoned farmhouse, police found no evidence that Isabel and David had been living there for more than a day or two. David was dressed in special scent-reducing clothing, so Isabel probably had some too. At least that explains why she was able to evade the tracking dogs after she escaped.

The police searched my cottage on the Braithwaites' property and found chocolate bar wrappers, empty water bottles, and odour-eliminating spray in the attic. The scent-reducing products were bought over the internet by David, which means the three of them worked together. David and Owen helped Isabel after she got out of Crowmont. Isabel and Owen planned the murder of James Gorden, bringing his body back to Hutton in a display of horror designed to shake me to my core. It must have been David who took the rest of James's body to the abandoned farmhouse after police had finished searching the area and moved on.

The thought of the three of them planning all this makes my stomach turn over in disgust. I'm sure the details will come out in due course, but for now I can't stop thinking about James. Where did they store his body? Did he remain in a car boot somewhere, rotting into the lining of the car? Or was he stuffed in a freezer and defrosted before being transported to the farmhouse? Did David carry his body up the path on the moors in the dark? Or did he manage to drive up there somehow? How close was I to all of this? If I'd looked out of the cottage window at the right moment would I have seen one or more of the Fieldings carrying the body of James Gorden through the night? I'm not sure I ever want to know.

And, at last, I finally know what happened to poor Maisie Earnshaw, an innocent victim who stumbled into the world of the Fieldings, a six-year-old girl who never deserved such a violent death.

During sleepless nights in the hospital I often think about contacting Maisie's parents just to talk to them about what I know, but I doubt it would offer them any peace. Sometimes I even think about contacting Anna Fielding, but I wouldn't even know where to begin. It's up to the police to find out if Isabel's mother was somehow involved in this whole mess.

One thing that keeps playing on my mind is whether James Gorden learned the truth about what happened to Maisie before he died. Did Isabel tell him? Or was James killed without ever knowing?

There are voices outside the hospital room. Since I arrived here, a police officer has been standing guard outside, which worries me because no one has told me what happened to Isabel yet. If they'd recovered her body, would I need a bodyguard? The wounds on my back itch as I wait to find out what happened after I made it to Seb's farmhouse.

When DCI Murphy walks into the room avoiding my gaze, I already know what he's going to say. "We didn't find her. We searched the area and we brought in tracking dogs to pick up her scent. There was a blood trail for a while, but then it went cold."

Not as cold as my flesh. "She survived?"

I can see that he's tired after the last few days. The stubble on his chin gives him a dishevelled, worried appearance, and his skin has taken on an unhealthy sallow complexion. I'm not the only one tormented by Isabel Fielding.

"It looks that way. It wasn't a straight drop down the gorge. There were a few protruding rocks and cliff edges. If she landed on one of them, chances are she would have walked away."

I turn my head away and stare out the window towards the minster. Isabel is clever and she knows how to evade capture. She has every chance to come back stronger after this.

"We're searching the Fielding property now."

"At least David died. He was dead, wasn't he?"

"Yes, he was dead when we found him. Tom hit the aorta when he stabbed him through the back. The boy did good."

Thinking about it only makes me feel sick. I hate what Tom had to go to save my life. Everything that happened to him was because of me. If I hadn't taken that job or been pulled into Isabel's games… if only I'd recognised what was happening to me, that I was ill and needed help. The regrets keep piling up, and I'm not sure I can ever forgive myself for them. But guilt is a burden I'm familiar with, and a load I can continue to shoulder to get through the day.

"We're searching Fielding's various properties for bodies. If what he told you in the abandoned house was true, he's been getting away with murder for a very long time. And as a man who owns a property developing business, he certainly had the opportunity to dispose of the bodies."

"And the Earnshaws? Did you tell them what Isabel told me?" They deserve to know what happened to their daughter.

"They'll be told." He pauses. "Anyway, how are you doing?"

I'm not sure whether he means the injuries on my back, or the psychological trauma of the last six months. "Sore. Waiting to get out of here so I can go home."

"About that." He pulls up a chair and moves it closer to my bed. "I strongly suggest you move away, change your name, and start somewhere fresh. I'm working on keeping your name out of the media, but you will need to give a statement about David Fielding's death, and so will Tom. But after all of that is over, keeping you safe will be the next priority. I can get you into witness protection."

"Tom too?"

"Yes, both of you. It'll move fast. I've set up a meeting with two officers in a hotel a few streets from here. They'll arrange everything. You'll be gone in less than a week, and you can't tell anyone where you're going," he warns.

Maybe Leah Smith could leave all that guilt behind. Maybe shouldering regrets could be a thing of the past.

I place my keys, purse, and mobile phone in the tray before stepping through the metal detector. I remembered to wear my wireless bra this morning so as not to set it off. The security guard hands me back my items, and I move through the hallway into a room set out like a break room, with cheap armchairs dotted around low circular tables.

He sits on the bright green chair, slumped over, but with his watery eyes directed up at me. Before I came, I told myself I wouldn't feel anything, that I wouldn't shed a tear for him because of the things he's done, but here I am with tears in my eyes and a strange desire to hold him. I know he feels the same way because he half stands, and then sits back down. The tears roll down his face and onto the veneer surface of the table.

"Leah."

I can't utter the word, so I just say, "I'm here."

"I never thought you'd come."

"I wasn't going to," I admit.

He sits silently, with tears rolling down his cheeks and his shoulders moving up and down as the sobs rack through his body. It's a wonder he manages to stay silent. After a while I can't look at him any longer, so I turn and brush away my own tears.

"It's good to see you," he says. "You won't believe me, but I've missed you. I've missed you both more than you could imagine. But it's good that I'm in here. They give me what I need to recover. I'm learning how to be a good man again."

I pity him, despite a growing sensation of rage burning and

bubbling beneath the surface. I can't help but pity him.

"You look well." He stumbles, his words growing less and less sure the longer we sit and stare at each other.

"I'm not," I say. "I'm not sure I ever will be because of what you did to me and to Mum."

His shoulders sag, but the sobbing has stopped. "I know. I'm sorry. For what it's worth. I know that's not enough, is it?"

"No. It isn't."

"But it's good to see you," he says. "Because I love you and I always have."

"Don't say that to me." I'm almost on my feet, but I tell myself to stay longer. This is about confronting what has held me back my entire life. I need to give it time.

"About the night I… I hurt you," he says, carefully looking away. "I wasn't in my right mind. I used to black out and wake up in different places. I know what I did, but I don't even remember doing it."

"That's no excuse," I say bitterly.

"I know. I did a lot I can never take back. I know now that I can never atone for my sins, but I can try, and I'll never stop trying."

"Good for you."

"I wish you all the happiness in the world, and I know you'll have more chance of finding it while I'm in here," he says.

"That's true."

"I'll never come out," he says. "And if they make me, I'll never try to find you."

"Then this is the last time we'll see each other."

"I love you, Leah," he says.

It's then that I realise he has cast a larger shadow as a memory than he ever did as a man. All I need to do is turn on the lights and chase out the darkness. "I love you too, Dad. I wish I didn't. I wish I hated you, but I don't. Sometimes I hate you, but deep down I think

I'll always love the dad you once were, and could have been if you'd been a stronger man."

Rose Cottage seems alive as I spend the morning moving around the rooms with Tom, gathering our belongings and cramming them into suitcases and boxes. Despite living to our means, we've managed to accumulate both stuff and memories—mugs from the farm shop, feathers from the chicken coop, pretty stones collected on the moors, and Seb.

But we can't take all of them with us, which is why, despite the Best of Britpop blaring out in the background, my heart still feels heavy. The fresh coat of paint and the tiny marks in the walls from where Tom hung his posters remind me of the life we could have had here. I may have been experiencing a psychotic break at the time, but that didn't change the *potential* I had to be happy here, with Tom, and with Seb, both of whom saved my life.

It's three days since I left the hospital. After meeting my dad for one last time, I went to a Travelodge just outside of York and received all the information I need to begin a new life. Tomorrow we travel to a rendezvous point at ten in the morning. I don't know where that rendezvous point will be. A man called Robert will telephone me with further instructions tonight at eight.

From there, the new life begins, and it doesn't include anyone from my old life, apart from Tom.

Partway through Sellotaping boxes, I leave the house to meet Seb, who gave me a home and a job when I needed them the most, and who never gave up on me no matter what happened. One of DCI Murphy's police officers waits outside the cottage to make sure Tom is safe, while I walk the main path down to the Braithwaites' farm. I want to walk our path along the moors, but Isabel has ruined those memories for me. The moors remind me of wild eyes disappearing into the darkness, and fingers stretching out towards me.

He waits for me in his Land Rover and drives us away from the farm. We're on our way into Hutton for a last lunch, but I can't wait that long.

"Pull over."

He turns to me. "What? Why?"

"Just do it."

When the car comes to a halt, I grab hold of his wax jacket in both hands and press my mouth against his for the first time. He's hesitant at first, but then his hands are in my hair, and his body presses against mine. Heat spreads through me so aggressively that I have to force myself to pull away. We're both breathless when we stop, but he takes my hands gently into his and kisses them.

The lunch we eat tastes like nothing. It's quiet and melancholy. We both know what might have been, but we both know I have to protect my son. The witness protection won't stretch to a non-family member, and I wouldn't ask him to give up his life for a "what if" scenario. And I can't tell him anything about where we will end up, because I don't even know myself. All he knows is that we're moving away and that we're going to be safe.

"Another time," I say, as he drops me off at the cottage. "Another place."

He nods and sighs at the same time. "Yep. I know."

"Do we get free eggs for the road? Or is that pushing it?"

"I'll be round with a dozen."

If I stop smiling, I might cry, and if I touch him again, I'll never leave this place. It has to be quick, and sting like a bastard, a waxing strip ripped from flesh. Seb must feel the same way, because the Land Rover makes a quick exit after I slam the door shut.

Tom is cleaning the cabinets when I walk in through the kitchen, sidestepping the spot on the doorstep where I found James Gorden's severed head. He takes one look at me and says, "You look like you need chocolate and Freddy Krueger."

"I think you're right. Do we have either of those things?"

"One last bar of Dairy Milk and Netflix on my laptop."

"You're a good kid." I ruffle his hair and pinch his cheek until he groans and squirms away.

It's not the time to tell him yet, but one day I will.

Our last night in the cottage is spent curled up on the sofa watching our version of a comfort movie, *Nightmare on Elm Street,* on Tom's tiny laptop screen, with police surveillance outside taking turns in shifts to make sure we're safe. It's a wonderful night, despite the circumstances, and my tetchy, frustrating, brave-as-hell teenage son makes me believe that there's a future for us after we've adapted to witness protection.

We have a chance for a new life.

The next morning, before we leave, Tom and I watch the postman dance with Pye the feral cat as we drink our last cuppa in the kitchen gazing out at the stunning views beyond the dry stone walls. I open the door and take the mail, apologising to the poor red-faced bloke with scratch marks on his calves.

"I know we shouldn't laugh, but…" Tom says as I shut the door and carry the post over to the table.

"It's okay," I reply. "After what we've been through, a little schadenfreude is acceptable."

Without paying much attention I slide my thumb into the corner of an envelope and tear it open. Inside is a folded letter of cream paper with a texture almost like linen. It's expensive art paper.

Carefully, I unfold the paper, already knowing what to expect. My heart is pounding, but I force myself to remain calm. This is okay. We've not made our new start yet. This is the last time it'll happen. The last time. The half-healed wounds on my back itch as though they've been recently opened again.

It's as beautiful as always, illustrated to perfection with an iridescent sheen across the wing. There are no words, simply a stunning drawing of a magpie. She didn't need to write any words— the picture says it all.

Isabel Fielding isn't done with me yet.